A gun went off and she jumped back. This followed by a lot of yelling.

She heard footsteps in the corridor outside. She waited until they were nearly upon her, then opened the door fully and stuck out her foot. One of Edward's girls hit the floor face-first and dropped the weapons she'd been carrying.

Linda jumped her. She knelt on the girl's spine then reached around the front of her throat with her right forearm and held the back of her throat with the left. Bending her wrist inwards she squeezed her arms together, restricting the carotid arteries. With the blood to her brain cut off, the girl kicked a couple of times then lost consciousness.

Linda got up and inspected the weapons the girl had been carrying. "Come to momma," she said as she picked up a sawn-off shotgun, two pistols, a Colt.45 and a Bowie knife.

Now she was armed as well as dangerous.

An Abaddon Books™ Publication
www.abaddonbooks.com
abaddon@rebellion.co.uk

First published in 2008 by Abaddon Books™, Rebellion Intellectual
Property Limited, The Studio, Brewer Street, Oxford, OX1 1QN, UK.

10 9 8 7 6 5 4 3 2 1

Editor: Jonathan Oliver
Cover: Mark Harrison
Design: Simon Parr & Luke Preece
Marketing and PR: Keith Richardson
Creative Director and CEO: Jason Kingsley
Chief Technical Officer: Chris Kingsley
The Afterblight Chronicles™ created by Simon Spurrier and Andy
Boot

ISBN: 978-1-905437-62-7

Printed in Denmark by Nørhaven Paperback A/S

THE AFTERBLIGHT CHRONICLES

DAWN OVER
DOOMSDAY

JASPRE BARK

Abaddon
Books

WWW.ABADDONBOOKS.COM

In the first decade of the new millennium a
devastating plague swept the planet, killing all
but those with the blood group 'O negative.'
Communities crumbled, society fragmented and in
its place rose the rule of tyrants and crazed cults
lead by dangerous religious revolutionaries.

This is the world of The Afterblight Chronicles...

CHAPTER ONE

Cortez hated the smell of whorehouses. It was so dishonest. Cheap perfume and stale sweat masking a fruitless search for satisfaction.

Cortez had always preferred torture to sex. He had little interest in the wares the girls were selling. Torture seemed far more honest to him. Just as intimate, but a hundred times more heartfelt and intense. There was so much more invested in torture.

Sex always left him feeling hollow afterwards. Empty, angry and unfulfilled. Torturing someone made him feel like a god. The men and women he was paid to torture came to worship him a little more each time Cortez touched them.

Cortez always thought it strange that in English fucking was politely called 'making love'. He had never made a woman love him by fucking her. He had made many women and men love him through torture. It wasn't long before they looked to please his every whim. To confide in him their deepest and most dirty secrets. Things they wouldn't even tell their closest friends and lovers, they would whisper into his ear between the pain filled sobs of shame. The timid admissions that lovers make to each other during pillow talk are nothing like the devastating truths he had extracted from his victims.

There are no misconceptions like there are with sex. No-one is thinking about a possible future together during torture. There were no tears when Cortez ended his relationship with his victims. They didn't beg him for one last chance to try and work things out. They looked at him with gratitude and relief. Some of them kissed his hand as joyous tears spilled from their eyes.

When they thought about the broken and agonising state their bodies were in, Cortez's victims realised there was no greater compassion a human being could show than to end their suffering. No lover's caress brought them anywhere near the relief Cortez did when he finally ended their lives.

And yet he had always been paid for this pleasure. Which, when he thought about it, made him little better than the women who worked in this brothel. They traded in their own tawdry and limited pleasures, much as he had. Taking lovers as he had victims, indiscriminately as long as he was paid.

He didn't betray it in his face or the way he stood, but it was this that annoyed him most about Greaves taking him to the brothel. Greaves was his paymaster. He went where Greaves asked him, irrespective of what he felt.

Cortez thought it ironic that even in these times, when Allah sought to test the faithful through plague and famine, that the world's oldest profession continued to thrive.

"What's your pleasure?" said a woman's voice over the intercom.

Greaves bent down to speak into the metal box, leaning against the reinforced steel door. "We're here to see Mr Edwards, the owner. About a... err, monetary transaction."

"Just a minute."

A CCTV camera, mounted above the door, swivelled round to get them both in shot. Cortez was impressed by the security. It wouldn't have come cheap. Seems sex sold well even after the world had ended.

Greaves straightened up and adjusted his glasses, looking out over the ruins of the traditional stone houses and churned up lawns of what had once been an exclusive suburb of Harrisburg, Pennsylvania.

"This part of town used to be real popular with the pharmaceutical execs you know," he said. "That's where all the money was out here. That and steel of course."

Cortez nodded silently. He didn't have anything of value to add. Greaves knew a lot more than he did. He was smart. Perhaps the smartest person Cortez had ever met. He was short and scrawny and he couldn't fight for shit, but the smarts Allah had granted him were as deadly as any weapon Cortez knew.

"They're taking their time aren't they?" said Greaves, taking off his glasses and rubbing his eyes. "Damn this pollen!" He swore and began rummaging for pills in the pockets of his greatcoat. He never took it off, even though it was high summer and the sweat stuck his mousey brown hair to his forehead.

"Okay, step inside," said the voice over the intercom.

The door buzzed and Greaves pushed it open. Cortez followed him into a cage of reinforced steel. Four shotgun barrels were pointed directly at them. Four dangerous women, with very little clothing, had a bead on them.

"Gentlemen," said a deep male voice from the shadows. "You'll be dead 'fore you even reach for your weapons. So I suggest you take out whatever you're packing – nice and slow mind – and toss it through these here bars. With the safety on."

Cortez didn't like the odds. He looked over at Greaves to see how they were going to play it. Greaves nodded for him to disarm. Cortez pulled out a Colt .45 from the holster under his robes and the sawn-off shotgun he had strapped to his back. Greaves pulled out the snub-nosed pistol Cortez had given him. He held it like it scared him.

"Is this how you put the safety on?" he asked, showing

Cortez the pistol.

All four women dropped a bullet into their chambers and aimed at Greaves. He went very pale.

"You need to press the lever forwards," Cortez told him, remaining calm.

"It's okay, it's okay," Greaves said holding the pistol away from him. "Don't shoot I'm not going to try anything." His hands shook as he fumbled with the safety before dropping the gun through the bars.

"Y'know fellas," said the man in the shadows. "There's a lot of cunts on sale in this place, but I'm not one of them. Think I don't know you're holding out on me? I wanna see *every* piece on the floor, in front of these bars."

Greaves looked confused and panicked. He turned to Cortez. Cortez shrugged, bent down and took the pistol out of his ankle holster. Then he reached into his belt and removed the Bowie knife he kept there.

"That's better," said the voice. Lights came on in the reception area revealing a hallway done out in plush velvet and gilt brocade. Edwards, the owner of the brothel, was standing at the bottom of a baronial staircase.

He was a big guy and, although he was carrying a lot of weight, he looked like he could move pretty fast when he had to. He was wearing shorts, slippers and a loud Hawaiian shirt. Beads of sweat stood out on his bald pate and what little hair he had was tied in a pony tail at the back.

Edward's arms were spread in welcome and he was smiling the type of broad smile you wear when you're just about to fuck someone good. "Welcome to the Pleasuredrome. Excuse the gals, they're not used to being up before noon and they're kinda tetchy until they've had their coffee."

The cage doors clicked, whirred and swung open.

Greaves entered and Cortez followed. Two of the women bent down to pick up the weapons, the other two kept theirs trained on the visitors.

"Can I you gentlemen anything to drink?" Edwards said, beckoning for them to follow him. "A little champagne perhaps, maybe something harder?"

The two women followed as they walked down a corridor off the main hall, shotguns still primed.

"I'll just have a glass of water," Greaves said.

Edwards chuckled. "Got ourselves a real party animal here gals." He slapped Greaves on the back. "Just busting your balls buddy, guess it is a little early in the day for some people, lightweights that is." Edwards turned to Cortez. "How about you big guy, what's your poison?"

"I do not drink." Cortez said. He trusted Edwards even less for his attempts to ply them with alcohol.

"Is that a South American accent I hear?" Edwards said, probing. "That's some beard you got there Fidel. You ain't one of the last surviving commies are you?"

Cortez started to lose his cool. He did not feel comfortable in this place of carnal sin and Edwards' attempt to rile him were beginning to work. "La ilaha illa Allah," he said aloud. Partly to put Edwards in his place, and partly to collect himself and ward off the stench of the wrongdoers. "Muhammadur rasoolu Allah!"

Edwards stopped at the door of his office. For a second he lost his composure, surprise burst out on his face. Then he pulled himself together and laughed as he unlocked the door. "Seems we got ourselves a Muslim girls." Edwards motioned for them to take a seat. "Don't have too many of those where you come from, I'll bet."

Greaves took a seat and leaned towards Edwards. Cortez remained standing. The two women kept him in their sights.

"Is that entirely necessary?" said Greaves. "You have our weapons. We're simply here on business."

Edwards waved a hand and the girls put their weapons at their sides. They stood at the back of the room, looking bored, irritable and tense. Not a good combination in armed women, Cortez noted.

"Don't mind them," said Edwards. "They're only hanging around in case you want to party when we're done. On the house of course." Edwards laughed when he saw their reactions. "What, you never had a blow job from a gal with a gun on you? Jesus, you guys like it vanilla don't you?"

Greaves cleared his throat. "Perhaps we should get down to business."

"Ah yes, I have some merchandise that you're interested in, I understand." Edwards leaned back in his chair and smiled his 'I'm gonna fuck you' smile again. "The big question is, how interested are you?"

"I believe I agreed a price with your associate," Greaves said. "I have the goods ready. Perhaps we could see her?"

"Now hold on there junior. You talked about the price with one of my lackeys. No-one said he was authorised to name an amount. Let's just say, what you've brought today, that's a down payment."

"What!" said Greaves sitting upright, his voice carried a sudden weight of authority. "We had a deal. I've upheld my side of the bargain. I expect you to honour yours."

"Hey, hey, calm down there junior," said Edwards holding up a placatory hand. "Now I understand how it is. You've gotten yourselves all psyched up. You probably went to sleep last night thinking about all the things you're going to do with her. And she is something, believe me. I don't go for Injuns much myself, but she is well worth a look. Whatever you've got in mind, hey that's fine with me, I'm not gonna judge you. Thing is though, you're wanting to buy this girl outright, not rent her, and I can still earn a fuck of a lot out of her. She's young, she's clean and she ain't injured any. That's a big chunk out of my profits and I need reimbursing. I got overheads you know, protection to pay. I put a lot of money into my girls."

"She's a slave," said Greaves with disdain. "You keep her chained to a wall and you feed her slops."

"Hey I'm not judging you, so don't you get all high and mighty with me you little pissant! We cater for a lot of exclusive tastes in this establishment. The slaves are a lucrative service. A lot of my customers will be disappointed to see her go. They might even take their business elsewhere. So you gotta make it worth my while. Hand over the goods you brought to trade and when you raise some more you can come back and we can talk about letting you have her."

"What if we just take our goods and leave?" Greaves said.

"Now that just ain't gonna happen," said Edwards with his biggest 'fuck you' smile yet.

The two women stepped forward and levelled the barrels of their shotguns at Greaves' temple.

That was their first mistake.

Before they could react Cortez stepped around behind them and grabbed the barrels of both weapons. He pulled them back and up, driving the butts into their faces.

He was right on target with the woman on his right. The butt hit the base of her nose. It exploded in a hot burst of blood and the bridge cracked, driving shards of bone into her brain. She was dead before her body hit the floor.

The woman on his left caught the butt on the side of her face. There was a crack as her cheek broke and her right eye rolled up into its socket. She fell to the ground, dazed and twitching.

Cortez swung both shotguns round and pointed them at Edwards, just in time to see him pull an ivory handled Magnum out of his desk. Cortez unloaded one shotgun and blew a hole in his left wrist. Edwards shrieked as blood and cartilage sprayed the floor, dropping the gun. He ducked behind the desk and grabbed the Magnum with his good hand, firing at Cortez's foot.

Cortez leaped back and Greaves cowered behind his chair while Edwards made a bolt for the door. He ran out into the corridor, screaming at the top of his voice. "Trixie, Fifi, Jezebel, Chelsea, get your skanky ol' asses out here! We got trouble!"

Cortez hauled up the unconscious woman. She moaned at the pain as she regained consciousness. "Where is the girl?" He demanded.

The woman shook her head. "What girl? I don't know who you mean."

"She's a Native American," said Greaves getting to his feet. "She's called Anna. We know you've got her prisoner here."

"I can't think. I'm hurt too bad."

"Take us to the girl Anna," Cortez said, leaning in close. "Or you will know what it really feels like to be hurt too bad."

"They're... they're all kept in the basement next to the dungeon," she murmured before passing out again.

Cortez walked to the door and stuck his head slowly round just as a stream of bullets tore up the frame. Jumping back he collided with Greaves.

"We can't leave," Greaves said, picking up his glasses.

"They've got us pinned down. We have to make them come to us." He thought for a minute. "How many of them did you see?"

"I was too busy dodging their bullets to count."

"Edwards called out four names. So there's at least that many coming for us. We're at the end of a corridor with no other exit. We're outnumbered and outgunned." Greaves hit Cortez with his fierce blue eyes. "There's got to be a way to turn that to our advantage."

Linda could have kicked herself when she came to. If she hadn't been too trussed up to move her legs and if her head hadn't felt like someone was doing all the kicking for her.

She was lying on her side on a cold stone floor. Her wrists and ankles were tied behind her. She arched her back to stretch her legs and relieve the cramp in her thighs. This tightened the rope and cut off the circulation to her hands. She felt for how it was tied with her fingers. Luckily it was a bondage knot that she knew. She found the right end of the rope and pulled. Her bonds uncoiled and she was free.

Thank God for pervy clients, she thought as she got to her feet and massaged the life back into her wrists. She was in a dark, confined space. She reached in front of her and felt what seemed like shelves and broom handles. She smelt bleach. Linda was in a broom closet. She'd been tied up and dumped in a broom closet.

Time to get some payback.

She fumbled her way over to the door and tried it. It wasn't locked. It opened on to a dimly lit basement. Across the way from the closet was a door marked 'DUNGEON', meaning she had to be in the Pleasuredrome. That's why she was tied bondage style. Sloppy of them really, her being a pro and all. They had to know she'd be able to get loose. They must have thought she'd be out for longer and were going to come back with better shackles.

She'd known there was something wrong with her clients the night before. They said they were visiting traders who wanted a three-way and they had a bundle of drugs to trade for it. She should have listened to her gut. They didn't seem that interested in her sexually and they knew their way around too well to be visitors.

They must have slipped her something after she had climbed into their car. She should never have taken a drink from them. Served her right for being careless.

Edwards had been after her to join his girls for a while now. Linda knew he didn't like independent competitors, but she never thought he'd resort to kidnap. She worked strictly downtown. Out of his way and away from his high-end clients.

Those clients had tastes that were too specialised for Linda. She had no illusions about what would happen if she couldn't get out of her current situation. She knew all about the girls he kept as slaves.

Linda walked slowly and quietly through the basement, scanning the gloom for any means of escape. It was a huge space, and covered more ground than the building above. It had obviously been specially excavated. The only doors she could find seemed to lead either into the well equipped dungeon area or into a series of tiny cells. She didn't want to think about who was kept there, or what the poor wretches were going through.

Something caught her eye over by the far wall. Linda peered at it, then turned away. Something drew her back however and she was glad it did. When she got closer she could see there was a hardboard panel nailed over a gap in the ceiling.

Linda fetched a wooden spanking paddle from the dungeon and pried the panel loose. About a metre above there was a grill leading to the outside. Linda pulled herself up and tried it. It was stuck fast. She tried to use the paddle to jimmy it but it broke. It would take more than one person to shift the grill.

Fuck! She was so close.

Changing tactics she hunted round and found the staircase. Making her way carefully up, she tested each step to make certain it didn't creak. The door at the top was locked, but only with a chub lock. Linda slid a thin section of the snapped paddle down between the door and the jamb, releasing the lever. Then she pulled the door open just a fraction and peeked out.

A gun went off and she jumped back. This was followed by a lot of yelling.

She heard footsteps in the corridor outside. She waited until they were nearly upon her, then opened the door fully and stuck out her foot. One of Edward's girls hit the floor face-first and dropped the weapons she'd been carrying.

Linda jumped her. She knelt on the girl's spine then reached around the front of her throat with her right forearm and held the back of her throat with the left. Bending her wrist inwards she squeezed her arms together, restricting the carotid arteries. With the blood to her brain cut off, the girl kicked a couple of times then lost consciousness.

Linda got up and inspected the weapons the girl was carrying. "Come to momma," she said as she picked up a sawn-off shotgun, two pistols, a Colt.45 and a Bowie knife.

Now she was armed as well as dangerous.

"Come on out honey," called one of the girls from up the corridor. "I got something for ya."

"I love you looong time," cried another. "Kill you quick."

Cortez was standing by the door. It was opened into the corridor to block the girls' view of the office. He said nothing and looked over at Greaves who was going through the drawers of Edward's desk.

"Seems Edwards has some exotic tastes." Greaves said, holding up a set of throwing knives and some shackles.

"I don't see how this helps us."

Greaves smiled and handed Cortez all but one of the knives. "I need you to use these to pin our dead friend here to the door," he said and gestured to the woman on the floor.

Cortez shrugged and picked up the body. Greaves applied the shackles to the unconscious woman.

Propping the dead woman against the door, Cortez held her left arm above her. Taking one of the knives he drove it through her wrist and into the wood behind it. He repeated this with her other wrist and both her feet. The body hung, crucified, against the door.

"Now give me a hand with this," said Greaves, struggling to lift the unconscious woman.

Cortez picked up the woman and Greaves directed him to hang her wrist shackles from the coat hook beside her friend. Kneeling, Greaves began to remove the screws from the hinges.

"Steady the door," he told Cortez. "Now we make them come to us. When I say go, we pick up the door and walk backwards to the far wall at an angle, using the door and the bodies as a shield." Greaves slapped the unconscious woman hard across the face. She groaned at the pain and came to. "Go!"

Cortez and Greaves lifted the door. They staggered backwards as a hail of bullets thudded into the wood. Most of them hit Cortez's side of the door. The bullets tore through but the corpse stopped any that might have hit Cortez.

As they reached the far wall two bullets connected with the woman Greaves was using for shelter, nicking her shoulder and smashing into the back of her thigh. "Aaaaah! Jesus – motherfucking – Christ!"

"Candy," called out one of the women from further up the corridor. "Candy is that you honey?"

Candy simply wailed in reply.

"Candy we're coming darlin'."

Cortez heard three sets of feet padding towards them.

"Come back you dumb bitches!" Edwards shouted.

"Now!" said Greaves, the second the footsteps stopped. He and Cortez kicked hard and the heavy oak door, with the combined weight of the two bodies, came crashing down on the three armed women. They collapsed, their guns clattering across the floor.

Cortez and Greaves ran over the door. Cortez grabbed two of the semi automatic weapons and Greaves picked up the other. They ran up the corridor firing indiscriminately.

Two women were caught by the spray of bullets. Their bodies jerked and flew backwards. Cortez and Greaves reached the hallway at the top of the corridor and looked around for more of them. There was no-one in sight.

Then Cortez heard an ominous click. He turned slowly to see Edwards with his Magnum at Greaves' temple. His wrist was wrapped with a makeshift bandage.

"Drop 'em big guy! Or your buddy here dies."

With great reluctance Cortez put down his weapons. Two of the women started climbing out from under the door behind them, moaning and cursing at their wounds. Three more came down the staircase, all of them armed.

"You sons of bitches are in some serious shit." Edwards said.

Linda had Edwards dead in her sights and she weighed up whether to pull the trigger or not.

She'd heard the catcalls and seen the gunfight in the corridor on the other side of the staircase. Edwards had hid and when the two men emerged he had got the drop on them. They were an odd looking couple. The runty one looked frightened and blinked through his glasses as Edwards held him at gunpoint. The big guy with him was a bit of an enigma – he was head and shoulders above everyone, including Edwards. He looked Hispanic, but he had a huge black beard and wore robes that looked Arabic. Linda had no idea what they were doing in this place, robbing it she supposed.

She kept Edwards in her sights as three more armed girls came down the stairs. Then she heard Edwards say: "We're gonna do far to worse to you than was ever done to that bitch you came to buy." That decided her. She wasn't certain why, but her gut told her which side she was on.

Linda unloaded the sawn-off shotgun into Edwards and blew his guts out the front of his body. Blood and ruptured intestines splattered into the wall opposite.

The girls on the stairs started firing and Linda ducked back. She heard the two guys return fire and a woman screamed.

Linda backed down the corridor as the men charged

towards it. She was standing next to the girl she'd tied up when they saw her. The big guy raised his Uzi and Linda raised her hands. The runt saw the girl at her feet, put his hand on the big guy's weapon and made him lower it.

"Were you the one who helped us?" the runt said.

Linda nodded. "I don't work here. I was a prisoner but I broke out."

"We need to get to the basement."

"It's this way." Linda showed them through the door. She locked it behind them and used the sawn-off to wedge it shut.

"That is my weapon," said the big guy.

It was the first time she'd heard him speak. "Listen," she said. "If we get out of this alive I've got two more you can have, free of charge. And trust me honey, I rarely give anything free of charge."

"How are we going to leave now?" said the runt. "Is there another exit?"

"There's a grill over there, but I couldn't shift it by myself. It leads outside."

The runt nodded then made his way down the steps with the big guy. Linda followed.

They headed for the cells. Linda watched as the runt slid open a hatch on each of them and peered inside.

"This is her," he said after the fourth one.

He reached into his greatcoat and pulled out a small device that he inserted into the lock. He fiddled with the end of the device for a few seconds and gave it a sharp turn. The lock clicked and he pushed the door open.

Linda was surprised by the runt's reaction. He stood in the doorway with his mouth open, stunned. He looked like a groupie meeting her favourite rock star. "I can't believe I've finally found you. You've no idea how long it's taken."

Linda looked past him into the cell. The occupant wasn't anywhere near as awe-inspiring as she seemed to the runt. She was a petrified Native American girl, half starved and in her late teens. The chains on her wrists and ankles ran through a ring in the ceiling and around a winch; most probably to allow the client to control what position she was in.

The girl shrank from the two men the minute she saw them. Greaves knelt down and tried his skeleton key in one of her ankle shackles but the girl kicked out in fear and knocked him on his back. "Shit," he said when he got up and looked at the key. "She snapped it."

"You want me to get her out of these?" the big guy said, holding up the chains. The runt nodded.

The girl tried to pull away from them while the runt tried to calm her. "Listen, Anna," he said. "It's okay. We're not here to hurt you. My name's Greaves and this is Cortez. We've come to get you out."

Cortez reached out to Linda's belt, and without thinking she pulled the bowie knife on him. "Getting a little fresh aren't we?"

Cortez stopped but he didn't pull back his hand. "You have my gun," he said pointing at the Colt.45. "I need it to break these chains."

Linda took it from her belt and handed it to him. "You know men usually have to pay to get their pistol in my trousers," she said playfully. Cortez met her flirting with a cold stare and turned away. *Obviously plays for the other team*, she thought.

Cortez caught hold of Anna's wrist. She cried out but her attempts to break free had no effect. He shot each of her chains off then picked her up like a child and flung her over his shoulder. She'd stopped fighting, but Linda could see that Anna's eyes were full of fear and mistrust.

"Hello... hello?" said a voice from another cell. "Is... is someone out there?" It was a woman with her face pressed against the grill. "Oh God you've got to take me with you. Please, I've got young children. There's no one to look after them. Please get me out of here."

Linda looked to Greaves who shook his head. "We haven't got time. She'll slow us down."

"And this one won't?" Linda said.

The door to the basement began to shake as something thudded into it from the other side.

"Quickly, show us this grill," said Greaves.

"Please," the woman in the cell called out. "Please don't leave me here. You don't know what they do to me... please..."

Linda tried not to listen as she showed them the potential exit. Cortez heaved at it but it remained stubbornly in place. The wood of the basement door splintered and gunfire raked the floor, inches from them. Greaves and Linda franticly joined the effort, and the grill gave as they heard the door give way and the first set of feet start to descend.

They scrambled through the tight opening. Anna first, then Greaves and Linda. A hand caught hold of Cortez's leg as he was leaving. He shot it away, shattering the knuckles.

They came out into a parking lot surrounded by a wooded copse. Greaves and Cortez, with Anna over his shoulder, raced to their vehicle then stopped in dismay. The tyres had been slashed.

"Quick, into the trees," said Linda. They followed her as armed women raced around the building and into the lot. The gun-toting prose tried to follow but weren't dressed for the rough terrain and soon lost their prey.

The copse continued in a steep ascent for a while and then gave out onto a highway. Greaves turned to Linda as they reached it. "We need a vehicle to get us out of the State. Can you help?"

"I may be able to but why would I want to? You boys look like you've got yourselves into a lot of trouble."

"Three reasons," Greaves said. "Firstly, Edwards had a lot of powerful friends who will want to get even with you for shooting him. Secondly I can pay you really well." He rooted through his greatcoat and came out with two gold coins. "These are Krugerrands from South Africa, they're pure gold," he said handing them to her. "This is just a down payment. And thirdly you'll be helping to save the world."

Linda nearly laughed out loud at that last statement but she could see from Greaves' eyes that he was deadly earnest.

"Follow me," she said.

Three hours and a lot of walking later they stood outside a lock-up on the north bank of the Susquehanna River. Linda unlocked the door and led them inside.

There, under a tarpaulin, was her baby. She tugged at the cover to reveal Bertha: A Fleetwood, 40E motor home, covered with customised bullet-proof armour plating. She came complete with onboard arsenal. There wasn't another vehicle like her on the road.

"Very nice," said Greaves inspecting the custom bodywork. "Where did you get it?"

"A grateful client. He didn't like his next of kin so he left Bertha and her contents to me."

She opened the vehicle up and Greaves and Cortez climbed in. Cortez put Anna down on a couch. She pulled her knees up under her chin and sat rocking, staring straight ahead.

"We've got enough gas in the tank to get us out the state," said Linda. "Where we headed?"

"Montana." Greaves said.

"That's on the other side of the country. We'll have to cross at least seven States to get there."

"I can make it very worth your while."

"Okay it's your money. So Anna, is she your relative, your lover or what?"

"We've never seen her before," said Greaves.

"So why'd you go to such trouble to rescue her?"

Greaves looked over at the traumatised sex slave. She was crying and shaking and snot ran down her top lip.

"Because," he said. "She is the future saviour of humankind."

CHAPTER TWO

At dusk the braves lit the meeting fire. Hiamovi held the talking stick above his head and everyone sitting on the rough scrub ground nodded their assent. He looked to the First Official of the Crow Council, Pauline Willowtree. She gave him leave to address the whole population of Crow Agency, the largest community on the Crow reservation.

He noted that, as was normal these days, at least a quarter of the faces looking up at him were white men and women. They were refugees from the cities. Survivors of The Cull, taken in and cultured by many of his people after their world was destroyed.

Hiamovi's heart beat faster, and that same cold feeling of anticipation and nerves, that public speaking always brought, spread outwards from his stomach. Before he spoke he let his spirit pour forth from his body to touch the spirit of the whole Crow tribe. His spirit went farther with each breath and there, at the boundaries of the tribe's collective spirit, he met the Great Spirit.

"Brothers and Sisters," he said, feeling the presence all around him. "In the days before the white man came – when the buffalo roamed these plains and there were hunting grounds for us all – in those days, when our Chiefs sought an answer to a problem that faced the whole tribe, our people would journey into the wilderness to find a revelation in dreams and prophetic vision."

The older members of the Crow nodded their agreement. The others leaned forward as Hiamovi paused, pulled in by the commanding tone of his voice.

"I too left my people and found myself lost in the wilderness. Not the wilderness of old, but the steel and concrete wilderness that the white man called his 'civilisation'. And I too received a revelation. One that was intended not just for my tribe, but for every one of my people and every one of our tribes.

"I wasn't searching for an answer. At that time I didn't care about the problems of my people. As far as I was concerned my people were my problem. They were the reason I had no self respect, no education and no identity. The reason I was left to rot on some reservation, living out my days in what I saw as a pointless existence. The truth is I hated myself. But I hated being a Cheyenne more."

Many seated in front of him shook their heads or drew a sharp breath. Not because they were disturbed by Hiamovi's disclosure, but because they had seen what he was describing all too often in the young men of their own tribe.

"Even though I was a chief's son I got into a lot of trouble on my reservation and when I'd used up every last bit of good will, I left. I left for the white man's cities, where I was even less happy and where I got into even more trouble. I'm not proud of it my brothers and sisters, but it happened.

"One night, on the road to Billings, I got into a fight. I was running drugs at the time. I was shipping across county lines for a connection I had in Butte. As a sweetener, for bringing him so much business, my connection had slipped me a package of grade A, home grown peyote.

"I pulled up at a station to get some gas in some little hick town on the way back from the deal. Because I'd taken the back roads to avoid being picked up, it was the first station I'd seen in a couple of hours. My tank was nearly empty but the owner claimed he 'didn't serve no

Injuns'. I was wired from the coke I'd been snorting. I felt paranoid and invincible at the same time, and I wasn't going to let this dumb redneck get the better of me. He'd picked the wrong Indian to fuck with. Trouble was, his brother-in-law, the local Sheriff, was using the can out back. He ran me in and impounded my vehicle before I could even throw a punch.

"They didn't find the coke when the Sheriff booked me – it was safely stashed in the bodywork of my car – but I knew it was only a matter of time before they did. If I was lucky, I was looking at a ten-year stretch in the white man's prison. A Native American doesn't have many allies in a white man's prison. Pretty much everyone wants a piece of him.

"I sat in that holding cell looking at a grim future. Then I remembered the peyote my contact gave me. The Sheriff and his men hadn't found that when they searched me.

"It wasn't a drug I'd tried before. But you know, when you're in a foxhole, you reach for whatever you've got. They could lock my body up, but at least I could set my mind free.

"I had no idea how much I was supposed to take. As this was my last chance to get high in what might be a while, I thought 'fuck it' and did the lot. Not an approach our ancestors would have approved of, but it got me where they wanted me.

"First the walls of the cell and my metal bunk started to feel like they were made of rubber. Then everything began to stretch out of proportion. My head got further away from my feet. The ceiling kept getting higher and higher and suddenly, in spite of where I was and what had happened to me, I couldn't stop laughing. I had to ram my fist in my mouth to avoid waking the Marshal on night duty.

"It was like someone had finally let me in on the joke that lay behind the whole illusion of my life. I saw the joy that powered all of creation and it was unbearably funny. I laughed myself into a state of hysteria and, without warning, the chord that held me to the physical plane just... snapped.

"The walls of the cell fell away. I was standing on the hunting grounds of my forefathers. I realised that I had never left. That the holding cell, and the white man's cities, and all the pain I had felt was only a bad dream.

"I felt the grass beneath my feet and the clouds in the sky and the trees that stretched to touch them, all reach out to welcome me home. I laughed again. This time out of relief. I let go of my fear and I let the laugh burst out, not caring who heard it.

"At that moment a whirlwind tore past me and snatched up the laughter. The laughter carried on but it was no longer coming from my mouth, it was riding away into the distance over a hill.

"Then I heard my laughter coming back to me. But as it got closer I saw it was no longer riding the whirlwind but was coming out of the mouth of a coyote. Not just any coyote, but *the* Coyote. The trickster god who trips you up so you learn the lessons only a fall can teach you. Lessons you won't understand until you let go of all your self importance, your vanity and the traps that your ego sets you. Lessons so valuable you have to hit rock bottom before they teach you to build yourself back up.

"Coyote stopped laughing and looked at me with gentle understanding. 'Come,' he said. 'There is someone who has been waiting to meet you since the day you were born'.

"Then he took me to a rock and he told me to climb it. It wasn't much of a rock to begin with but with every handhold and foothold I found, the rock grew a hundred feet taller until I cried out in despair that I would never reach the summit. Not even in a hundred lifetimes.

"A great laughter came from below. It was Coyote's laughter, and as it travelled up the face of the ever-growing rock it seemed to lift me up, reminding me that I was trying to conquer the rock, as the white man tries to own and conquer the land, because I was afraid of it. If I were to stop fearing the rock it would lift me up and carry me to the summit. I did this and within two steps I was at the top.

"The rock was now higher than all the world and I realised it was Tunkashila, the first land to break above the waters, called by my ancestors: 'Grandfather Rock'. I was so high that I was seen by First Man, son of night and the blue sky and also by First Woman, daughter of daybreak and the scarlet sky of sunset. They smiled when they saw me, as though they had been waiting for me to arrive so they could begin the ceremony. They took the sky in their hands and parted it as if they were opening the flaps of a teepee.

"Beyond the sky I saw a great light spilling out. This light was the source of all life. It was the force that pushes the corn up through the earth and the child out of the mother's womb. It was the purest form of love, that gives the gift of life to all creatures of land and sea and asks for nothing in return, except that we be mindful of each other. This light was the Great Spirit.

"I was afraid to be seen by this light. I felt ashamed and unworthy to be touched by it. I wanted to dig the biggest hole in Grandfather Rock and hide in it. To cover myself over with dirt so that it might never know of me, for I had turned my back on my people. I had spat on their ways and disgraced their name. I had been trapped by the white man's drugs and his money and I had been put in a cage.

"Tears of shame and self pity ran down my cheeks. I hoped that they would form a lake at my feet so I could drown myself. For here was the Great Spirit, of whom my people had spoken for generations. Whom I had spoken of in scorn and disbelief and yet here I was, humbled by the truth and made wretched.

"Even still, the Great Spirit lifted me up and told me, with a patience more infinite than the rock I was standing on, that my shame was nothing more than vanity itself. No different from the disbelief I had clung to, and just as foolish. So I let it go.

"I have no idea how long I spent with the Great Spirit. It felt as though a lifetime passed in the Great Spirit's world with every breath I drew in or let out. Yet only a heartbeat had passed in the world of man.

"I learned many things in that time. The Great Spirit told me He had been waiting until I was at the lowest point in my life before he contacted me. Just as he had been waiting until our people were at their lowest point before he came to their aid.

"Then the Great Spirit showed me our land before the white man came. When we were free to hunt and fish and tend our corn. Next he showed me how the white man came to our shores. Like a virus. Entering our land like bacteria. Only a tiny amount of them needed to enter our lands before the whole continent was overrun, spreading through our lands like a disease, destroying our way of life. Breaking their treaties and murdering our women and children.

"But, the Great Spirit told me, our people would recover from this disease. We would not die from it. No matter how many churches the white man built. No matter how many times he proclaimed that his god alone was the only god of the world. The Great Spirit tends everything that lives on American soil. For He is that life and springs eternal from it. He was here before the white man came and He will be here after the white man has gone.

"Then the Great Spirit showed me how a single ear of wheat fell from the hands of the first white settlers and grew to be a tall stalk. 'This is the white man who feeds from my soil,' he told me. 'And this is how I will withdraw the life so that the white man will no longer prosper here'. And the Great Spirit withdrew his life from the soil around the roots of the wheat and it withered and died. Then He showed me a famine strike the roots of fields all across the country. 'And so shall the white man fall,' the Great Spirit told me.

"Finally the Great Spirit showed me a bundle of wheat. It was tied together with twine and it rested on a single stalk of corn which was bending beneath the weight. Pressed to the ground and nearly broken. He told me that the white man had not beaten the human beings because of his lies, or his brutality. The white man had beaten the human beings because, while we prided ourselves on the independence of our tribes, the white man came together to found a nation. One stalk of wheat cannot break a stalk of corn, but a bundle can bring it low.

"The Great Spirit cut the twine holding the bundle together. The wheat fell apart and the stalk of corn sprang back up to health. Before my eyes a thousand stalks of corn sprang up out of the earth and then a thousand more, all grown to full height. They were packed together tight enough for me to walk across the tops of the corn. The Great Spirit joined me and, as we walked, He told me that he was going to bring a plague to the white man and wipe him from our lands. I was to raise up a nation of

Native Americans in their place. A United Tribal Nation in which all tribes were equal and worked together to reclaim our rightful place on the hunting grounds."

Hiamovi paused for a moment to take a drink of water from his flask. His throat was dry from so much talking. The only sound was the crackle of burning wood and the wind in the distance. The whole audience waited eagerly for him to speak again.

"I came to on the floor of my cell. I've no idea how much later that was. I couldn't hear a thing. No Sheriff shouting abuse. No activity in the other cells. Nothing.

"I sat for hours in my cell without doing a thing. When I got too hungry I tried calling out. That didn't help me any. No-one answered.

"After a night of hunger pangs, wondering if this was all some head-fuck on the Sheriff's part, I finally heard some activity in the front office. I started hollering as loud as I could. When I stopped and listened I heard a man cussing. Then he stopped swearing and broke down in tears. It was one of the Sheriff's men. I recognised his voice from when he had been stomping on my head.

"He burst into corridor outside my cell and pulled his gun on me. He seemed crazy with grief. 'You,' he said. 'You brought this to town, I don't know how, but you did.' His arms shook as he took aim. Before he could squeeze the trigger he started to retch. He put his hand up to his mouth and blood and bile spilled out between his fingers.

"He dropped down on all fours in front of my cell and threw up all over the floor. Again and again, unable to stop himself. Gallons of blood spilled from his mouth. He broke wind and the back of his pants were stained red.

"He died right there in front of me. When the son-of-a-bitch had been beating on me I had wished him dead a hundred times over. Then I watched it happen and I vomited. I half expected to see blood. But it was just liquid and whatever was left of the last cheeseburger I ate.

"I didn't know what was happening but I saw a chance to escape. I knotted the sheet from my bunk and used it to drag the Marshal's corpse over to my cell. I frisked his pockets for keys but didn't find any. So I took his gun and shot off the lock. It took five bullets, and I nearly lost a toe when one ricocheted but eventually I forced the door open.

"I walked out of that place with one bullet in the Marshal's gun. I looked around the town and there were corpses everywhere. The whole town looked as though it had just dropped where it stood. People had been out posting mail, jogging or walking the dog when it had hit them. Some of the pets were now feeding off their dead owners. All around me was living, or rather dead, proof of what the Great Spirit had told me. His first promise had come to pass.

"I took the Sheriff's car and drove into Billings. What I saw there was the same as every town I passed through. Nothing but white folk lying dead. The course that the rest of my life would take became clear to me in that moment. I'd met the Great Spirit, and He'd made good on His word.

"I made my way back to the reservation where I was raised and rejoiced to see so many of my kinsmen alive and well. I realised it was time to accept my destiny. I began preaching the Great Spirit's wisdom. I was living proof that He had come to redeem His people. I accepted the mantle of Chief and I took the name Hiamovi, a traditional Cheyenne name.

"From these seeds the United Tribal Nation was born.

Today our membership includes citizens from every tribe of this land. We have built a network that ships supplies from one side of the continent to the other. We have greatly expanded the territories enjoyed by the Native American and we have made them safe from looters.

"We respect the autonomy and the individual customs of each tribe we help. We seek only to offer you the strength and security that comes from allying yourself to our cause. Your problems become our problems and our might becomes your might, if you join with us.

"Our ambassadors have already visited you with supplies, medicine and other necessities. These are gifts. Tomorrow I will leave you to discuss our offer. My men will return in three moons to hear your decision."

Hiamovi stepped forward and lowered his voice. He was going for the clincher. His audience craned their necks.

"I am of mixed parentage. My great grandfather was a Chief of the Crow tribe. His name was Plenty Coups. He lived in a time when we still carried the coup-stick. And when he threw his stick into the soil it meant that he, and those who stood with him, would fight to the death to protect the territory it staked out. It was a line you didn't dare cross.

"Now is the time to plant our coup-sticks once again. To fight to the death to reclaim what is rightfully ours. To sweep the white man from these shores and redress the wrong done to our forefathers. To build a truly great future for our children with the blessing and protection of the Great Spirit!"

Hiamovi's men let out a fierce war cry and leapt to their feet. All the young braves and most of the young squaws followed suit. Many of them danced on the spot, their voices raised in defiance of the white man and in praise of the Great Spirit. Even those among the Crow who came from the white man's world. They now identified so heavily with their adopted culture that they too railed against the injustice of how their new brothers and sisters had been once been treated.

No-one else saw it, but the clouds of dusk parted over Hiamovi and the pure, bright light that was the Great Spirit spilled down on to the Crow tribe that danced to his words.

Two days later Hiamovi sat cross-legged on the floor of a lodge near Yellowstone. Sitting with him, in a circle, were the other five members of the United Tribal Nation's inner council. A brave stood guard by the door.

"We have tremendous support among the young and the recruits," said Cheveyo. By 'recruits' he meant those survivors who had been taken in by the tribes after The Cull. "Our numbers grow with every day that passes."

Cheveyo was a Hopi chief of the Bear clan. As was now customary in the UTN, he had adopted a name that was traditional to his tribe. He was a cautious idealist whose counsel Hiamovi had come to respect. Cheveyo was ten years Hiamovi's senior and there was no greater devotee to the cause of the UTN.

"Yes," said Hinto, a Dakota chief responsible for liaison and coordination of the North West tribes. "But rebellious youths and disaffected white men aren't going to win us the support of the whole tribal community. We need to sway the Elders to our cause. They're the key to the tribal councils. Without the tribal councils we don't have the endorsement and the support we need from any of the tribes."

"It's the Elders that are causing us the most problems,"

said Amitola. A prominent Sioux, Amitola had proven his organisational skills running the UTN's supplies and communication network. "They're the most resistant to our agenda. They lived too long in the old world, when the white man ran things. They don't realise the extent of the change. They're scared of losing the power they have and they're scared of what the white man might do."

"The white man's just as scared of what we might do," said Huyana, she was the daughter of the head matriarch of the Miwok. Huyana ran all the intelligence and information networks within the UTN. "That's what makes him dangerous. That's why the Elders need to join us and organise against the threat they pose."

"The white man lives among us," said Onatah, an Iroquois Matriarch by birthright, she spoke on behalf of the women of the UTN. "We're all likely to have one as a grandchild if the Great Spirit sees fit to grant us a long enough life. This isn't a racial matter anymore. It comes down to lifestyle and belief. That's what matters to the tribes now."

"That's why we have to emphasise our grass-roots campaign," said Cheveyo. "We're winning the hearts and the minds of the tribes. The Elders won't be able to hold out against the popular pressure of their own people. Sooner of later they'll be forced to ally themselves with us. Our greatest asset is our message and the man who delivers it." Cheveyo indicated Hiamovi, who nodded graciously. Cheveyo always looked to strengthen Hiamovi's position in these meetings and Hiamovi was appreciative of this.

"We need to get Hiamovi to speak to more tribal gatherings," Cheveyo went on. "If they believe in him they believe in all of us. No one can fault him as a leader when he speaks. No one is a better embodiment of the principles of the UTN. And it's the principles we're founded on that will eventually inspire all the tribes to come together under one banner."

"You won't win the tribes over by just making pretty speeches," said the brave standing by the door. Everyone turned to look at him. He was not the tallest of braves. He was maybe five-foot eight in height, five-nine at a push. He was stocky though, with a powerful upper body and sturdy, muscular legs.

He had no authority to speak at this meeting. Indignant, Hinto was about to reprimand the brave for addressing the council, but Hiamovi raised his hand. He wanted to hear what the brave had to say.

"Principles are all well and good, but only a handful of people will fight and die for their principles," the brave said. "If you want the tribes to stand together side by side with you then you've got to terrify them. You've got to make them think that they, their families and their whole way of life is under threat. They need to believe that the only thing that can protect them from this threat is the UTN. Then they'll do anything to join you."

"You don't found any kind of lasting powerbase on fear," said Cheveyo. "Fear turns to anger and when the people you're leading find out you've mislead them, that anger is turned on you."

"It isn't misleading to say that our lodges and our tribes are under threat," said the brave, his face radiating defiance. "Every day our borders are attacked by one klan or another and our belongings stolen by scavs. You think that threat is going to go away if we all simply hold hands? The stronger we get the more of a target we become. We're not misleading our people when we tell them they ought to be afraid. Fear is what unites us."

For the first time since he'd known Cheveyo, Hiamovi saw anger in his face. "Who are you to address the council in this way?" Cheveyo said. "What right do you have to speak to us of these things? Who do you think you are?"

"I am Ahiga and I have the right of every man who's prepared to fight and die for the principles you're so fond of. Why don't you tell me what right you have to address this council? Because you maintain your power by flattering our leader with honeyed words. That is the Hopi way. A Navajo earns his standing through the truth of his actions."

"How dare you!" Cheveyo sputtered. Ahiga's words had blindsided him. Hiamovi, and the rest of the council were well aware of the long standing feud between Navajo and Hopi. It went back centuries, to when the two tribes were forced onto reservations that bordered one another. There had been many bitter territorial disputes over the centuries. Disputes not even a devastating plague could resolve.

"This is not the place for such divisive talk." Onatah said. "The UTN transcends all tribal disputes and differences. We are all brothers and sisters in the cause."

Ahiga raised his hands in deference. "I beg the council's pardon, I don't want to disrespect you or the UTN. I simply want to exercise my right as a loyal follower to have my voice heard."

"You have no right to be heard by this council," said Cheveyo.

"I have the right of challenge," said Ahiga. "You spoke of principles and their importance to the UTN. Isn't one of our principles that we uphold and honour the customs of all the tribes within our nation?"

"Yes, but no tribe has a custom allowing foot soldiers to slander a council member."

"No," said Ahiga. "The Cheyenne have a custom though,

one that is shared by the Sioux and the Blackfoot. When a member of the tribal council is unfit to hold his seat another member of the tribe can replace him if he beats that council member in a fair contest of wills."

"I am not unfit to be on the council," said Cheveyo. He looked around the rest of the council for support. "This is nonsense, let us end it now."

"Your words prove you are unfit," said Ahiga. "You want us to build a powerbase and defend ourselves with nothing more than speeches. You want to put our leader in constant danger by forcing him to appear out in the open at all times, where any of our enemies could reach him. That's why I'm challenging you for your place on the council."

Cheveyo had the look of one who has just woken to find the world has become a nightmare. He turned to the rest of the council and Hiamovi. "Are you going to let him continue? Do you not see what he is doing?"

Before Hiamovi or the council could respond, Ahiga said: "Hiamovi, your people the Cheyenne have a rite called the Challenge of the Four Arrows. I ask your permission to challenge Cheveyo to this rite."

All eyes turned to Hiamovi. He took a moment to consider the situation. He was impressed by Ahiga's impertinence. He liked the brave's courage in addressing the council so brazenly, in seizing the initiative. Hiamovi had an intuition, as he often had about these matters, that Ahiga would become important to his plans in the future. Cheveyo was an old friend however. Hiamovi had come to depend on the Hopi's wisdom, even if, in this instance, he agreed with Ahiga about Cheveyo's views.

Hiamovi turned to Cheveyo. "Old friend, I do not want to lose your wisdom on this council. I do not want to turn my back on our customs either. So I will allow the challenge with one proviso. Ahiga is not challenging you for your place on the council, just *a* place. If he succeeds he may join his voice to ours. If he fails you will have silenced him."

"And if I refuse?"

"Then you will be a coward," said Ahiga.

Cheveyo's stiffened with indignation. His fate had been sealed.

Somewhere off in the distance, out of the hearing of the rest of the council, Hiamovi caught the sound of a coyote laughing.

CHAPTER THREE

Downtown Laramie had changed a lot since Samuel Colt had last blown through. They'd stopped crucifying non-believers outside the railway station on Superior Court for one thing. The gallows on North Third Street, one of the busiest in Wyoming just a few years ago, seemed to have fallen into disuse too. It looked as though scavs had half dismantled it when Colt and his honour guard drove past. Laramie had done some serious moral back-sliding, Colt was sure of that much.

Same could be said of the Good Shepherds. Time was when they were one of the fiercest, most effective branches of the Neo-Clergy. Raised, like most of the top Klans, from a street gang into part of a ruthless international organisation. When the plague had finished wiping the sinners from God's green earth, the Neo-Clergy had risen like a beacon from the ashes of a dead and corrupt world. In its heyday the Apostolic Church of the Rediscovered Dawn, to give the Neo-Clergy its proper title, had controlled three continents. That was before the forces of Satan had brought it low and killed their leader John-Paul Rohare Baptiste.

Jack Mills ran Wyoming back when the Neo-Clergy were in power. There was a man Colt could do business with. A man who made God something to fear again and had terrified the whole state with His holy name.

Not like Benny Cooper. Benny grinned his shit-kicking grin and offered Colt the semi- automatic. "D'ya wanna have a little fun with 'im, 'fore we finish 'im off?"

Colt looked at the godless wretch on the ground. He was pissing blood from at least twenty wounds and still he begged for his life. He was already on his way to see

Satan. No amount of pleading could stop that.

The man's brothers lay dead at his feet. Their blood congealing on the floor of what used to be Laramie's biggest mall. When the Neo-Clergy took over it became a stockade. Worship of the Almighty Dollar turned to worship of the Lord. Now Benny was in charge, it had turned to worship of idiocy.

Colt declined the offered weapon. "I'm not here for fun."

"Suit y'self," said Benny and put one in the wounded man's gut. He doubled over, trying to scream, but the lack of a stomach wall and the blood in his throat stopped him. He would be dead within the hour.

The entertainment had started soon after Colt and his men arrived. They'd pushed some prisoners into a lower level of the mall and blocked off the walkways so they couldn't get out. Then Benny and his guests had leaned over the balcony of the upper level and picked them off with their rifles.

"We're gonna show Colorado we know how to hold a party," Benny had said with a fool grin on his face.

Colt knew he was just trying to show him how big his dick was now that he'd stepped into Jack Mills' shoes.

"Take these bodies an' hang 'em up in Optimist Park." Benny said. "Let everyone see what happens when I don't get ma tributes."

"But Boss," said one of his lackeys. "We didn't bring these guys in for not paying their tributes."

"Did I ask for your opinion boy?" said Benny, pissed at being corrected in front of his out-of-town guests. "'Cos if I wanna hear it, then I'll tell you what it is." Then, to emphasise this, he smashed his rifle butt into the man's face. "Now git."

"Yeff fir," said the lackey, spitting blood and teeth as he

got to his feet and left.

"Maybe you gentlemen'd like to accompany me to ma office," Benny said and walked towards an armour-plated door in the far wall. Colt joined him and motioned for Simon Peter, his number two, and one other soldier to follow. The rest of Colt's men stood to attention. Dressed in full Neo-Clergy uniform they looked every bit the crack team they were. Not like the bunch of yahoos Benny Cooper had around him.

As they walked down a corridor to what had once been a manager's office, Colt got the measure of Benny. He was around six-five and broad across the shoulders, with long red hair. Benny wouldn't have been allowed it like that when he was in the Neo-Clergy. Nor the cowboy hat and boots he and all his men wore. All ways of showing their independence from the past. That would change soon.

Two other men flanked them as they approached the office. Tom Eastman, head of the Crazy Eight klan from Casper, walked like he knew how to handle himself in a fight. Next to him was Carl Jennings, head of Cheyenne's Lonesome Rancheros Klan. Colt knew Carl of old. He was a pastor's son who had done a tour with the marines before The Cull. They had history in the Neo-Clergy and Colt was prepared to give Carl some latitude. With his buzz cut hair and his sharp angular nose he could have been Simon Peter's brother. They were even the same height. The only thing that distinguished them was the long scar down Carl's left cheek.

Benny showed them into the office and sat in the big leather chair behind the desk. The walls were covered with hunting trophies, weapons and even a pair of severed human hands, mounted on wooden plaque. There wasn't a crucifix or a Bible in sight. Benny was in need of moral education. Colt was just the man to give it.

"Why don't we get down to business?" Benny said, leaning back and putting his feet on the desk. "I think we all know why our friends from Colorado are here."

Colt drew himself up straight. He had not taken the tiny stool he had been offered. It would have put him at a lower height to everyone else, so he remained standing while they lounged.

"I'm not a man to waste words," Colt said. "So I'll come to the point. The whole country's gone to hell since John-Paul Rohare Baptiste died. While he was alive and the Neo-Clergy was strong the people had a chance. There was order. Things got done. Now, wherever you look there's degeneracy, sin and disorder. There's never been a time when the country had more need of the Neo-Clergy. I intend to answer that need. I've been building the organisation back to its old strength. We've taken control of Colorado and New Mexico, as you know. We're also running most of Utah. Now we're ready to welcome Wyoming back into the fold."

Benny, Carl and Tom all exchanged looks. "As all three of you used to be in the Neo-Clergy," Colt went on, "I'm prepared to let you keep control of your Klans. But things have got to change. You'll have to start paying dues and recruiting foot soldiers for central HQ. Full uniform will be worn at all times and daily prayer meetings are compulsory, not just for members but everyone in your territories."

"Well that's mighty generous of you," said Benny. "But y'know, the Neo-Clergy ain't too popular round these parts anymore. What with all that talk about John-Paul drinking kiddie blood and all." Benny was talking about a rumour that had plagued the Neo-Clergy since it had lost its grip on power.

John-Paul Rohare Baptiste was the founder and glorious inspiration for the Apostolic Church of the Rediscovered Dawn. Years after the The Cull had struck down everyone whose blood group wasn't 'O' negative, this one man had miraculously survived the levelling. By the laws of science he should have been dead. The blood in his veins should not have kept pumping through his heart as it was not O-neg. Yet the divine grace of the Lord had kept him, and him alone among all the other people with a different blood group, alive. Kept him alive in these Last Days to lead the Neo-Clergy and save God's people.

Satan was covetous of God's miracle though and he wanted the last of the souls the Lord had left alive. So he struck down John-Paul, scattered the Neo-Clergy and put about the rumour that their leader had survived not through a miracle, but by blood transfusion using blood from the children the Neo-Clergy had taken from their parents to mould into God's future warriors.

"That was a damn lie," said Colt, seething with anger that a former member of the Neo-Clergy could repeat such slander. "John-Paul was a man of God. A walking miracle, kept alive by the blessed grace of the Lord."

"Even so," said Tom. "There's a lot of folks glad to see the back of the Neo-Clergy. And I'm inclined to agree with 'em."

"Which is why we've been forced, by popular pressure mind, to join forces and keep you out of Wyoming," said Benny. "Now we know you gotta lot of men under your command. But we also know you gotta lot of trouble out in Utah. Which is why you're over here recruiting. Together we're more'n a match for whatever you can throw at us. So you best keep out of Wyoming from now on. We've gotten to like things they way they are and we don't want no-one else muscling in on our rackets."

"So that's how things are," said Colt after a long silence.

"That's how things are."

Colt looked at all three men in turn. None of them met his eye. He turned on his heel and marched out of the office. Simon Peter and the soldier followed him.

"You drive careful now," Benny called out as they left.

Colt was mighty pissed. Simon Peter could tell that. Maybe more pissed than he had seen him in a while. He got quiet when he got angry. And that was frightening, Like waiting for a lit fuse to blow.

Simon Peter could feel him seething in the back seat of the SUV as he turned onto Route 287 out of Laramie. Even with his back turned to Colt, Simon Peter could feel his mood, like heat from a furnace. The two foot soldiers sitting either side of him could feel it too. They looked away, watching the road intently.

Wyoming was practically Colt's backyard. It looked bad in front of the other States if he couldn't bring them back into the Neo-Clergy.

Simon Peter knew the only way to get Colt out of his mood was to get him to scheme. He had to be careful how he did it though. "Permission to speak sir."

Colt waited a while before answering. "What do you have to say?"

"Sir, I don't trust those Wyoming boys. I'm fixing to go in there and gun down every one of 'em. But I know you got a smarter way of handling this. I was hoping you might tell me, 'cos otherwise I'm so pissed I'm likely to kill the next inbred local we see. Just to see the look on his stupid face."

"At ease soldier. Don't you worry none about them Wyoming boys. They're going to get theirs."

In the rear view mirror Simon Peter saw Colt crack his knuckles then stroke his bald head and clean shaven chin. This was a good sign, it showed he was thinking. Colt was a big man and when he sat up he made even a roomy vehicle like the SUV seem small.

"I got me a plan for dealing with this, but I want to see you show me some initiative. What do you think I'm gonna do?"

Simon Peter knew this game. He knew how to play dumb and show the right amount of deference. "Well I don't have your experience sir, but I'm guessing that until we can subdue Utah, which ain't anytime soon, we don't have enough troops to take Wyoming back into the fold. So are you planning to cut off their supply lines and starve 'em out?"

"And what supply lines would those be? They grow or scavenge most everything they need right there in Wyoming. Had to since The Cull came down. You're gonna have to do better than that."

"What about sabotage? Are you thinking of guerrilla tactics? Sending in small parties to take out their fuel depots and food stores."

"It'd crossed my mind. There's always the risk of them getting caught though. Could compromise us if they torture the men for intelligence or try and ransom them. Not to mention the excuse it would give them to counter-attack. You ain't doing too good at this."

A light came on in Simon Peter's head. "Maybe you ain't fixing to use force at all."

"Really?"

Simon Peter thought for a minute about the best way to sell his idea. "Maybe you're gonna mount a 'hearts and minds' campaign. Try and win over the people them Wyoming Klan's rule. They seemed to put a lot of stock in how unpopular the Neo-Clergy was. What if that were to change? What if there was – how did Benny Cooper put it? – 'popular pressure', that's it. What if there was too much popular pressure from their own people to keep us out?"

Colt grunted, he was impressed. Before he got a chance to say anything though, Simon Peter lost control of the vehicle.

The back end took off and the wheels left the road. A wave of blistering heat came from behind. Simon Peter saw flames in his rear-view mirror.

He put his head between his knees and clasped his ankles. The front end of the SUV hit the ground and crumpled.

The vehicle fell on its side, the windscreen shattered and covered Simon Peter in shards of glass. He lifted his head and looked into the back seat.

The back windscreen was gone. A piece of flaming metal debris was sticking out the back of one soldier's head. His eyes were vacant. His cap was alight and blood ran out of his nose and mouth.

"Help me get Reverend Colt out." Simon Peter shouted to the other soldier.

"That's alright, I'm fine," Colt said. He pushed the dead soldier aside, kicked the back door open and climbed out. Simon Peter and the other soldier followed him out the wrecked SUV.

Bullets raked the vehicle the minute they were out. They ducked behind it and took shelter. Simon Peter saw that the vehicle behind them – part of their small convoy – was now a flaming mass of twisted metal and burning flesh.

The van that had been riding in front pulled alongside and three soldiers jumped out. "Sir, thank God you're alive," said the first.

"What in hell just happened?" Colt shouted.

"Rocket took out the rear vehicle sir. Came out of nowhere." More gunfire thudded into the vehicles and everyone took cover.

A gang of four motorcyclists tore by, firing Uzis. One of them had a rocket launcher strapped across his back. They must have been hiding just out of sight, waiting to launch this ambush.

Simon Peter pulled out his pistol and unloaded half the clip. The other soldiers followed suit, returning the biker's fire. Simon Peter caught the last rider in the shoulder. The biker jerked backwards and the bike skidded out from under him as he hit the ground with a crunch loud enough to hear above the gun play.

The other riders circled back, just out of range, as their fallen comrade screamed out to them. They charged back towards him, providing cover with their Uzis.

This was not a wise move. Colt had trained his men well, which meant Simon Peter and the surviving soldiers were crack shots.

Someone took out the front tire of the lead bike. The rider went right over the handlebars and smashed into the road. His corpse jerked and spasmed as a torrent of bullets ripped into it.

The second biker caught a bullet full in the face. It cracked his visor and sent his brains flying out of a hole in the back of his helmet. He carried right on past them without stopping and rode straight into the fiery wreck of the burning vehicle. His gas tank exploded as he hit.

The remaining rider turned three-sixty and fled.

"Someone get after him!" Colt shouted.

Without thinking Simon Peter ran over to the rider he had taken down, who was still screaming about his shoulder. Two in the face put a stop to that.

Simon Peter kicked the motorbike into life and jumped on.

He took off after the escaping biker and caught up with him a mile down the road. The man knew how to ride and Simon Peter was only on him because he'd taken a lot of stupid risks. As he began to draw level the rider turned into a side road which led to a wooded copse. Simon Peter followed.

He pulled out his pistol and let off a few shots. The biker zig-zagged across the road and Simon Peter tried for his tires but didn't have any luck.

The rider took his bike off-road and tried to lose Simon Peter by taking sharp turns through the trees. Simon Peter took a gamble on the biker's next turn and drove straight at the point he thought the rider would hit. He was spot on and ploughed straight into him at nearly fifty. At the last minute he leaped and caught hold of the biker around the waist. They went straight into a tree trunk. The biker caught the brunt of the impact. Simon Peter fell backwards and the man landed on him. A sharp pain shot up his spine and he kicked the biker away.

He sprang at the man and tore his helmet off, then punched him twice in the face before he noticed the ribs sticking out of the biker's chest.

"Who sent you?" he screamed. "Who are you working for?"

The man just shook his head and coughed up blood.

Simon Peter punched him a few more times, but the biker couldn't have talked even if he wanted to. Simon Peter was so pissed at him after chasing him all this way that he just walked away and left the man to die slowly. He wasn't going to put the son of a bitch out of his misery.

Half an hour down the interstate he found Colt and the other men. Colt wasn't too pleased when he heard what Simon Peter had to say. He remained ominously silent for about five minutes then said: "We don't need no confirmation. He'll deny it of course, but we know who sent those men to kill us. And he just signed his own death warrant."

CHAPTER FOUR

Linda had never ridden with anyone as irritating as Greaves. For a guy who had survived the worst plague in history he sure was allergic to a lot of things.

Every five minutes he was either taking some pill or sucking on some inhaler. The huge greatcoat he never took off was an Aladdin's cave of pharmaceuticals. It had a million pockets and each one of them rattled with some kind of medication. Shame it stunk worse than a flatulent skunk.

"Ah, New Harmony," he said as they passed a bullet-riddled road sign. "Site of America's only socialist community. Founded in 1825 by Robert Owen."

"Wasn't he a blues singer?"

"A British industrialist actually," said Greaves, missing Linda's bored sarcasm. "It didn't last long. Socialism never caught on in the States. It's one of those European things."

"Like soft cheese and not bathing?"

"Quite."

Wherever they drove he'd come out with these gems, straight out of some 'Big Boy's Book of Facts'. Greaves was a walking almanac. Still, that did prove useful at times. He could scavenge them just about anything with what he knew.

As soon as they hit Indiana, Greaves took them to the waterfront on Lake Michigan. He blew a lot of hot air about how it used to be one of the industrial centres of the world. Then he lead them to an underground fuel depot with enough gas to fuel an army of Berthas. They drove away with enough gas to get them all the way to Montana.

God knows how Greaves knew where all these things were. It was like he never forgot anything he read or heard. He was obviously one of these freakishly intelligent mutant types you hear about. The kind of guy that can only form relationships with cyber-porn. Greaves probably hadn't had his pipe cleaned since the Internet disappeared. No wonder he had to keep swallowing so many pills.

After fuelling up, he had taken them south in search of some cave complex, even though it was miles out of their way. They followed the River Wabash south for a while then headed out on the highway to Kentucky. Greaves directed Linda west as they hit Crawford County. Only then did he tell her they were looking for the Wyandotte Caves.

That was his way of keeping control of everyone. He told them just enough to keep them going where he wanted them to, then found them just what they needed, hidden somewhere no-one knew about.

All except for Anna. Greaves treated her differently, like some bashful kid in the company of royalty. He really tried hard to be gentle with her, this wasn't something he was used to. Not from the way he acted with everyone else. Watching him around Anna was like watching someone who'd read a book on kindness without ever having been shown it.

All Anna did was snivel mostly. Occasionally she'd start praying in that strange 'olde worlde' language she used, sounding like she was a refugee from the *Little House on the Prairie*.

In the two weeks or more that Linda had been travelling with the three of them she hadn't seen Anna do anything to justify Greaves' strange belief that she was going to save humanity. Maybe it was just a little quirk he had.

Like those otherwise normal people who believe their dog controls the weather.

Still, it was an easy job and the rewards seemed to be good. She'd drop Greaves and his little band in Montana, let them save the world or whatever, and make off with her payload.

First Greaves wanted to go exploring caves though.

Cortez was sleeping when the motor-home pulled up. He could drop into a deep sleep for five minutes and wake alert and refreshed, it was a technique he had learned in the jungles of El Salvador during his time in the Mano Blanco.

Cortez had learned many things in the Mano Blanco, like what made a real man. The men he had run with knew what real men were and wasted no time in showing him. Many of them had been part of the paramilitary Organizacion Democratica Nacionalista, or Orden for short, before the government shut it down in '79. This hadn't stopped General Medrano, its founder. He knew how to keep his country in line. He simply streamlined the organisation and turned it into an even more lethal machine: the death squads of the Mano Blanco.

Cortez was just a young hooligan from a coffee plantation when he joined. He was good at hurting people and it didn't worry him. The Mano Blanco hardened him, focused him and taught him everything he'd ever needed to know.

Such as not questioning your employer when he wants to go exploring caves. This was something that the whore did not realise. She knew how to fight he'd give her that, but she didn't know her place or when to keep her mouth shut.

"So," she said as they stood outside a fissure in the rock face that Greaves said was a secret entrance. "You mind telling me why I've got to crawl down this hole in the ground?"

"There are twenty-three miles of passages down there," Greaves told her. "More than half of them were used covertly by the CIA. There is a weapons cache, a Black Ops archive and nearly a quarter of the entire Colombian annual cocaine export hidden down there."

"Well why in hell are we wasting our time chatting?" said Linda and crawled into the hole.

"What about the girl?" Cortez asked Greaves. "It is not safe to leave her alone in the vehicle."

"Go get her. She'll have to come with us."

"The passage splits here. We need to take the left fork. It goes down for a little way then comes out onto a proper walkway."

Linda was glad to hear that last part. She'd crawled nearly half a mile on her hands and knees so far. As she took the left fork Greaves put his hand on her butt. "You might wanna find another hand hold. Or you won't have any hand left to hold it with."

Greaves snatched his hand back and dropped his torch. It was the only one they had. Everything went black for a minute and Linda heard Anna whimper behind them. Then Greaves fumbled the torch back on.

Sure enough they did come out onto a walkway. "Down this way," said Greaves. They followed him through a series of tunnels for about ten minutes until he came to a stop. He bent down and started to mess with what looked like a fuse box. There was a loud clunk and lights came on. "Auxiliary generators still have some juice in them."

They were standing inside a stone corridor lit by strip lights. There were two metal doors in the wall up ahead of them. "This area was specially built," Greaves said. "It's where all the admin was done. We need to get into these offices."

"Is this where the coke is?" Linda said.

Greaves shook his head. "We'll get to that later. This is more important."

Greaves had Cortez shoot off the lock on the first door. Linda could tell he still missed his skeleton key. Behind the door was an office with a few desks and some filing cabinets. Greaves began to turn the room upside down.

"What you looking for?" asked Linda. "Maybe I can help."

"I need to find a certain memory stick. It has a specific serial number on the side."

When they'd checked and re-checked every inch of the room and turned up nothing Cortez shot the lock off the other door. The office behind that was pretty much the same as the last, with the exception of the corpse at the desk.

The first thing that hit Linda was the smell. The body had rotted down to the skeleton in most places. It was still wearing a sharp black suit and most the back of its skull was gone. A rusted pistol sat in its lap. This guy must have known what was going to happen to him when The Cull hit, even down here. So he chose the quick way out.

Greaves didn't even seem to notice the corpse. He just went about his frantic searching. Cortez on the other hand picked up a Zippo lighter from the desk and stared fiercely at it. It was the first time Linda had seen him register anything like an emotion, other than when he was bowing towards Mecca five times a day.

Cortez put the lighter down and began frisking the corpse, going through its pockets until he found a wallet. "You won't find anything there," said Greaves. Cortez ignored him. He stood still, looking at the wallet. Linda couldn't imagine why.

"Thank God," said Greaves bending over a drawer. "It's here."

He stuck the memory stick in his pocket. Linda stepped out into the corridor with Anna to get away from the smell of rotting flesh. Away in the distance she heard footsteps echoing through a stone chamber, and voices calling to each other. Linda looked over at Anna. "Did you hear that?" Anna nodded.

Linda stuck her head back into the office. "Guys, I think we've got company."

"Impossible," said Greaves. "This place was above top secret. I'm the only living person who knows about it."

"Well I just heard voices and footsteps nearby."

"Stay here and look after the girl," Greaves said to Cortez. Then he turned to Linda. "We better go and investigate."

It was John Tannenbaum. *In the name of the Prophet*, thought Cortez. *This is what happened to the son of a bitch.*

He paid little attention to Greaves and Linda as they tooled up and went out into the corridor to search for the intruders. He paid even less to Anna as she crept into the office and hid behind the filing cabinet. Cortez was thinking only of Tannenbaum.

So this is how he ended up. Holed up like a rat in a cave, hiding from the plague. And when he found that he wasn't safe from it miles under the ground, he bit down on his gun barrel like a coward.

When Cortez had realised who the corpse was, he couldn't believe it. A man he never thought he'd see again. A man who had such an impact on his life.

It was the lighter that gave the bastard away. It had been the first thing that caught Cortez's attention when they met all those years ago. '92 had not been the best time for Cortez. The civil war had ended and El Salvador was preparing for its first election in decades. The military chief of staff Colonel Rene Ponce had made sure no-one in the death squads would be brought to trial for what they did. That didn't change the fact that Cortez was out of a job. For years he'd been part of something, had purpose. People had been scared of him. He was powerful.

Then it was all over. He was faced with being a simple shit-kicking peasant again. A know nothing nobody who had to stand in line like everyone else.

He was in a bar getting drunk when he caught sight of the lighter and someone watching him. It was Tannenbaum. The lighter was Marine special issue. Even without it Cortez knew Tannenbaum was American. The American military worked real close with the death squads. They trained them and provided intelligence. Tipping the squads off to which teachers, labour leaders or even priests had leftist sympathies and ought to disappear. Cortez had met a hundred Yankees at that point. He even liked a few.

Tannenbaum approached him with a bottle and a job offer. Seemed he'd been checking out Cortez's credentials and liked what he'd heard. Tannenbaum worked for the CIA, he referred to it as 'The Company.'

Things might have gone quiet in El Salvador but there were a lot of other places in Central America where a man of Cortez's talents might prove useful. His trial run was abducting an American journalist who was getting too close to things she wasn't supposed to know about. He passed with flying colours. No-one ever found the body.

For nearly a decade Cortez ran Black Ops for the Company. He became an expert in torture. They trained him up, but he got so good that soon he was training others.

Then in the new millennium Tannenbaum told him that no one was interested in commies anymore. Marx had had his day. Now it was Mohammed they were worried about. They had a bunch of prisoners being held on non-American soil. That meant they could practise 'enhanced interrogation techniques' on them without worrying too much about the Geneva Convention.

It sounded like another routine assignment. What Cortez didn't know was that his whole life was about to change.

Linda had never seen Greaves so agitated. He was such a control freak. Everything had to be planned out meticulously in advance. Everyone had to be told what to do, but only when the time was right. If anything or anyone deviated from this, then he got mighty antsy.

They were lying down on a ledge that overlooked a central chamber. They'd gotten there by a round-about route that Greaves took to keep them out of sight. They'd passed a stash of high explosives on the way and Linda had even helped herself to a little something when

Greaves wasn't looking. After all, a girl never knew when she might have to kick things off with a bang.

There were stacks and stack of crates in the main chamber. A party of about seven men with torches were tearing off the lids and drooling over the weapons they found inside.

"See Frankie, I told ya," said a scrawny looking guy with a limp. He looked like a scav and most of the fingers on his left hand were missing. "There's caves and caves of this stuff. You've no idea the things I could direct you to."

"Ya done good this time Vinny," said Frankie. He was taller and broader than any of the others. He looked Italian and acted like he was some kind of Klan boss. "I might even let you live when we're through with you."

"Aw come on Frankie. Look at the size of this haul. This has got to make us quits. Way I figure it, you probably owe me now."

Frankie grabbed him by the front of his jacket. "Don't push your luck dickwad." He threw Vinny to the floor and wrinkled his nose? "Jesus you stink. When's the last time you took a bath."

Vinny giggled nervously and waited until Frankie's back was turned before he got up and brushed himself down.

Linda was just about to get up herself when she heard a voice say: "Don't either of you fuckers move!" A shotgun barrel was pointed right at her head and another at Greaves.

Five minutes later they were kneeling in the middle of the chamber in front of Frankie and his boy with their hands on their heads.

"Good thing I sent two men out to case the joint ain't it?" Frankie said. Then he turned to Vinny. "I thought you said no-one else knew about this place."

"They don't," said Vinny, starting to shake. "I swear to God I'm the only one."

"They was armed too boss," said one of the men who'd got the drop on them.

Frankie didn't look happy. "I swear to God Vinny, if you were trying to double cross me."

"No Frankie no. I could never... how could you even think... "

"Cut it out Vinny," said Linda. "The games up. He's on to us. I told you Frankie was too smart.

"Oh, so it all comes out now," said Frankie, smacking Vinny across the face with the back of his hand.

"Frankie, on my mother's grave. I don't know who these people are. I have never seen them before."

Frankie raised his fist. "Still you lie to me, right to my face you lie!"

While Frankie and the rest of them were distracted, Linda stood up and took her hands off her head. "That's enough," she said in a commanding voice. "Now I want all of you to drop your weapons and lie face down on the floor."

Everyone pointed their weapons at her. Frankie was non-plussed. He turned to Linda with a smile of bemusement. "And do ya mind telling me why we'd want to do that?"

Linda lifted her top to reveal the belt of gelignite she was wearing. "'Cos I'll blow everyone of you to hell if you don't."

Cortez heard a scuffle behind him. It was Anna behind the filing cabinet. She was praying. He went over to where she was hiding and bent down. "Are you alright?"

"Are you going to sacrifice me to Satan now?" she said.

Cortez was stunned by the question. "Why do you think I'd want to do that?"

"Well that's who you worship isn't it? That's who you're talking to when you do all that praying on your mat."

Cortez shook his head and laughed. There was something so child-like in the way she asked the question that he couldn't take offence. "No. I abjure Satan and all his works. I worship God, just as you do."

"But don't you hate Jesus?"

Cortez shook his head. "Muslims recognise Jesus as a great prophet. We revere his teachings. We also believe he will return in the last days, transported bodily down from heaven to slay the Anti-Christ at the gate of Ludd in the Holy Land."

It was Anna's turn to look shocked. Cortez recognised that look. He knew what it was like to re-think all your prejudices about Islam. He'd been there himself.

When he first worked for them, Cortez had a lot of respect for the CIA. Without them he'd have been nothing. They killed all that on his last assignment though.

He was transported to a secure facility in the back of a van with no lights and no windows. Not even the guards there were allowed to know its location. The US government wanted full deniability on its existence.

They kept the suspects who were brought to him in cages too small to stand up or sit down in. At first they were just glad to be out of them. Their relief didn't last long once Cortez's got his hands on them. What did seem to last was their inability to tell him anything. No matter how much pain he inflicted.

To begin with Cortez wondered if his paymasters were

testing him. Did they distrust his loyalty? Were they trying to see if he could tell a genuine terrorist from a loudmouthed idiot? The people he had worked with before always knew something, even the nuns and the priests. They could usually call up one tiny bit of information to make the pain stop. The name of a neighbour with sympathies, a deal they'd heard about in the street, anything. The suspects Cortez were sent weren't even aware of what they were supposed to be telling him.

Neither were the officers Cortez reported to. At first they wanted to know about the network of secret underground caves that the suspects used. When Cortez failed to get even a shred of evidence out of his subjects, and when the troops on the ground in Afghanistan also failed to turn up anything, command changed their minds.

Next they wanted to learn everything they could about the suspects' terror cells and how they were organised. Who the suspects reported to, how they were recruited, where they met and what they were planning. When, once again, Cortez was unable to uncover any information of note, the officer in charge starting asking for things on the strangest of whims.

Finally they decided they wanted to create double-agents and to get some of the suspects to turn. They were going to do this by getting the suspects to foreswear their religion and convert to Christianity. Cortez was ordered to get them to turn their back on Islam and accept Jesus as their personal saviour. This was where he met his biggest failure yet.

Given enough pain most people will say and do just about anything you want them to. Including spit on their religious icons and call their god a cock-sucking motherfucker. But not the Muslims Cortez worked on. They would sooner give up their lives than their faith.

Cortez had never come across such conviction and strength of purpose. It actually earned the poor wretches his respect and grudging admiration.

One of the men they were holding was an Imam. A much revered holy man, who was a great inspiration to the other prisoners. If Cortez could break him, the officers reasoned, then the other men would soon fall into line.

Cortez had worked over some tough bastards in his time but no-one had ever held out on him like the Imam did. He was easily into his sixties but he took everything that Cortez did to him and never gave an inch.

Cortez changed tactics. He decided to learn a little something about the Imam's faith, so he could have something to use against him. As he tore off the Imam's finger nails, worked heated knives into his nerve endings and broke the Imam's toe bones to grind together the jagged ends, he questioned the teachings of Islam. Slowly it dawned on Cortez where the Imam got his strength and endurance. It was his faith. Cortez had never seen anything so powerful.

After a few sessions Cortez forgot about the torture altogether and just asked questions, tending to the damage he had earlier inflicted on the Imam. He now came to see the man as wiser, braver and more saintly than anyone else he had ever met. The Imam's words felt the same to Cortez as water feels to a man about to die of thirst. Something ugly, black and misshapen began to come to life inside Cortez. Something he had long thought discarded. His soul.

Finally Cortez asked the Imam how Allah, in all His perfect love for mankind, could allow a man as devout as the Imam to fall into the hands of a person like Cortez. The Imam smiled and said: "Because He knew that you, above all people, needed Him the most. The evil that we do and the harm that befalls us does not come from Allah. We ourselves are responsible for that. The loving grace of redemption, that comes from Allah alone."

Cortez felt something wet run down his cheeks. He thought at first that he must have accidentally cut himself, but when he put his hand to his face he found it was tears. He hadn't cried since he was a child. Now he couldn't stop himself. He had a lifetime's worth of tears to shed over a lifetime's worth of sins.

He fell to his knees in front of the Imam and offered him his knife. When the Imam declined he held the knife to his own throat and offered the Imam his life in recompense for what he had done. The Imam stood slowly, in spite of the pain, and took the knife from Cortez.

He placed his hands on Cortez. "Do you bear witness that there is but one God and his name is Allah?"

"Yes."

"And do you bear witness that the Prophet Mohammed is the messenger of Allah?"

"I do."

The Imam told Cortez to go and shower. Then to leave the compound and to do no more harm to his Muslim brothers.

Cortez stood in the staff shower. The water rarely came out hot, but this time it was ice cold. It didn't matter. Cortez was washing away his former life of sin. The shower was a declaration of faith. He was stepping over a line into a new life. He left the shower and walked out of the compound. No-one bothered to stop him. The world seemed as though it had been created anew. Everything was golden and full of the divine grace of Allah.

Cortez hired a boat and sailed across the Gulf of Mexico. He left it adrift a mile off shore and swam to the coast of Florida. Then he went to pray at the first Mosque he could find. Two weeks later, on the run as an illegal alien, he discovered that although he had never met anyone from a terrorist organisation, he was listed as one of the most wanted members of Al Qaeda.

"Are you out of your mind?" said Greaves, as Linda stretched a line of wire between two crates of high explosive. "Do you know how volatile gelignite is?"

"Not as volatile as seven crazed Klan boys with guns. I merely chose the lesser of two evils."

"It could go off at any moment, you've only got to make the slightest wrong movement." Linda had noticed that Greaves got real sweaty when things didn't go his way. "Will you at least take the belt off?"

"Not until I've set this wire. And me wearing this gelignite was the only thing that got us out of a cave full of pistol packing maniacs intent on killing us."

"Yes, and you left them surrounded by crates of weapons and ammo. It doesn't matter that you took their weapons, any second now they're going to get up off the floor and arm themselves to the teeth. Then who do you think they'll come looking for?"

"So why do you think I haven't taken the gelignite off?" said Linda, answering Greaves' no-brainer with another. "And hold that torch steady. This is even more volatile, especially if I can't see what I'm doing."

She looped the wire around the pin of a grenade and gently pulled it taut. The wire ran across the entrance to the side chamber where they had found all the high explosive. She set it shin high to avoid detection. "We better grab the others and get out of here. We'll be safe if we use that secret entrance you showed us won't we?"

"I doubt it," said Greaves as they ran back to the corridor where Cortez and Anna were waiting in the office. Linda left her belt of gelignite back with the tripwire.

Greaves poked his head round the door of the office and shouted for Cortez and Anna to follow them as quickly as they could. Linda figured that when Frankie and his Klan boys did arm themselves and come looking for them, they'd split up and cover as many tunnels as they could. This meant that one of them was bound to stumble through the side chamber with the explosives and trip the wire. It was just a matter of time.

They had no idea how long they had. As they reached the fissure Linda heard voices approaching in the tunnels below. The Klan boys were gaining on them. What was it about Greaves and Cortez? All she seemed to be doing since she met them was running from people intent on killing her.

They were only a few metres from the entrance when the tripwire set off the grenade, which set off every other high explosive packed in the chamber.

It started as a low rumble vibrating through the tunnel they were crawling along. Then came a searing blast of heat and suddenly the rock around them seemed to be screaming as the tectonic structure of the whole cave system started collapsing.

Everything shook. Linda felt as though she was moving in every direction at once. The seemingly immoveable nature of the stone which surrounded her for miles just melted. Nothing was fixed. Everyone screamed but the din of the earth quaking drowned out the sound.

And finally it ended.

They had all bounced quite a distance back down the fissure. Up ahead of them a cave-in had blocked the entrance. Cortez crawled up towards the rubble and started to move it with his hands. "It's alright. I think I can shift it."

They crawled up to join him, dragging the rubble away. An hour and a half of sweating, cursing and scraping the skin off every knuckle later they finally saw daylight.

It was raining when they crawled out of the cave mouth. By some dumb luck Bertha hadn't been buried by the landslide set off by the explosion. Her armour plating looked sleek and welcoming with the rain running off it. Linda couldn't believe how relieved she was to see her baby.

It might be dumb to get all emotional over a big bus like Bertha but Linda had no family left, no network of friends, no-one she could depend on. Bertha was the one thing she had for protection. And she was a beautiful juggernaut. A dream to handle and a danger to anything that got in her way.

"So," said Linda. "All that coke and all those guns we left down there?"

"Buried," said Greaves. "There's no way we'll get them back. That much explosive would have brought down half the cave system. We're lucky to have gotten out alive after your reckless stunt."

"We wouldn't have gotten out at all without my reckless stunt. I hope your little memory stick was worth risking all our lives."

"And a hell of a lot more," said Greaves patting his pocket. "This is going to show us the way to salvation."

Cortez waited for a moment by the entrance he had cleared in the rubble while the others returned to the vehicle. He was not pleased that they lost such a large haul when the cave collapsed.

The guns and drugs could have been bartered for a lot of things. Greaves seemed to think that they got the most important item though. Cortez trusted he was right.

Cortez was pleased to leave Tannenbaum's desiccated corpse lying down there, covered by the ruins of the Company base. He felt as though a part of his life he deeply regretted was now safely buried and laid to rest.

CHAPTER FIVE

This was not a custom of Cheveyo's people, this was a Cheyenne custom. The ritual was to take place in Cheyenne territory between a Hopi and a Navajo. Such was the blurring of the tribal ways in the days following the Great Purification, as the faithful awaited the Fifth Age of Man.

Cheveyo had been challenged. He had not accepted to save face or defend his territory, the usual reasons a brave faced the challenge of the Four Arrows. Cheveyo had accepted to safeguard the Fifth Age of Man and to win back the soul of his leader. Cheveyo believed Hiamovi was a forebear of Pahanna, the White Brother of Hopi prophecy.

The Hopi, which means people of peace and truth, were considered the record keepers of the Native Americans. Cheveyo had been taught since an infant about the Tiponi, the four sacred stone tablets given to the Hopi by Massauu – the Great Spirit – which contained nine prophecies. When the Chief, who was guardian of the Tiponi, fell into evil ways his two sons stole away with the tablets to protect them. The elder brother walked east towards the rising son and the younger brother, Pahanna – which means White Brother – walked west.

When his father, the corrupt Chief, died, the elder brother returned with his tablets and the prophecies they contained. Everything they foretold came to pass. From the arrival of the white man, and the roads and railways he built, to the great plague that wiped him out. This was the time known as the Great Purification. The prophecies state that the Earth will be purified of the evil ones and two forebears will come forward to bring the people together to welcome the return of Pahanna bearing the lost tablets. This will then bring about the Fifth Age of Man, a time of great peace, prosperity and spiritual awakening.

The prophecies also stated that even after the Great Purification, Pahanna may not return. If man fell back on his old ways of greed, corruption and hunger for power then all would be lost. Cheveyo saw all those qualities in Ahiga, in everything he did and everything he said. What's more he saw how Ahiga's ideas impressed Hiamovi. To keep Hiamovi from squandering his destiny, and to ensure the Fifth Age would come about, Cheveyo had accepted the challenge.

As the sun rose Cheveyo stood by Ahiga's side on a flat plain surrounded by woodland, on a Cheyenne reservation in Montana. Behind them Hiamovi and the inner council of the United Tribal Nations bore witness to the challenge.

The rules were simple. Four arrows are fired and the challengers race to where each arrow lands. The first arrow is fired by a neutral party. Whoever reaches that arrow first will fire the next one.

Before the contest the challengers both choose two sectors of land. They prepare hidden traps and snares within these sectors to catch their opponent out. When one of them reaches an arrow before their opponent, that brave fires the next arrow into their own sector, to lure their opponent into the trap they have prepared. It is a contest of stealth and cunning as much as strength and courage.

Cheveyo said a silent prayer to Massauu, the Great Spirit, as Avonaco, the neutral Cheyenne brave, drew back his bowstring and aimed the first arrow. Cheveyo asked to be as swift as the deer, as wise as the owl and as cunning as Coyote.

Cheveyo and Ahiga leapt forward the minute they heard the bow string twang. Cheveyo had stolen a slight lead on Ahiga by the time the arrow had completed its arc and hit the ground. Although he was probably ten years older than the Navajo, his body was leaner and less heavily muscled, built for speed not combat.

He increased that lead by tiny increments as they advanced on the fallen arrow. There it was, sticking out of the ground by another bow and arrow, where the plain gave way to the woods. With his heart pounding and the air burning his lungs, Cheveyo reached it first. He grabbed the bow, aimed the arrow into his first sector, deep in the woodland, and let it fly.

Ahiga crashed into him as he let the arrow go and held up his hands with a mocking smile as if to say it was an accident. Cheveyo knew it was an attempt to ruin his aim.

Ahiga charged into the woods. Cheveyo followed, content to hang back and stay on his tail so as not to give away the exact location of the arrow. As soon as he could, Cheveyo lost Ahiga and circled round to the safe route he had planned.

Padding quietly through the trees without disturbing the undergrowth he made his way to a small clearing. In the centre stood the trunk of a tall conifer tree. The top part of the tree had been chopped off about fifteen feet from the ground. The arrow Cheveyo fired stuck out of the top, right in the centre of the trunk's rings.

The remaining branches that stuck out of the trunk had been cut back to the length of a few inches to make hand holds. As Cheveyo entered the clearing Ahiga sprang out of the undergrowth and pushed past him, knocking him to the ground.

Ahiga leaped and grabbed hold of the lowest branch, hauling himself up and reaching for higher hand holds. He made his way around the trunk as he got closer to the top and the arrow.

Seconds from the top Ahiga swung himself up to a branch that came away in his hand. He flailed madly and reached out for another handhold. That too came away as did the other branch he was hanging on to. They had been sabotaged to break under his weight.

Ahiga fell and hit the ground in the exact spot that Cheveyo had planned, crashing through a light covering of saplings, twigs and loose dirt into a ten foot pit with sheer earth walls. The fall knocked the air out of him. He tried in vain to climb out but the soil of the walls just crumbled and he slipped back down with every attempt.

Cheveyo grabbed hold of the lower branches and hauled himself up by the safe hand holds that he had carefully memorised. He picked up the bow and the third arrow that were lying next to the second.

"Well help me out then," Ahiga called up to Cheveyo, before he pulled back the string of the bow.

"And let you continue with the challenge? Would that be wise?" There was nothing in the rules that said a challenger should free his opponent from a trap.

"It would be fair and honest. I thought the Hopi were a people of peace and truth. Or is that just a lie you tell, to keep your squaws and their mothers happy?"

"I will let you continue," said Cheveyo. "But not because you call the honour of my people into question. We of the Bear clan have a tale. It concerns a snake and a hare. While the hare was feeding on a root, the snake crawled through the long grass and made ready to pounce. Misfortune struck the snake however and a dead branch fell from a tree, pinning him to the ground.

The snake called out to the hare to use his powerful back legs to kick away the dead branch and free him. The snake promised he'd be so grateful he would never harm another hare. The hare was a kindly soul and instead of running he came to the snake's aid and kicked away the branch, whereupon the freed snake opened his jaws and swallowed the hare whole.

"The hare's soul went to heaven and Massauu the Great Spirit called the hare to him. He asked the hare why he had freed the snake and placed himself in danger. The hare replied that if he had not freed the snake then the sin of murder by neglect would have fallen on his shoulders, and that would have meant not joining the Great Spirit in the afterlife. 'The snake has enjoyed a meal,' the hare said. 'But I will enjoy an eternity with my creator, which is a far greater prize'. For this reason the Great Spirit exults the hare above all other animals. Only the hare was brave enough to do the right thing in spite of the danger he was in."

"A pretty tale," said Ahiga, only half hiding his sneer. "But when are you going to free me?"

Cheveyo drew back the bow and fired the third arrow. Then he swung himself down from the top of the trunk. He tied a vine around the base and lowered it down to Ahiga before sprinting off after the third arrow.

Cheveyo could feel himself flagging as he sprinted towards the copse. His breathing was harder and his limbs felt heavier. He had little energy in reserve and he could hear Ahiga crashing through the trees, gaining on him. He did not sound like he was slowing at all.

He circled round the copse, looking for a side entrance.

The one he had to take to retrieve the arrow without setting off the trap. The arrow had landed just where Cheveyo wanted. He had been practicing the shot for two days before the challenge.

It had hit the top log in what looked like a random pile. There appeared to be only one way to approach the pile. In actual fact the logs had been carefully balanced so that when someone stood in what seemed to be the only spot to remove the arrow and then pulled it free they would trigger the logs to fall. This would release a counterbalance that was holding a wide noose of interwoven vines and ivy in place.

Disguised by the ivy, the other end of the noose had been thrown over a branch and tied to a strong sapling, bent to the ground. When the noose was released the sapling would spring back up and the noose would close about the ankles of whoever grabbed the arrow, yanking them off their feet and leaving them dangling upside down.

Cheveyo trod carefully as he walked towards the arrow, but froze as Ahiga burst into the copse. He assessed his chances of lunging for the arrow. Ahiga didn't seem to see Cheveyo from where he was standing. He shot quick glances around the copse. He looked wary, then left the way he had come in.

This put Cheveyo on guard. He couldn't see or hear anything so he ran for the arrow. He had his hand out to grab it from the pile when a branch smashed into his shins. He fell forward and instinctively pulled his knees up to his chin, crying out with the pain. Cheveyo rolled on to his back and saw Ahiga standing by the log pile, holding the dead branch.

Cheveyo started to stand as Ahiga caught hold of a low branch, pulled himself off the ground and grabbed the arrow. Cheveyo remembered too late where he was now standing. Before he could jump the noose snapped about his ankles. His feet went from under him and he hit the ground face first. He was dragged through the mud and up into the air as the sapling whipped back.

His shins throbbed and his face ached as he flailed around, suspended from the branch.

Ahiga smiled up at him with malevolent satisfaction as he picked up the last bow and arrow. "Not a bad trap Hopi. Shame you didn't have the guts to make it work. You know what gave you away? The vine you threw down to me was the same you used to make that noose. The minute I recognised the vine I knew what your trap was. Your own stupid charity undid you."

"Very clever," said Cheveyo, trying to find what grace and dignity he had left. "Now fire your arrow and cut me down."

"Cut you down?" Ahiga said with a derisive laugh. "Cut you down? What sort of idiot would I be if I cut you down just when I'm about to win?"

"It would be the honourable thing to do."

"Let me tell you something about honour. The Navajo also tell the story of the hare and the snake. Only we have a different ending. The hare is not called before the Great Spirit. His soul is eaten by demons because his actions were neither brave nor wise. He died of stupidity and his offspring have no souls because of it. That is why my people hunt and eat the hare. It is a gift from the Great Spirit. It has no bravery and no soul, therefore killing it is not a sin. And leaving you to hang there is no dishonour."

Ahiga fired the last arrow out of the copse and back on to the plain where they had begun the challenge. Then he flung down the bow and raced after it.

Ahiga was standing with the inner council around the fourth arrow when Cheveyo limped out of the wood and across the plain. He had twisted his ankle when he had eventually freed himself from the noose.

"Join us Cheveyo," said Hiamovi with a conciliatory smile. "In welcoming the newest member of our council."

"I will not," said Cheveyo, desperate to save the UTN from the duplicitous Navajo. "His victory is dishonourable."

"Dishonourable?" said Hiamovi turning to Ahiga. "Is this so?"

Ahiga looked to Cheveyo. "In what way is my victory dishonourable?"

"You know."

"Did I break any rules?"

Cheveyo shook his head. "No but..."

"Then how have I won dishonourably?"

"Through your underhand tactics and your disgraceful conduct, you..."

"Enough," said Hiamovi. "It pains me to say it Cheveyo, but the dishonour seems to be yours. You lost the challenge on fair terms and yet you refuse to gracefully accept the outcome. I am disappointed in you."

"Old friend," said Cheveyo with a hint of pleading in his voice. "Please believe me when I say there is too much at stake to let the UTN fall into the hands of this scurrilous Navajo."

"Please Cheveyo," said the matriarch Onatah. "Accept your defeat with good grace. There is no need to fall back on old grievances between tribes."

"It's not about that," Cheveyo tried to explain.

Hiamovi raised his hand to silence him. "Your conduct is unbecoming to this council. You have forfeited your right to sit with us for four months. After that you will apologise and we will consider readmitting you."

With that the council all turned their backs on him and walked away. Cheveyo's shoulders slumped. His chin touched his chest and the fight drained out of him. Like rain water from a leaky barrel it seemed to run out of him into the dry plain at his feet.

A cold fear filled his stomach as he thought about the coming of the Fifth Age of Man, of all it meant to humanity. A week ago it had never felt closer. Now it couldn't have been further away.

CHAPTER SIX

Colt sat in the boxing ring of the Daniel Ritchie Centre for Sport and Wellness. Once the jewel in the crown of the Denver University campus, and now another part of the head quarters of the resurgent Neo-Clergy.

Colt had moved the Colorado branch of the Clergy into the university soon after the Apostolic Church of the Rediscovered Dawn first rose to power. The arboretum surrounding the campus and its location, seven miles south of downtown made it eminently defendable. The halls of residence made a great barracks and there was plenty of space to administrate a state wide organisation. This was one of the reasons why Colt's branch of the Neo-Clergy had maintained control of Colorado.

Colt didn't spend much time around the boxing ring. His men held regular bouts. It helped them blow off steam. Betting on the matches was a sin however and strictly forbidden. He had chosen it today as the site of an important meeting.

He was alone when Simon Peter walked in and announced that the Prophet had arrived. Colt told him to show the man in. He entered flanked by two of Colt's best men. "Mr Kinnison," said Colt, with a genial smile. "Or should I call you Prophet?"

"You can call me Robert if you like, Mr Colt."

"That's Samuel to you, seeing as we're on first name terms now. Come on in."

The Prophet climbed into the ring. "You didn't bring me all this way to spar did you Samuel?"

"No," said Colt, with a smile. "Though I understand you used to box a little yourself when you were at college. Amateur State champion for a while weren't you, bantam weight division?"

"You've been doing your homework I see. And how about you Samuel, did you ever don the gloves?"

"I was a welterweight, back in reform school. Southpaw as it happens."

"Lost my only fight to a southpaw. Couldn't box clever enough to get around his left hook. Legs just went from under me and I hung up my gloves soon after."

"The Lord had something else in mind for you."

"That He did," said the Prophet. "That He did."

Robert Kinnison smiled a broad smile. He had charm and charisma aplenty, but he carried himself with enough gentle humility that it wasn't overpowering. It was hard not to like or trust him straight off. Colt guessed he was around five-nine in height, in good shape too, with a lean muscular figure that looked like he was in his late twenties and not his late forties. An African American whose grey beard and salt and pepper hair, made him look like a backwoodsman. His weather beaten skin and the calluses on his hands added to this impression.

Kinnison was right about Colt doing his homework too. Colt had done extensive research on the Prophet. His network of informants had been digging up everything they could.

Before The Cull Kinnison had been a ranger at Yellowstone National Park, one of the few African Americans to ever hold the job. He was also a conservationist who taught workshops in back-to-basics wilderness survival and ran a programme to get kids from inner city ghettos out into the forests to explore nature. It was on one such outing that he was caught in a landslide and fell into a coma, a matter of weeks before the Cull tore through the country.

According to rumours, while in the coma his soul

left his body and was called before the Almighty. Upon meeting his creator, Kinnison was charged with bringing all of God's children back into the fold.

Kinnison woke three months later in a hospital in Buffalo, Wyoming. It was full of rotting corpses. He left the hospital and began to round up the survivors, preaching of the visions the Lord had sent him. He gathered together a band of followers and led them out of the city and on a long trek to his beloved Yellowstone, stopping along the way at places like Worland, Powell and Cody to pick up more followers.

Together with his people he formed a commune in the heart of Yellowstone. With his specialist knowledge of survival he was able to keep them alive through the hard winter and, with the visions he had received from the Lord, he was able to sustain their souls. Word spread of his commune and their numbers slowly grew. Kinnison came to be known as 'The Prophet.'

When the Neo-Clergy fell, Wyoming cried out for the word of the Lord, and the Prophet stepped in to fill that need. He travelled to the towns and communities of the survivors, and preached of the prophecies. His followers handed out fresh meat, herbal remedies and animal pelts to those who came to listen. The Prophet's grass-roots following became so large and he became so loved that gangs like the Good Shepherds couldn't suppress or profit from him. The people of Wyoming protected him from the gangs, no matter how great the cost to their own lives. This was why Colt was so anxious to meet him.

"They tell me you have the gift of prophecy Robert," Colt said. "Did you foresee this meeting?"

"Well now, it don't exactly work that way. I don't hold no truck with crystal balls or any of that gypsy nonsense. When the good Lord sees fit to contact me, He don't ʃive me no specifics. He gives me what you might call a ɔroader picture. But to be frank Samuel, I don't need to read no tea leaves to know what you called me here to talk about."

"Is that right? And just what might that be Robert?"

"Well. I hear tell that you're re-building the Apostolic Church of the Rediscovered Dawn."

"You hear right."

"I also hear that you got run out of town when you went to take Wyoming back into the fold. Now the Good Shepherds have formed an alliance with the Crazy Eights and Los Rancheros to keep their former masters out of the State."

"So they can continue their Godless rule? I would have thought as a man of God you'd want to put a stop to that."

"As a man of God I want to save as many souls as I can."

"I'm all about saving souls. I want to drag this country up out of the sewer it's fallen into. I want to put the fear of God back into the hearts of every man woman and child."

"Well now," said the Prophet. "See I've had the great privilege of actually meeting God. And I can tell you from my own personal experience that He ain't nothing to fear. Less, of course, you got sin in your heart."

"Are you insinuating something Robert?"

"There's a lot of blood on your hands Samuel. But is there Jesus in your heart?"

Colt's hands clenched into fists. If any other man had asked him that he would have knocked him to the ground and made sure he never got up again. But there was something about the Prophet's gentle, penetrating stare that seemed to look right into him, leaving him searching for his certainty all of a sudden. Searching to see if Jesus really was there in his heart.

"I don't mean no disrespect by my question Samuel. As I said before it don't take no crystal ball to guess why you've brought me out here. You want me to help you take Wyoming without taking too many lives, 'cos I've got the ear of the people."

"And will you?"

"Well that all depends on what I'd be party to. Now don't get me wrong, I've read my Bible. I know the Lord can be vengeful and, at times, calls upon his followers to exact vengeance. He brought down the walls of Jericho and drowned Pharaoh's army in the Red Sea. Those Good Shepherds and their like, well it wouldn't be the worst thing to happen to Wyoming if they were brought into line. But would the Neo-Clergy be the best people to do that?"

"I can't think of anyone better. We picked this country up off its knees when The Cull hit it. We spread the word of God to every State and beyond."

"There was a lot of fear back in those days. A lot of it was of the Neo-Clergy. You spread the word of God but did you put the love of Jesus in their hearts?"

"Well now maybe I need someone like you for that."

"How do you mean?"

"You can't stop the rebirth of the Apostolic Church of the Rediscovered Dawn Robert."

"Don't reckon I can."

"But maybe you can influence its course. Maybe you can put that love of Jesus in people's hearts. In our organisation's heart."

"I'm listening."

"You ever heard of the Tomorrow Show?"

"I've heard tell of it," said the Prophet. "I never saw

one, but wasn't it the television show the Neo-Clergy used to broadcast?"

"Yes. The only television show to be broadcast anywhere in the Western hemisphere since The Cull happened. Five years we were on the air until Satan cut us off. Turns out my boys came across the group of technicians responsible for running the show. Living as a gang of scavs they were. They reckon that all the hardware and the networks are still in place to get the show up and running again. All it needs is some repairs and a little reconstruction. We're even gonna build a signal booster out by Montana. Thing is though, we don't have no one to present our broadcasts."

"I see," said the Prophet.

"Think of it. If you were the face of the Tomorrow Show, how many people could you reach with word of your prophecies? How many hearts could you fill with the love of Jesus?"

"You make a mighty persuasive case."

Colt grinned, a big knowing grin. Turns out the Prophet had a price after all. He'd worried Colt for a while there, with his probing stare and his heartfelt questions. But now it seemed he could be bought. And that made him a man Colt could do business with.

Colt offered the Prophet his hand. "Do we have a deal Robert?"

"You know Samuel," the Prophet said, pausing before he took Colt's hand. "You asked me if I'd foreseen this meeting. Well the Lord is kind of particular about what he shows me. I wasn't too certain until now that this was what I'd foreseen. But I did see this handshake and it's significance. You're aiming to redeem the souls of an entire broken nation. One soul sits at the centre of all those souls and influences their fate. That's your soul

Samuel. That's the one soul the Lord has sent me here to redeem. If I accept your hand, you have to accept Jesus as your personal saviour."

With that they shook hands and said their goodbyes, leaving Colt to wonder what he'd really bought with his promise to promote the Prophet's preaching.

CHAPTER SEVEN

"We'll be reaching the Big Sioux soon," said Greaves. "Iowa's bordered on two sides by rivers; the Mississippi on the east and the Missouri and the Big Sioux on the west. Just over a hundred years ago this all used to be prairie, probably won't be long before it goes back that way. The grass used to be higher than –"

"Oh for fuck's sake," Linda said slammed her hands against the wheel. "Don't you ever give it a fucking rest? It's like you've got Tourette's or something."

"Tourette's syndrome is a brain disorder characterised by involuntary swearing," said Greaves. "If anyone's exhibiting signs of that it's you."

"There you go again. That's exactly what I'm talking about. It's like it's involuntary with you. Every five minutes, no matter where we are you come out with this constant stream of facts straight out of Ripley's Believe-it-or-Die-of-Boredom. Why don't you tell us something we actually want to know? Like how you know where all this secret government stuff is stashed. Or what you're taking us to Montana for."

Greaves went quiet and stared out of a side window. He was trying to do wounded silence but it came across as more of a sulk. Maybe she'd gone too far. If it was involuntary like she'd said then he probably couldn't help himself, or perhaps it was his twisted idea of small talk. He probably thought they were bonding over a fascinating fact or two about the local geography.

"I'm sorry," Linda said. "I'm just wound a little tight. You've got to admit you're not the safest guys to be around. I've been saving your lives and getting shot at since I met you, and I think the least you could do is give me an explanation of what you're up to."

"You're paid well enough," said Greaves. "I don't see why I need to explain anything."

"You've given me a load of gas for Bertha and a bunch of coins that I can't spend 'cos no-one uses them as currency anymore. Don't think I'm not grateful for the things you've dug up for me, but honestly, your people skills are lousy. If you want me to continue putting my neck on the line you've got to talk to me. And not just about the mating habits of the local wildlife."

"How do I know I can trust you?"

"Because I've saved your scrawny ass enough times and I haven't pulled over and dumped you in the middle of nowhere, in spite of you being the passenger from hell."

Greaves shifted uncomfortably in his seat. Linda changed her tactics. "And what about Anna? Don't you think you owe her an explanation? You drag her out of that cathouse and haul her across half a continent, as if she hasn't been through enough, because you claim she's going to save the world. Yet you haven't got the decency to tell her how she's supposed to do that. Or the rest of us who are supposed to be helping her."

"You're right," said Greaves. "She has been through a lot. She doesn't need to be burdened with anymore unnecessary information."

"Please," said a voice from the back. "Mistress Linda is right. I would be very beholden to you sir, if you would be so kind as to tell me why you think I can save the world."

Linda and Greaves both turned around in surprise. Linda nearly took Bertha off the road. Greaves had no idea how close she'd been to pulling over and throttling him for being so pigheaded. He suddenly got all flustered and bashful as Anna put him on the spot. To be fair to him, it was the most any of them had ever heard her say.

"Well you see, erm Anna, it's that you're..." Greaves swallowed and tried again. "Look, perhaps I better tell you a few facts about my past. As long as that's okay with certain PMT sufferers?"

Linda let that last quip go. She was too interested in what he had to say.

"Before The Cull I was a scientist. I specialised in genetically engineered bio-weaponry and worked for a secret laboratory run by a branch of the shadow government. My employers were above top-secret and answerable to no-one. The work we did was right on the cutting edge of science. Our branch was so far ahead of our contemporaries that few people outside of the lab could comprehend what we were doing."

"What were you doing?" said Linda, hoping he'd get over himself and get on with it.

"We were constructing super-viruses, far deadlier than anything mankind had ever seen. The AB virus that wiped out nine tenths of the population was strictly amateur hour in comparison to what we were working on."

"So what did you do?" said Linda. "Go on, impress us."

"We created many viruses. Some of them so infectious you just had to catch someone's eye to come down with it."

"No way."

"Way," said Greaves, looking very pleased with himself. "We could vary the exact symptoms from person to person and time to the minute the moment they would expire. The holy grail of the whole project was to create a virus that was self-aware. In the decade before The Cull we succeeded.

"The virus was not only a living entity, capable of almost infinite self replication, given enough organisms to infect, it was also unstoppably virulent. What's more, it could mutate to attack the actual DNA of any organism it infected. Nothing could ever develop an immunity to it."

"Let me get this right," said Linda. "You created an intelligent virus?"

"Not intelligent. A virus by its nature can never develop a central nervous system. Therefore it's never going evolve a brain to deal with all that sensory information. Without a brain it can't have proper intelligence. We were able to make it self aware though, thanks to the creation of a biogenic field."

"What's a biogenic field?"

"All multi-cellular life forms emanate a bio-electrical field as a by product of the biochemical energy they use. We were able to prove it was this biogenic field that drives their survival mechanisms and gives them a sense of themselves as separate entities. We went on to create a virus that can generate a unified biogenic field. A virus capable of seeing itself as separate from anything it infects, and of fighting to protect its survival.

"We even solved the problem of intelligence. If the virus was able to interact in a malignant fashion with the DNA of other organisms then it could also interact in a benign way. It could borrow not only the central nervous system of another organism, but also its intelligence. If the host organism were human this would give them direct control over the deadliest weapon ever created. They could choose whoever lived and whoever died anywhere on the planet.

"There were other things we coded into our 'Doomsday Virus'. Things not even our superiors knew about. The

Doomsday Virus would alter the DNA of its human host and keep them alive indefinitely, making them virtually immortal. Not only that but it could grant immortality to anyone they infected by altering their DNA. They would have the power of a god."

"So if this stuff infects you," said Linda. "You become a god right?"

"No. You die. There were so many determinate factors involved in becoming a host to a the virus that the likelihood of anyone being born with all of them was statistically impossible. So we had to genetically engineer a host from scratch. There were many trials and more errors than I dare admit, but eventually we were able to successfully create five human embryos capable of becoming a host to the virus.

"It was at this point that those of us working on the project realised our lives were in danger. The people we worked for thought they had what they wanted and, in order to maintain security, planned to expunge anyone with knowledge of the project. So we took the infants we had created, when they were nine months old and hid them where they wouldn't be found.

"I parted ways with my colleagues after this. Eventually they resolved the issue and most of them resumed working for the shadow government, coming in from the cold they call it. Before they could retrieve any of the child hosts The Cull hit and that was the one variable we could never have accounted for. It never crossed our minds that someone else would unleash a virus that attacked blood groups. That one simple mistake lost us four of the five hosts.

"Only one host had the Diego antigen. The single gene SLC4AI, most commonly found in certain ethnic groups such as Native Americans, that makes them immune to the AB virus that caused The Cull. That host had been placed in an Amish community as a tiny baby."

"Why sir," said Anna. "You're talking about me."

"That's right Anna," said Greaves as though he were congratulating a bright child. "Did you never wonder why you were the only Native American girl growing up in an isolated community?"

"My momma and poppa never spoke about such matters. My poppa did say God had picked me out with a special plan in mind though."

Linda was so wrapped up in the conversation that she nearly missed the turn. A lot of things were starting to make sense, such as why Anna spoke in that quaint, old fashioned manner.

"After The Cull there was only one record of your whereabouts," said Greaves. "I got to it before they did. When the first outbreaks of the AB virus occurred, I realised what was going to happen. I knew it would quickly take out most of the population and I knew what would be valuable in the sort of world that would exist afterwards.

"So as civilisation slowly came to an end I spent every day that I could hacking into classified government databases, not to mention a few private ones. I found out where all the secret stashes were. Our former government and its branches had been stockpiling all kinds of things for years, from weapons to drugs and gold. I tracked down the sites that weren't likely to be looted and I've been living off them ever since.

"I used the same technique to find you Anna. By the time I got to you of course, you weren't there. I've been looking for you ever since. Now that I've finally found you, we need to get to Montana."

"And what, pray tell," said Anna. "Is in Montana?"

"The only surviving strains of the Doomsday Virus. They're in a laboratory run by my former colleagues."

"You mean they survived The Cull?" said Linda. "How the fuck?"

"They are sponsored by an organisation with more resources than the combined former governments of the world," said Greaves, dismissing her. "You don't think a minor thing like the death of nine tenths of the population is going to stop them do you?"

"Sir," said Anna. "I don't hold to understand even half of what you've told us. So forgive me if I have this wrong. But you are saying that I was made by men and not of a mother and father, and that this was done so I could control a disease that could kill everyone left alive?"

"Or make them live forever, its your choice."

"Why, that is the work of the Devil!"

"No Anna, no it's not," said Greaves. "It's the work of science. Don't you see? You could create a new Eden. You could rid the world of all those who want to oppress others and enslave them. You could reward the just with life everlasting. There are enough natural resources left on the planet to turn it into a paradise. One that we could enjoy for all eternity."

There was silence for a long while after this. Linda, Cortez and, especially, Anna simply sat and tried to process everything that Greaves had told them. Tried to comprehend what it meant to their tenuous alliance and the outcome of their journey.

Anna looked more terrified than Linda had ever seen her. She crawled to the back of Bertha and curled up on her bunk. Her frightened prayers could be heard for the rest of the night.

CHAPTER EIGHT

Two miles south of Lame Deer, on the North Cheyenne reservation, Ahiga motioned for them to reign in their horses. They were on a rise covered with Ponderosa pines. To their right and below the Tongue River rolled through the valley. Up ahead of them was the site of a sacred burial ground reserved for Chiefs. It was this that Ahiga had taken Hiamovi and the two other braves to see.

The burial ground was in a clearing on top of the largest hill in the area. Through the binoculars Ahiga handed him, Hiamovi could see there were about a hundred or more white men and women on the hallowed ground. They had already erected makeshift dwellings and seemed to be engaged in constructing a large metal tower.

"Do we know what they're up to?" said Hiamovi.

"They're Neo-Clergy," said Ahiga. "That's some sort of a television transmitter they're building."

"Why was I not told of this sooner? This is happening on my tribal territory."

"You've been travelling great Chief. The affairs of the UTN have demanded all your attention. The Neo-Clergy only appeared a week or so ago. They brought the building materials with them and set to work straight away. This is the first chance we've had to show you."

"I thought both television and the Neo-Clergy were dead."

"They're making a come-back. The Neo-Clergy never lost Colorado, now they're moving out across the south and Mid-West. There are pockets of resistance among the white man, mainly in Utah and Wyoming. Seems not everyone was that happy when they were in charge. They're gaining control of most towns and settlements in Kansas and Nebraska though, mostly without a shot being fired."

"Why are they building a transmitter so far from their territory?"

"They are hoping to restart their television broadcasts," said Ahiga. "I don't know if you ever saw it great Chief, but they used to send out a broadcast called *The Tomorrow Show* for an hour every week. It was a big part of the strength of their organisation. My sources tell me that they hope to use it as a propaganda tool to overcome resistance in areas holding out against them."

"But why are they using our land?"

"Two reasons. First, they're testing us. They want to see how much of a threat we might be in these early days when they're vulnerable to attack, when they don't have the kind of network and resources they used to. My sources also tell me that they don't have the manpower to take Wyoming and North and South Dakota by force, not to mention Montana. With this signal booster they can reach most states west of Wisconsin and Mississippi. As soon as the white man knows about the broadcasts they'll be able to tune in on just about any workable television set, as long as they've got a generator."

"Tell me brother, these sources you mention. I've been hearing mutterings about them. Some of our brothers and sisters are suspicious."

"Great Chief –"

"It's flattering that you want to call me that Ahiga. But most people in the UTN just use my name."

"Doesn't Hiamovi mean Chief of Chiefs in the language of the Tsistsistas?"

"It does," Hiamovi said. He was impressed Ahiga knew the name his people gave themselves. It meant 'like hearted people', Cheyenne came from the Sioux's name for them: Shahiena. "Let us get back to your contacts."

"Great chi... Hiamovi. Many in the UTN have a past they're not proud of, I'm no exception. The fact that you overcame your past was a big part of why I joined, like a lots of members. You showed us how we could be Native Americans and powerful with it. To be proud of our heritage without slinking back to our reservations with our tails between our legs. My contacts come from the days before The Cull. I lived in Boulder. In my teens. I used to run with one of the gangs that formed the Neo-Clergy when they took over Colorado. I know some of the guys involved and from time to time I get in touch. It helps to find out what they're up to."

"And what do they want from you?"

"The same thing, information. I don't give them anything real, that they can use. I just make stuff up that they want to hear."

"How do you know they don't do the same?"

"Because I check everything they tell me," said Ahiga. "I don't bother telling anyone the stuff we can't use. I know these guys, I know how their minds work. So do you Chief."

Hiamovi nodded and turned back to the men and women on the burial ground. Through the binoculars he could see about twelve armed men. They were all wearing a uniform of white robes with a red 'O' on them, which was the Neo-Clergy symbol, and hats that looked like a cross between a beret and religious 'kippah'. These were soldiers.

"They've deliberately chosen a burial ground," said Hiamovi. "They must know we're going to be outraged. Those are the noblest of our ancestors they're desecrating."

"I think they chose that site for it it's height and the

range it'll give the transmitter," said Ahiga. "These men care little for our ways and customs. I don't think it crossed their minds to check if we held this land dear."

"I'm not so sure. Do you think they could be drawing us out? Are they trying to lure us into a trap?"

"I have scouts out combing the surrounding area. None of them have reported reinforcements. I think this is all there is in the way of any troops. They just have those men there to protect what they're doing, not to incite an attack."

"And you think we should attack. Am I right?"

"This is the perfect opportunity to unite the tribes behind the UTN. To show them what a threat the white man is becoming to our way of life. If we let them march onto Cheyenne land and take whatever they want, where are they going to stop? Nothing unites people like a common enemy."

"Or destroys them."

"You're right of course. But only if that enemy is stronger than us. The Neo-Clergy are vulnerable and won't be expecting a full scale retaliation. We could strike a blow for the cause and inspire many to take up arms alongside us. Once they know what a threat the white man's becoming, and once they've seen how bravely we vanquished them, they'll flock to us. They'll have to for their own protection. Nothing brings safety like large numbers."

Hiamovi was silent. So Ahiga pressed his advantage. "I know your people, the Tsistsistas, fought for this land. When all the other tribes were accepting the tiny reservations given them by the white man, you were still fighting. Time and again they tried to take you down, to capture your people and move them back to land they'd designated for you. Time and again you escaped their clutches and beat them back. You forced them to give you this land. That's the only reason there's a Cheyenne reservation in Montana. You beat General Crook, General Custer and the whole of Fort Robinson. It's time for the Cheyenne to show the rest of our people how to hold back the white man again. To finish what our ancestors started and to make this whole land ours once more."

Hiamovi liked what Ahiga had to say. There was undoubted wisdom in his words and this did seem to provide an opportunity to increase their power base. "What the white man does here is an outrage," he said. "Don't think it doesn't sicken me. They will have to be stopped. What did you have in mind?"

"Let me take a hand-picked team of our best braves and make a surgical strike. We'll take out the soldiers, destroy the transmitter and chase the rest of the interlopers off our land."

"Very well. You have my blessing."

Hiamovi signalled to the other braves standing watch to mount up and they all turned to ride back the way the had come.

"This is a great day," said Ahiga.

"Let us hope so," said Hiamovi, turning to take one last look at the burial ground while the others rode ahead. "Let us hope so." He reached out with his soul to feel the comforting hand of the Great Spirit. To ask for His guidance. It wasn't there. It had been some moons now since had last felt the Great Spirit's presence. Or heard the call of a Coyote.

CHAPTER NINE

Colt stood at the foot of the tower and looked up. It wasn't even a quarter finished but it looked impressive. It was going to be the largest working transmitter operating anywhere in the world. It would give them dominion over the hearts and minds of most of America.

"Is there any sign of the Prophet yet?" he asked Simon Peter. Dusk was falling and they were low on rations.

"Sir, our men met his party about ten miles further down along the Tongue River. We know they're coming but the batteries are dead on their radios. Those things are difficult to repair nowadays and even harder to replace."

"Ain't that the truth," said Colt. He looked around the camp at the volunteers helping with the construction. Some of them he knew from Colorado, faithful members of his flock. Most of them he'd never seen before. "That Prophet sure brought us a lot of help didn't he?"

"Seem to be a lot of people anxious to hear his words sir. They're not all from Wyoming neither. Some of them are from Montana too. Prophet's got followers as far as Laurel and Miles City now."

"He's about to have a heap more. More importantly, so are we."

"They're proving useful with the construction sir. We couldn't have got this far without their sacrifice."

"They're going to sacrifice a good deal more yet and prove a powerful sight more useful." They both smiled. Simon Peter was a stand up guy. One that could be trusted. He caught the meaning of Colt's words straight away.

There was a cheer from the borders of the camp. Everyone stopped and turned to look, dropping their tools to crowd around the Prophet and his party as they entered the camp. Simon Peter and Colt exchanged looks and raised their eyebrows.

The Prophet's party were carrying two freshly killed deer, pheasants and even chickens. Colt felt himself drooling as they were taken off to be butchered and the fire pits for the spits were dug.

The crowds of volunteers flocked around the Prophet. All of them wanting to shake his hand or simply touch his clothes. The Prophet just grinned and dealt with the attention far better than Colt would have.

Colt didn't bother to approach the Prophet. He let the man come to him. He wanted the people in the camp to understand the hierarchy.

The Prophet pushed his way through crowd and walked up to Colt. "Good to see you again Samuel."

"And you Robert." Colt shook the Prophet's hand.

"That's a mighty impressive job you've done on the tower. Ahead of schedule so I hear."

"Couldn't have done it without your fan base here. You sure know how to raise a crowd of people."

"Ah now, that ain't my doing. These are the last days Samuel and people are hungry for the truth. The words of Jesus, well they're just about the most beautiful things anyone has ever said. They remind us that no matter how low a man sinks, no matter how far he's fallen, God's love is still there with him, waiting to lift him up soon as he asks. What you see here today, that's God's love in action."

"So long as it don't form no union, it sounds good to me."

The Prophet laughed, took off his hat and mopped his brow. "If you'll excuse me, I've got a cook-out to attend to."

"Knock yourself out."

The Prophet replaced his hat and tipped it to Colt as a sign of respect before leaving to busy himself with the evening meal.

"There'll be more singing and clapping this evening then," said Simon Peter. "And a whole shitload of hymns." Colt looked sternly at him. He swallowed hard. "Don't get me wrong now sir. I love God and I love my country, but there's a limit to the amount of hallelujah's a decent man can stand."

"At ease man. Let 'em have their fun. They won't have much to sing about soon. Walk with me," he said to Simon Peter as he strode away from the camp into the surrounding woods. Colt looked over at two of his men, Fitch and Golding. Fitch, the tallest of the two, had a lean and muscular frame, a shaved head and a moustache Colt didn't care much for. Golding was carrying a lot more fat, but it didn't slow him down and he was dangerous in a fight. Both of them knew how to get things done, that's why Colt used them

They were lounging against some logs and leapt to their feet as soon as they saw Colt. He signalled for them to follow him.

Colt looked at the setting sun's rays as they broke through the pine trees. "You know boys, God couldn't have picked a more beautiful spot for us to start our campaign. It's a shame them Injuns have been desecrating it with their heathen rituals for so long."

"They'll get theirs soon enough," said Fitch in a low growl.

"That they will," said Colt. He looked the wood over to make certain none of the pilgrims were around to hear them. Then he turned to address the three men. "Did you speak to that Injun you've got on a leash?"

Fitch nodded. "Tom Lightfoot you mean? He was a

banger with the 57th Street Gang, back before The Cull, same as me and Golding. Mean son of a bitch too. When the dying started he upped and went back to his own people, started calling himself Ahiga. Rides with this bunch by the name of UTN now."

"United Tribal Nations," said Simon Peter. "They're like to cause us a mess of trouble soon."

"Not if we play it smart," Colt said. "Fact is, they could prove mighty useful." He turned to Fitch and Golding. "So your man on the inside. Is he down with the program?"

"Oh yeah," said Fitch. "We still got some shit on him. He's our pet redskin. He's going to attack at dawn three days from now. Soon as the Prophet's gone."

"Leave a skeleton crew guarding the camp. Have the rest of the men and the technicians fall back with the Prophet's party. When the Injuns are done have them roll in and sort out any survivors."

"Will the tower be safe sir?" said Simon Peter. "These redskins won't do it any damage will they?"

"I doubt they have the resources."

The sun disappeared and dusk threw the woods into shadow. The smell of roasting meat wafted over from the camp. In the deepening gloom Colt felt his stomach growl.

"The love of God in action," he muttered to himself with a wry smile and wandered back to the gathering.

CHAPTER TEN

It started in her dreams.

Anna was at a barn raising. She'd come in her parents' buggy. Her poppa was the community's master carpenter and could have built them the finest buggy in the whole settlement, but it was a sin to store up and possess fine things for yourself when your brother's and sisters in God hadn't any. So poppa built them a buggy no better than anyone else had. For God made all men humble in the end and poppa's gifts were for the whole community, not just his family.

Anna was helping her momma and the other women prepare the food for the noon day meal. The women were chattering about who was courting whom and who had been seen riding home in whose buggy after the Sunday evening hymn singings. There was a lot of concern for poor Katy Lapp whose third child had been taken ill and wasn't expected to last the summer.

Anna kept glancing over at poppa who was overseeing the raising. She knew that pride was a sin but she was so proud of him and how clever he was. They had been there since daybreak and already they had the frame built. Come evening the Beilers would have a brand new barn for storing their tobacco crop. No-one in the community used the tobacco themselves, that would be worldly and would lead them into sin. The tobacco was grown for sale to the outsiders.

Anna shuddered when she thought of the outsiders. They lived in a world full of so many traps, built by Satan to keep them from God. Anna had never seen an outsider and never wanted to.

Except for when she was in chains, like the Israelites

in Babylon. And an outsider was inside her. And it hurt so bad. And he just laughed when she cried and begged Jesus to stop it all. And he pushed harder and deeper into her...

And...

And...

And she was peeling carrots for the pot. She put down the knife and started shaking, for Satan must surely have sent her a vision. It was because her thoughts had strayed from righteousness to the ways of the outsiders. She had let down her guard and Satan had slipped in.

But the pain had seemed so familiar. As though the moment had a hook inside her soul and was tugging her back to a memory of loss and degradation. She had to escape it. She looked to her poppa. Her kind and gentle poppa who was her rock and her protector.

He was nowhere to be seen. She ran to the barn which was suddenly finished, except it wasn't a barn anymore. It was a building that shouldn't be anywhere on the settlement. A building where she had been held prisoner.

What was the Pleasuredrome doing on the settlement? Where had the community gone? Why wouldn't her legs work properly and let her run after them?

And there were angels in the sky.

And there were demons coming out of the Pleasuredrome, all wearing the face of Mr Greaves. Mr Greaves, heavenly Lord, what was he doing on the settlement?

The angels in the sky started to call to her. They were mighty pretty. They looked like the fallen woman Linda, who talked with such a dirty mouth. But they were angels and filled with the grace of the Lord.

The demons called to her too. Neither of them called out loud. They spoke directly to her body and her soul, as though she could only hear their call in the pit of her stomach and the marrow of her bones. They pained her and they transported her into ecstasy with their calls. She knew not if it was the angels' or demons' calls that transported her and she feared the truth.

Anna reached up her arms to the angels, and she tried to call back to them but her mouth wouldn't open. She tried.

And she tried.

And...

And she was sitting up in her bunk, drenched in sweat, inside the fallen woman's motorised vehicle. She had been dreaming. Sweet blood of Christ it was only a dream.

Then Anna felt an unbearable pang of loss as the memories of the first part of the dream came back to her and she remembered that she would never see her momma, her poppa or any members of the community again.

It was the dead of night but Anna couldn't get back to sleep. She looked around the sleeping area. Mr Cortez was sleeping on the floor under a blanket. He had been kind to her of late. She prayed often that his soul would be saved from enslavement to the devil called Mohammed. Even still, she fetched him his mat when he stopped to pray five times a day. His beard reminded her of the men of her community. Except that they were forbidden to have moustaches because military men wear moustaches.

Cortez had told her that God and the entity Allah, to which he prayed, were one and the same. She wasn't sure if that wasn't simply the dissembling of Satan the arch liar, but she hoped that it wasn't.

Cortez told her he had once been a bad man. He had hurt people without caring about it. Then Allah had interceded and showed him the way. She still held out hope that he could be saved.

Anna lay back down and wondered if she could sleep again tonight. Then she heard the call again, just like in the dream. Only this time she wasn't asleep. Merciful God, she was wide awake but she could hear the call.

It was stronger this time. There were no angels or demons yet she could feel the call pulling at her whole being. She sat upright. No, she was pulled upright, like a puppet. The power of the call was so great it was moving her body and she couldn't stop it.

Anna's heart beat faster and her stomach lurched. What if she had become infested by some demon? What if consorting with heathens and helping them in their prayers had opened her up for possession? Could Lucifer now control her every action?

The call got stronger and Anna felt her body respond with a deep yearning. As though it had waited all her life for this. Maybe this wasn't the work of the Dark Lord. Maybe she was being called by God.

Anna knew she had to get out of the vehicle and away from the others. She climbed quietly off her bunk and reached for her clothes. Mr Greaves had bartered her a selection of frocks and under garments about a month ago.

He tried so hard to be nice and she knew it didn't come easy to him. She couldn't help but find him deeply unsettling though, there was just something about him that made her flesh creep. He believed the strangest things about her. He wanted her to catch some disease so she could save the world and make everybody live forever.

Anna didn't understand a word of what Greaves spoke about most of the time. When he told her she was really born in a laboratory, and made by the worldly crafts of scientists as a sort of a bride for a virus, she became so afraid and confused she couldn't think. All Anna could do was pray for days and days, asking guidance.

The call hit Anna again, washing over her like a wave. It was so strong that she found herself outside in the dark with no memory of having left the vehicle. The call was inside her, tugging at her. It was under her skin whispering to her flesh.

It was pitch dark outside. Anna had no shoes and no will of her own.

It was Cortez that woke Linda. The big guy was up and on his feet before she'd even blinked the sleep from her eyes.

"What's up?" she croaked, wishing she had a cigarette and a shot of bourbon. "What's happening?"

"Anna is not in her bed."

Greaves fumbled with his glasses and nearly fell out of his bunk. "Are you sure?" he said.

"See for yourself," Cortez pointed to her bunk. "I woke up when I heard the door shut. There's no sign of her anywhere."

"Where's she gone?" Greaves said. "Why has she left?"

"Who knows," said Linda. "Maybe the john's backed up. What are you so worked up about?"

"We're out in the wilds of Nebraska," Greaves said, getting all antsy. "We don't know this territory. We don't know what's out there. We've no idea what kind of danger she's in."

"You're the walking encyclopaedia," said Linda. "I thought you'd memorised every square inch of the USA."

"I'll go and look for her." Cortez said. "She is probably close by."

He left Bertha and Linda caught Greaves scoping her butt. She realised she hadn't dressed yet. All she had on was a slip and a pair of panties. "Hold that thought," she said with a smile. "You might need it next time you're alone with a box of tissues."

Greaves pulled a face and turned away. The pills in his pockets rattled with agitation.

Linda got dressed and Cortez came back inside. "She isn't anywhere nearby. It's dark but I checked everywhere."

"Listen," said Linda. "I'll go look for her okay? She can't have gotten that far."

"How come you want to go?" said Cortez. "Don't you want to stay here and look after your vehicle, seeing as it means so much to you?"

"What and stay locked up with encyclopaedia boy? I don't think so."

"It's pitch black out there," said Greaves. "How are you going to find her? What if you get into trouble?"

"There's a little something I've been saving for just such an occasion." Linda opened a cupboard and pulled out a reinforced steel trunk. Unlocking it, she took out a hunting rifle with telescopic sights, some ammo and a pair of night vision goggles.

"You didn't tell us about those," said Greaves.

"Hey, a girl's gotta have a few secrets, right?" Linda also grabbed a snub nosed pistol and a large hunting knife, just in case. Once she was safely tooled up she took off into the night.

Linda had parked Bertha on an old picnic site near a river that, according to Greaves, was called Dismal – it looked it too. Still you never could tell when it came to names. The road signs a few miles back said: 'Welcome to

Hooker County', so Linda thought she'd be right at home. Shows you how wrong you can be.

There was dense woodland either side of the site where Bertha was parked. A small road ran by it and on the other side was a steep rise that was also wooded and seemed to go up quite a ways.

Linda slipped on the night vision goggles and shapes appeared out of the dark. The world suddenly looked green and phosphorescent, like she was in an old computer game. She started to look for any kind of tracks Anna might have made. For a second she felt thirteen again, out with her father hunting game on the shores of the Tionesta Lake.

That was before she had found out what a motherfucker her father was. Back then she was desperate for his attention.

Her brother wasn't interested in their father's passion for hunting, so Linda pestered and pestered him to bring her along. Eventually he agreed. He taught Linda how to shoot, how to handle knives and how to track all kinds of animals.

Those were the happiest memories she had of him, before she discovered drugs and boys. And before she found out about the three mistresses he bankrolled.

Linda scanned the ground for footprints. It wasn't easy in the dark, but it wasn't impossible either. Anna wasn't wearing shoes. Linda could tell this because she'd kept to the softer earth. This meant she was more likely to leave tracks, but the tracks would be less distinct than the tread mark of a shoe.

The tracks led up to the road and stopped. It took Linda a while to pick them up again, but it was fairly straight forward once she did. They started again on the rise. Anna wasn't trying to cover her trail so she wasn't too hard to follow. Whenever the foot prints disappeared Linda looked for bent or broken branches and strands of hair or fabric caught on a twig. These were more difficult to see in the goggles' monochrome glare.

There didn't seem to be any logic to Anna's movements. Linda wondered if she might be sleep walking. Her trail led all over the place. Eventually it came out at the top of the rise in a clearing that overlooked the picnic site where Bertha was parked.

Anna was pacing backwards and forwards muttering to herself in her weird accent, which sounded half American and half Dutch. She looked startled when Linda walked into the clearing, like a little rabbit caught in a juggernaut's headlights. Linda realised she must look pretty scary to someone who had never seen night vision goggles, so she took them off.

"What the hell are you doing out here? I've been following your trail across the whole hillside."

"I'm mighty sorry to have put you to any trouble," Anna said. "I've been praying to the Lord for guidance."

"Oh really? Well next time you needing guiding use a compass like the rest of us."

Anna just blinked at her. Linda realised the poor kid probably had no idea what she was talking about. She felt a sudden surge of sympathy. "Look, you can't just take off like that without telling anyone where you're going. What are you playing at?"

Anna hung her head. She looked like a scolded school girl. "I'm sorry. I wasn't aiming to be a vexation to nobody. It's just that, well, do you know what it's like when you feel like you hear a calling, but not with your ears, and suddenly you aren't the one who's in charge of your body and you've just got to keep on walking until you're told not to?"

"Well, now you come to mention it," said Linda. "I haven't the faintest idea what you're talking about." The minute she saw the dejected look on Anna's face, she regretted being so flippant. "So like, you're hearing voices and stuff? Is that it?"

"No, not voices strictly. It was like some kind of calling that woke me up and just took over my body. I thought at first it was the Devil come to claim me for his own. But then I began to hope it was the Lord calling me to the top of the mountain to take me away from all my troubles. Then when I walked a ways up here I knowed it for what it truly was."

"Indigestion?"

"No, it was that disease that Mr Greaves keeps a harping on about."

"Really? So like, that shit's for real then?"

"I'll thank you kindly not to cuss please."

"Well excuse me! You can't blame a girl for being surprised though. I mean, we all know that Greaves has got some kind of weird computer brain, but a lot of the stuff he comes out with, it's kinda out there don't you think?"

"I'm sorry, I'm afraid I don't follow what you're saying Mistress Linda. He comes out with what stuff where?"

Linda felt like she was talking to someone from another century. "I mean the things he says, they're a bit hard to believe."

"Oh yes. I was afraid to believe them, mighty afraid. I think his so called science is the work of Lucifer. Then I felt this – how does he call it? – Doomsday Virus calling to me."

"What? All the way from Montana? That's more than two States away. How can that happen?"

"I do not know Mistress Linda," said Anna, her eyes

filling with tears. "But it knows I am coming. It's alive, it is truly alive and it's waiting for me. And I'm scared." She broke down, her whole body heaving with sobs like a little lost girl. "I am so, so scared."

Linda didn't often feel compassion. It made you vulnerable. Compassion was a luxury from another time and another life. She was a survivor. She dropped whatever endangered her without a thought. She'd let her compassion go without mourning its passing. Until now, standing on a hillside as a full moon came out from behind the clouds.

This fragile woman had clung on to her dignity and her beliefs in the face of unimaginable abuse. And now the only certainty in her life, the very rock to which she had clung, was crumbling away. Thanks to men like Greaves with their test tubes and their theories. They had raped her all over again, shattering everything she held sacred.

Linda put down the rifle, took off her jacket and draped it over Anna's shoulders. Anna shivered and Linda pulled her close, then she too started to cry. For a stinking world that had started out as a piece of shit and just kept getting worse. For every two bit, lousy bastard who had ever paid to shoot his load inside her. Fuck the lot of them, she thought and gave in to her estranged compassion.

The moon was high when the girls finally stopped crying. They stepped away from each another, awkward at the unexpected intimacy. Linda wiped her nose on the back of her hand. "Listen," she said. "We need to get back. You know what an old woman Greaves is."

Anna smiled. "Come now, that is an insult – to old women."

A joke. A smile and a joke. Linda had never seen her do either before. Anna was suddenly, and quite surprisingly, beautiful.

From where she stood on the rise, Linda could make out Bertha way below them. "I think I can work out an easier route down the hill," she said. She bent to pick up her rifle and scanned the terrain.

Something caught her eye. Was that a movement near Bertha or had she imagined it? She peered hard. She hadn't imagined it. Something, no someone, was moving around Bertha, several someones in fact.

Linda brought the sights of the rifle up to her eye and took a closer look. There were two men crouching next to Bertha's fuel tank, siphoning off her gas. Linda drew a bead on both of them, to make certain she had them in her sights, then she scanned the surrounding area to see if they were alone. She spotted at least four others at the perimeter of the site. From the confident way they moved there was likely to be more of them nearby.

It must be a gang of raiders. Linda had no idea there was anyone in the whole county. They'd stopped at a small town called Mullen a few miles up the road, to see what they could scavenge. The place had been picked clean, nothing around except for a few skeletons. That was why they'd chosen to stop just up the road. The raiders were probably passing through themselves.

Linda only had a clear shot at the two men by Bertha's fuel tank, but she didn't dare fire in case she sent the gas up.

"Is there trouble Mistress Linda?"

Linda shushed Anna and waited for the men to finish.

When the two had filled their container they started to lug it back to the woods. Linda got the taller of the two raiders in her sights. Slowly she emptied her lungs, waited till her heart beat was regular and squeezed the trigger.

It was a perfect head shot. Daddy would have been proud. The bullet went clean through his right temple and took the left side of his head with it. Brains and blood burst out of his shattered cranium, framing it in a crimson halo. The man crumpled.

The second raider leaped with shock. He dropped the container and stared wildly around. He started to fumble in his belt for what looked, at Linda's range, like a Colt .45. He never got it out. Linda had already made the shot and put two in his chest.

He jerked backwards and splashed down into a spreading pool of his own blood.

Bertha's passenger door flew open and Cortez charged out. Bullets smashed into the ground around him and ricocheted of the side of the truck. He turned and ran back for cover. Cortez slammed the door and the shutters went down, protecting the windows.

The armour plating would repel all but the highest calibre bullets. Greaves and Cortez were safe inside for the moment, but they were sitting ducks. They couldn't go anywhere with an empty gas tank and they couldn't see more than a few yards beyond Bertha in the moonlight.

They could use the headlights but that just made them more of a target. Chances were the raiders knew this terrain better than any of them. All they could do was sit tight till dawn.

Linda meanwhile could provide covering fire, picking off any of the raiders who might try and attack. If she was careful, night and the cover of the trees would stop them from making her position.

She paced around the edge of the bluff, looking for the best sight lines. She picked three separate spots that would allow her to cover the area surrounding Bertha. Then it was just a matter of waiting for the sun to rise.

"Please, Mistress Linda," said Anna. "You're frightening me. Whatever is the matter and what are you shooting at?"

Linda looked over at her. The poor girl looked more scared than ever. She was shaking while gnawing on her thumb.

"It's okay. Everything's going to be fine. There's a few men prowling round Bertha. Raiders who were trying to steal her gas and anything else they could get their hands on. I took care of a couple of them but Greaves and Cortez can't do much to defend themselves while it's still dark. Looks like we're going to be here for a while. Might as well make ourselves comfortable."

"Took care of... you mean you killed them?" Anna looked horrified. "That's a sin. That means... "

"I'm going straight to hell. Pretty much where I was bound anyway."

"You shouldn't joke so Mistress Linda. We are on this Earth but a short time. Your soul will be tortured in hell for eternity."

"Well it can't be a lot worse down there than it is here at present. Fact is, things have got so bad here who's to say we haven't all died and gone to Hell already? Maybe Hell's just opened up and annexed the Earth and everyone left on it."

Anna was silent for a time while Linda scoped the trees surrounding Bertha through her rifle sights. "Perhaps it is a sin," said Anna, in a quiet voice. "But I must confess I have wondered similar things myself, many times."

"I think lots of people have. I'm no expert on these matters, but I don't think that's a sin. It's just hard to believe in a better tomorrow when all you dream about is yesterday and what you fear most is what you'll wake up to tomorrow."

"But you've got to believe. Why, not to believe, that's the worst sin of all. Not because you cheat God, but because you cheat yourself. Without faith you can't be redeemed and without redemption there isn't any possibility of hope."

"Wait a minute," said Linda, scanning the trees below. "You just said you thought you were in Hell. Where's your redemption there?"

"There isn't any redemption in Hell and that's how I know we're not in Hell. In spite of all my wondering, I still believe. That's not been taken away from me. I can still be redeemed. I can still hope. In Hell there isn't any hope, because you're never going to get redeemed, there's nothing to believe in. And in a way, Mistress Linda, maybe you are right. Maybe Hell has annexed, as you would have it, a bit of this world. Because I just realised you don't have to die to go to Hell. All you have to do is stop believing. Give up all hope and you are already there."

Linda caught a movement in the trees. A pair of legs running. Nothing she could fix on or aim at. They were planning something, but what? "You mean after all that stuff you've just been through with the Doomsday Virus, you still believe?"

"Even though I know I was made by men, using Lucifer's tools, to be offered up to some disease that can take over the world, I still have my faith. So I'm not in Hell. I have being praying to the Lord for guidance and He has delivered it unto me."

"Good for Him. Let's hope He delivers us from this shit we're up to our necks in."

"Your language is not becoming. And you said

everything was going to be fine."

"Yeah, well, that was before you got all religious on me. Now I'm the one needs reassuring."

"You're going to kill again aren't you?"

"Only so we can stay alive. I know you might be bound for heaven, but right now, if I die, I haven't got the slightest hope of being redeemed. So I'm fighting for my body and my soul. Anyway I didn't think you Christians were against killing. Isn't God always striking people down and stuff?"

"I cannot speak for other Christians. I was raised in an Amish community, we are committed to a lifestyle of peace and non-violence. We don't believe you can positively resolve any situation using violence."

"Which is cute," said Linda. "Until someone's busting to pop a cap in your butt. Then it kinda loses its appeal, 'cos it seldom works."

"We don't choose non-violence because it always works. We choose it because of our commitment to Jesus Christ and the truths that he preached."

There, down in the shadows, Linda almost missed him. One of the raiders was creeping up on Bertha from behind. It was a blind spot from inside. The raider was carrying something. She was too far away to tell what it was. It could be a grenade, or it could be a smoke canister.

That's right, thought Linda. *Just a little further and you'll be in the moonlight.* The raider took two more steps and she had a clear aim. She put two in his gut. He was knocked to the floor with his hands on his midriff. Blood pissed through his fingers as he tried to keep his stomach wall from falling out.

The raider was screaming in pain and calling out to his comrades. Linda could feel Anna wince without looking at her. Just as Linda hoped, his cries drew one of his companions out. The man bent down to pick up whatever the fallen raider had dropped. Linda caught him at exactly the right angle. The bullet tore through the top of his head and out the back of his neck, severing the spinal column. Death was instantaneous.

Unlike the poor bastard lying on the ground. He was writhing and jerking and calling out: "Jesus fucking Christ help me you mother-fucker help me! Oh God you cunt, you cunt no, No, NO!"

"Speaking of other Christians," said Linda. "I bet that's not a prayer you Amish often used."

Linda felt Anna's hand on her shoulder. "Please, he doesn't have to suffer so," she said and Linda could tell from her voice how much strength she was summoning to remain calm and gentle. "Killing is wrong, but this is worse. I know you can put a stop to it." She was right. No-one else was coming to help him. Linda was just torturing the wretch out of spite. Two more bullets answered the man's prayers.

"Mistress Linda, do not think me impertinent, but I have need to ask you a question."

"Shoot," said Linda. Then remembered Anna would not pick up the irony. "I mean go ahead, ask."

"Do you hate your father?"

"Doesn't everyone?"

"No. I loved mine very much."

"Well you're the lucky one. Mine was a bastard. What's that got to do with anything?"

"There was a girl in my community, who shunned all her brothers. No matter how respectfully and piously they treated her. From the oldest to the very youngest, she turned from them all. Hatred burned in her bosom for every man. Her father hanged himself in his own barn. This is unusual within our community. Later we discovered it was through guilt. His wife had died some years before and he had done his daughter a great... disservice."

"Really?" said Linda. "Well my father never did me that 'disservice'. Not physically anyway. Mentally that's another matter. See, when I was a little girl I was like the son he always wanted. The son my brother refused to be. It was my father who taught me to shoot so well. We used to go on long hunting trips together. Then I became a young woman and he couldn't help noticing. Nothing had changed for me, but it had for him. He didn't like spending nights alone in a cabin with me. Not out in the middle of nowhere. So suddenly he just freezes me out, doesn't want to know. Even sent me away to a private school. I mean how extreme is that?

"This all suited my mom fine, of course. All she did all day was hang out with her country club friends, getting drunk on Martinis and high on whatever pills her doctor prescribed. She hated not having a daughter she could dress up and parade around at her society functions. She hated that I liked my father more than her. She hated most things. Top of her list were common folk and my father. Didn't hate the money he made though.

"Anyway, I get good grades at this exclusive school, so I figure I deserve to party a little. Some of the other girls from my school used to hang out at this bar called Nabokov's. Named after an author who wrote this book called Lolita, you probably won't have heard of it, it's about an older guy who falls for this young girl. Anyway that was the whole point of the joint. It was basically a place where older guys with money could, you know, cruise younger girls, buy them expensive drinks and maybe take them home." Linda looked up from her sights and glanced over at Anna. "You're not following any of this are you?"

Anna's brow furrowed. "I got a little lost when you mentioned bars of Nabokov. Is this a type of metal?"

"No," said Linda taking a deep breath. "A bar is a place where people meet to drink alcohol, to talk and maybe take someone back to their home."

"To marry?"

"Not exactly. To do what married people do, but without the same level of commitment."

"To fornicate."

"Yes. If they get lucky. Anyway, I'm having fun doing this for a while, then who should I run into at this club but my own father. And I don't just run into him at the bar or the cloak room or nothing. No, I run into him in the ladies room. I open the door of the cubicle and there he is. Snorting coke and getting blown by a girl from my school, two years younger than me." Anna was wearing that puzzled expression again. "Listen, I don't need to go into it, but those are two very bad things okay?" Anna simply nodded and let Linda continue. "The next day at school this girl comes looking for me and starts making out like she wants us to be friends. She tells me my father offered to put her up in her own flat and everything, saying he's already got three other women like that. So when I got home I confronted him with this."

"How did he respond?"

"He went ballistic. He called me a whore and a junkie for hanging out in a bar like that. Can you believe the nerve of the guy, after what I caught him doing? So we have this big stand up row and he throws me out on my ass. Literally picks me and throws me out onto the lawn. Then he opens my bedroom window and starts throwing all of my things out. Clothes, CDs, make-up, books, all of them right there on the ground. And my mother, she just sits there and watches. Sipping her early morning Manhattan and popping pills, like nothing is happening."

"So you had nowhere to live?"

"Nope," said Linda. "And then I found out who my friends were. None of my school friends would take me in, or the 'good families' I knew. I ended up in a YWCA hostel, with no income. Then I bump into a guy I knew from that bar I was telling you about. He buys me dinner and tells me I could be making good money just doing what I used to do for the fun of it. He gets me a couple of clients and before I know it I've got a swanky uptown apartment and the names of the most powerful men in the State in my address book. I got to travel the world executive class and basically had a ball."

"Had a ball. That means you were happy, am I right?"

"More or less."

"You enjoyed the things those men did to you? I am sorry to say I know a little about that myself. I find it hard to believe that it made you happy."

"Yeah, well my situation was different. I had a choice about what I did. I wasn't chained to a wall. Besides there were worse things I could have done with my time."

"There were?"

"Well yeah," said Linda getting a little riled. "As soon as people started dying in their millions I found that out. Turned out that while there wasn't a lot of demand for IT specialists or stock brokers anymore, people in my line of work could still get by. Only the rewards were a lot less and the risk was a lot greater."

"Is that when you started killing people?"

"Only, as I've said before, to stay alive."

Linda caught a movement down by Bertha. The door to one of her exterior storage compartments opened slightly and something fell out. It was long and black and it rolled under the van. It was Cortez. Damn it, he was a cunning bastard. She ought to have known that he and Greaves weren't just going to sit there and do nothing.

They must have dismantled one of the dividing walls and slipped into the outer storage compartment. Then jimmied the lock from the inside. If they'd done any permanent damage to Bertha she'd make them pay for it.

Linda could just make out Cortez commando crawling along the underside of the vehicle. He came out right by some trees, completely in shadow. There was no way the raiders could have seen him. He was taking the fight to them.

Close combat, in the dark, in dense woodland. Didn't matter how well the raiders knew the terrain, this was now Cortez's territory. Poor bastards didn't stand a chance.

"Mistress Linda," said Anna. "I have only known you a short while so forgive my impertinence, I don't claim to see into your soul but would you permit me to make an observation about you?"

"Go ahead. Knock yourself out. It'll help pass the time I guess."

"I know you say you had a choice about your erm... career. Is that how you would have it?"

"That'll do."

"And I know you say you only killed to stay alive, but I wonder if you would grant me the indulgence of offering another explanation?"

"You have such a quaint way of talking. But you don't have to keep pussy footing around, get to the point."

"Alright, I think you fornicate with other men to win back your father's love. You went to this place Nab, err..."

"Nabokov's."

"Yes, you went to Nabokov's to find men your father's age. To give to them what you couldn't give to your father. The very thing that you felt made him withdraw his love for you. Then when he banished you from his home, once again over the very same thing, you kept looking for his love from other men. You gave them what you felt had kept you from your father. However, they could not give you the love that your father withheld. It says in Corinthians 6:18: 'He that committeth fornication sinneth against his own body'. You started to kill men out of anger at your father. You were angry that he stopped loving you and even angrier at what this had made you do to yourself."

Linda put down her rifle and just stared at Anna. She looked away, nervous and self conscious. "Pray forgive me Mistress Linda. I fear I have spoken out of turn. The circumstances are unusual and I forgot myself. You were being so kind and I..."

"No, no," said Linda. "That's okay, I'm not cross, I'm... well I'm flabbergasted. I mean I thought you were this retard. I'm not being rude or nothing, but all you did was whimper and pray all the time. Then suddenly it's like you just look right into my soul. You're a regular little Freudian aren't you?"

"Freudian. Is that like an Episcopalian?"

"Not exactly. But it's kinda like a religion to some people."

A scream of intense pain stopped the conversation. It came from the woods around Bertha. Both Linda and Anna jumped. Several short bursts of gunfire followed. Linda scanned the woods through the rifle sights.

A single raider bolted towards the road. A machete shot out of the trees. It was so fast Linda only made out what it was when it had buried itself in the man's head, cleaving the back of his skull. The man stopped running and reached up to touch the handle. Only then did he realise he was dying and keeled.

Cortez strode across the clearing wiping blood off his big Bowie knife. He picked up the container full of gas and took it back to Bertha. Greaves came out with a funnel and they refilled the tank.

"Come on," said Linda. "I think it's safe to go back now."

The moon was low and the sky was getting lighter. Dawn was on its way. The bluff, the woodlands and the river below, everything looked different in the light of the approaching day. Especially, thought Linda, the brave and astonishing young woman with whom she'd spent the night.

CHAPTER ELEVEN

This was about payback, plain and simple. That's what Ahiga told his braves. Payback for four hundred years of oppression, treachery and barefaced lies.

The white man stole this land from them. Their forefathers had to live with that because the white man had the numbers. Now the Great Spirit had cut the white man down to size. It was time to take back what was rightfully theirs, to send a message to each and every white man left alive.

Don't fuck with us no more.

What Ahiga didn't mention, was his own personal payback. He hadn't told them of the eyes. Those beautiful brown eyes, with their long lashes, that still looked up at him every time he closed his own to go to sleep. He'd said nothing of the gun barrel he'd placed between the lips of the eyes' owner, or the guilt he'd carried ever since. This was where the payback started. Where old scores were finally settled.

There were two sentries posted on the trail up to the burial ground. Neither looked as though they could even hold a gun, let alone fire one. The two scouts he'd sent to scope out the defences had returned and asked him to accompany them.

There didn't appear to be many men guarding the area. Their defences were minimal. The two scouts, Hastiin, a young Navajo Ahiga had chosen specially for the mission, and Akecheta, a Sioux who was a crack shot, were wary. They wanted to check with Ahiga that it wasn't a trap.

Ahiga came with them so as not to arouse their suspicion. He already knew it wasn't a trap. He had been briefed on when and how to attack by Fitch and Golding.

He assured the two braves there was nothing to worry about. The Neo-Clergy had sent most of their men off to guard Colt and the Prophet as they left the camp.

Besides, they were arrogant and complacent. They didn't think anyone would dare attack them.

The two braves seemed satisfied with this explanation. Ahiga sent Hastiin back to order the rest of the braves to advance. Then he gave Akecheta the go ahead to take out the sentries.

Akecheta took two arrows from his quiver. This was going to be done old school. They'd come packing plenty of heat as back up, but the initial attack was to be done in honour of their ancestors. They had a point to make today.

Akecheta released his bow string and the first arrow struck the left sentry clean in the chest. The shot was perfect, a thing of beauty. The sentry tried to swat it like an insect. Then he looked down and saw the shaft poking out of him. He turned to alert his comrade but dropped dead before the warning could reach his lips.

The other sentry dropped his weapon in fear and surprise. He stared wildly about him, panicking. He bent to pick up his rifle then, half way down, decided against it and just ran. Akecheta sent an arrow after him, which thudded into his back making him fall forward, twitching.

Ahiga and Akecheta walked up the path to make sure the sentries were dead. The second one was twitching and crying. He rolled over on to his side and looked up at Ahiga. "Please Mister. Please, I don't wanna go see Jesus just yet. I've survived a lot. You don't know what I been through and I ain't even kissed a girl yet."

Ahiga knelt by the man. He reached over and cradled his head with his right hand, pulling the man up onto his knee. Akecheta's arrow protruded from the front of the man's robes, which were soaked with his blood. Ahiga supported the man's chin with his left hand.

"Aw thanks mister," the man said. "I could tell you was a good sort, straight off I could tell. I'm a good judge of character see and I took one look at you and –"

Ahiga pushed forward hard with his left hand and pulled back with his right. The man's spinal column snapped with an audible crack. Ahiga pushed the body away and stood up.

Akecheta thanked him for finishing the job, to which Ahiga nodded. They waited for the rest of the braves to join them.

There was a sacred and ceremonial path all the way up the giant mound to the burial place. The chief at Lame Deer had explained in great detail all about the path, and the way to proceed along it to bury the fallen leader. Ahiga did not like him. He was a bore and a weakling. Like the idiot Hopi he'd gotten rid of.

There were also secret ways up to the burial ground. Ways that hid whoever followed them. However, warned the chief, bad things happened if they were misused. Ahiga had ignored his mewling and demanded the routes off the chief. The man was a coward and he gave them after making only the feeblest protest.

Ahiga and his war party moved quickly and quietly in pairs. When they got to the perimeter the pairs split up and circled the Neo-Clergy camp. All the braves were trained in guerrilla warfare and stealth tactics, but the camp guards were practically asleep.

In the centre of the burial ground was a large steel tower. The Clergy had dug up sacred graves for the foundations and poured concrete inside, to anchor the legs of the tower. These white devils had desecrated the most holy land and now they were nonchalantly climbing the tower, welding new pieces to it, even whistling and joking.

Ahiga could see anger and resentment on the faces of the braves as they looked on from cover. That was good. They were starting to hate smart. Theirs was a dispossessed generation who had finally been given a cause, a target for all the discontent and alienation they'd felt growing up.

On the eastern side of the camp were the living quarters: tents mostly, plus a few benders – temporary structures made out of bent twigs and reeds, an old woodsman's trick. In the centre of this area was a large log cabin which must have served as a central food hall, although it looked as though it had only just been finished. Beside it there were barrels of water.

Nine armed guards were visible in the camp. Eight of them were in pairs, patrolling the grounds, while the ninth was idling against the wall of the cabin. The other hundred or so occupants were all unarmed, just over half were women and children. They looked happy and content in their work, oblivious to the danger lurking all around them.

It was just as Fitch and Golding had said. Ahiga knew they thought they were playing him. They imagined they still had something to hold over him, even after all these years.

The only thing that held him to them was his need for revenge. To redeem himself and win back his manhood. Manhood they had stolen. Not with their threats or their innuendo, or even the terrible thing they had made him do. But the man he had done it to, had shown him what real bravery and what real manhood were.

In giving in to Fitch and Golding he had fallen far short

of that mark. That was what he could never live down.

This was where they got theirs. They were the ones being played. This was where it started and it wouldn't end well for either of them.

Ahiga raised his arm and his bowmen readied their weapons. On his signal they stepped forward and let fly, raining a volley of arrows down on the unsuspecting camp guards. Five of them fell on the spot.

Two civilians got caught in the volley. An old man took one right in the eye and his head snapped back, as though he was looking at the sky, trying to pinpoint where the arrow came from. Then he toppled over. A young woman was hit in the shoulder. She stepped into the trajectory at the last second and fell to the ground screaming with pain.

Her hollers were drowned when Ahiga fired his pistol in the air. The braves charged into the camp whooping and calling the ancient war cries. They were dressed in ordinary western clothes. They had no feathers in their hair, or war paint on their faces, but they looked terrifying.

The effect this had on the camp was immense. Everyone tried to flee or run for cover but soon found they were surrounded and hemmed in. There were shouts, sobs and general pandemonium. Someone even called out: "Indians!" They honestly said that. Like some corny old movie from days gone by.

One of the guards fought back straight away, unloading his rifle into the oncoming warriors, wounding two and killing another. When his ammo was spent he picked up his weapon like a club and charged, but was soon overwhelmed. Five braves beat him to the ground with the butts of their rifles. He raised a hand in surrender, to show he was done. This didn't stop his attackers. They had come for blood and nothing was going to deny them. They cracked his bones, ruptured his stomach and caved in his skull.

One guard raced out of the woods by the log cabin with his trouser still round his ankles, a shit smeared leaf in one hand and a pistol in the other. He saw what was happening and tried to bolt back into the bushes. Two braves caught him, disarmed him and threw him face down on the ground. They shot him twice in the ass and once in the back of the head with his own weapon. His last earthly act was to empty his bladder.

"When you gotta go, you gotta go," said one of his killers and laughed.

The remaining guards threw down their weapons and put their hands in the air. The rest of the camp's occupants were herded together into a group. The men put protective arms around their women folk, who pulled their children to them. They watched in fear as the guards were brought before Ahiga and made to kneel.

"Don't think you stinking heathens will get away with this," said one of the guards and he spat at Ahiga, hitting his boot. Ahiga brought the boot up into the man's face, kicking him to the ground. Then he picked the man up by his hair and pulled out a knife. Hastiin and Akecheta took hold of the other man and drew their own blades.

"Please," a woman called out from the huddled crowd. "For the love of Jesus, please don't"

"I have no love for your Jèsus," said Ahiga and he sliced open the man's throat. Hastiin and Akecheta did the same. Ahiga stepped into the warm arc of blood pumping from the severed artery of his victim, bathing himself in its crimson spray. He roared with delight. The primordial cry of a victor, standing over the corpse of his enemy. The rest of the war party did the same. They were elated. They were victorious. They had payback.

Ahiga raised his hands. "Silence!" he commanded. The war party stopped roaring. Ahiga turned to the huddled mass of civilians. The adults shook and the children cried. "I said silence!" Some parents put their hands over their children's mouths. Others tried to shush those old enough to understand.

"When your forefathers first came to these shores," said Ahiga, "my ancestors welcomed them in peace. When they starved because they couldn't hunt or grow crops, my ancestors fed them. And how were we repaid? With lies and bloodshed as you built your cites and stole our land. Then your cities failed, your people died and once again you could not feed yourselves. Then who did you turn to for help? My people once again. And once again we fed you and looked after you and taught you our tribal ways. How have you repaid us for this kindness? You come on to our most sacred land, our most holy burial ground, and you desecrate the corpses of our most honoured ancestors. Did you think we would just lie back and take this? That we would let you trample over what little dignity we had left? Well, you were sorely mistaken if you did."

One of the older men stepped forward from the crowd. He clutched a cap to his chest and his head was bent in submission. "Please," he said. "We have obviously made a grave mistake. We did not know this land was holy. We would never have come here if we did. We'll put right any damage we've done and we'll leave straight away."

"Liar," said Ahiga as Hastiin stepped forward and punched the old man in the face. He spun round and spat out a tooth as he hit the floor. A group of braves gathered around and stomped on the man.

"You knew exactly what you were doing," Ahiga said.

"We will not tolerate your presence here a second longer. You will watch as we undo the wicked grievance you have done us. Then you will gather up your dead, who are not fit to be laid on this sacred ground, and we will escort you off the reservation. We do not kill unarmed men, women and children and this is what puts us above you and your kind."

There were surprised mutters amongst the war party and Ahiga silenced them with a gesture. He knew that Fitch and Golding had hoped for a full scale massacre, but he wasn't going to play into their hands. They were pawns in his game, he was not a pawn in theirs. He was going to do something they hadn't counted on.

Ahiga signalled for the braves with the TNT to get to work. Both were former construction workers. One wasn't even a Native American. He was the only one in Ahiga's party who wasn't. He'd been living with the Navajo in New Mexico since The Cull so he could be trusted. The two of them had lugged the TNT in a reinforced steel container all the way from Lame Deer. Now they fixed it to the base of the tower and the concrete foundations.

The crowd of Neo-Clergy volunteers were herded over to the far north side of the burial ground. While the half finished tower was primed for demolition, the other braves set light to the log cabin and living quarters of the camp. There were gasps and sobs from the crowd as favourite teddies and treasured family Bibles went up in the flames. The braves guarding them quelled the noise.

The detonation wire was connected to the explosives, reeled out to a safe distance then hooked up to the detonator. Ahiga himself did the honours.

The noise was deafening. The ground shook and a wall of heat came off the inferno that engulfed the tower, stinging Ahiga's eyes and nose.

The tower came crashing down on the sacred earth. The blackened steel of the structure seemed to scream as it buckled and fell apart. Flaming girders, rivets and chunks of molten metal rained down, scattering impromptu funeral pyres across the cemetery.

A cheer went up from the braves, it was an awesome sight. They had laid the white man's schemes low. The tower had been like a giant middle finger raised to the Native Americans. A huge metal dick showing the white man's power, and they had just chopped it down, unmanning the whole Neo-Clergy.

The braves separated the men folk and forced them at gunpoint to pick their way through the flaming ruins of the tower and drag the corpses out. Acting on Ahiga's orders, Hastiin filled a blood stained quiver with arrows that he pulled from the dead bodies.

Then he led the crowd down the mound, following the traditional path. The survivors of the attack were forced at gunpoint to mourn the death of their villainous scheme, and mourn it Native American style.

"You should be pleased old man," said Ahiga to the chief.

The weakling just sighed and looked solemn. This was how Elders exerted their power over the younger braves. The sombre silences, the shunning and withdrawal of approval. It wasn't going to work on Ahiga though. "You had the white man camped out on your most sacred site, trampling on your traditions and your territory. I just got rid of him for you. I've given you back that land."

"I heard the explosion," said the chief. "What kind of a state have you left the land in? Do you honestly think we will ever be able to use it again to honour our dead?"

"That is the white man's doing. Not mine. At least now you have the chance to rebuild."

The chief gave him a sad look, full of the pain of betrayal. Ahiga knew the old man was holding back what he wanted to say, but his look was far more eloquent. Ahiga could feel the anger building inside him. He choked back the bile that was rising in his throat and marched out of the chief's quarters.

He would have started to beat on the old man if he hadn't. He'd seen that self same look only once before in his life and he did not want to be reminded.

It had come from those beautiful brown eyes as he squeezed the trigger. They were the only eyes he had ever loved and he had stolen the light from them forever. He had done it out of fear. Not the fear of knowing it was kill or be killed but the fear of being revealed in front of the gang. The fear of being thought less than a man. What ate him up inside was that he hadn't felt like a proper man since.

Ahiga heard footsteps approach. The tread was familiar, without turning round he knew they were Hastiin's. The brave stopped a respectful distance from Ahiga and waited without a sound.

After a time Ahiga collected himself and said: "Is it done?"

"I placed the quiver and the detonator inside the meeting hall as you instructed. Even a half-assed search will turn them up, but they'll stay hidden unless someone thinks to look."

"Speak of this to anyone and you're a dead man. You know that don't you?"

"Of course," said Hastiin. "I believe in the UTN. I believe in Hiamovi and what you're doing to bring our people together. I'm honoured to be a part of it."

"Good. When the time comes, I'll see you right by this."

"I appreciate that," said Hastiin. "But just being a part of something bigger than myself – something that matters – that's enough of a reward."

"Leave me now," said Ahiga and Hastiin went.

Everything was now set in motion. An old Greek pimp had once told Ahiga that when the gods want to punish us they give us exactly what we want. The saying had always stuck with Ahiga. Fitch and Golding were going to get what they wanted. It was going to punish them more than they could possibly expect.

It was getting near dawn and Fitch was pissed. He'd been driving up and down the road bordering the reservation since he'd heard the explosion. He had no idea what kind of stunt that sick faggot Ahiga had pulled, but he was going to make him pay when he found out.

"Where are these stinking Bible bashers?" he said. "Can't that freaking Injun get 'em to the borders of his own reservation?"

"T'aint his reservation," said Golding, who was riding shotgun in the jeep. "These are Cheyenne. He's a Navajo. He told me that."

"Whatever. They're all redskins. Should've killed 'em back when we had the chance."

"Have to make do with happy clappers for the time being."

"Yeah, freaking Christians. Them I'll kill for free. Bug the fucking shit outta me."

"Don't let Colt catch you saying that. He's real big into

his religious shit."

"I know. That's his problem. Christianity, that's what we push to the masses. T'aint what we swallow. First rule of dealing: don't get high on your own supply. We start believing in all this turn the other cheek, peace on earth bullshit and we're fucked."

"Naw. Colt's more of your eye for an eye, tooth for a tooth kinda Christian. Strictly old school, old testament. He told me that."

A horn blared behind them, from one of the two troop carriers following them. Fitch checked his mirror. The driver of the last vehicle was leaning out the window waving for them to go back.

Fitch pulled a U-turn and swore as he hit a pothole. He drove past the troop carriers, executing three point turns. Up ahead, on the right hand side of the road, about a hundred or so volunteers were coming out of a small copse of Ponderosa Pines.

"Goddamn it," said Fitch. "He hasn't killed a one of them. First the explosion now this, what the fuck is that cock sucking Injun playing at?"

"Wait," said Golding. "I see a few bodies. Our boys though, worse luck."

"You didn't expect he'd let them live did ya?"

"S'pose not."

Fitch pulled up and jumped out. The other two vehicles were just pulling up when the volunteers spotted them. The troops climbed out of the carriers. Thirty men armed to the teeth.

The whole crowd ran towards them with their arms out. Some of them bawled tears of joy. Fitch thought they might fall down and kiss his feet. They swarmed round him, the women tugging at his clothes while their scrawny ass kids screamed. Everyone was talking at once. Fitch pulled out his pistol and fired it into the air.

"Alright," he hollered. "That's enough, I can't make out a word you're saying. You," Fitch said pointing to a tall, thin man who had hold of a corpse by the ankles. "What the fuck was that explosion we heard?"

"That was the tower," said the man. "The Indians blew it up. Had dynamite and everything." The man tilted his head at the corpse he was carrying. "Killed this one and nine others."

"Anyone else dead?" said Fitch. "Apart from our men?"

"Couple I think. Few of us are wounded too. Do you have a first aid kit with you?"

"Oh we got just what you need. Don't you worry 'bout that none."

The troops formed themselves into a line spanning the road, guns at the ready.

"How bad's the damage to the tower?" Fitch said. "There any chance of repairing it?"

The man shook his head. "We'll have to start again from scratch. The whole thing's destroyed. Set light to our things too. All we got is the clothes on our back."

"You won't need nothing where you're going," said Golding.

The volunteers started to look nervous. A few of them began backing up the road or slinking into the trees. "You guys are here to help us aren't you?" said the tall man. "We're gonna finish off the work on the tower ain't we? So the Prophet can get his word out."

"We're gonna finish off the tower," said Fitch. "But first we gotta finish up what them Injuns left undone."

"Listen," said the man. "I don't quite follow what you're saying. You need to send us some place we can get seen to."

"We're going to send you some place alright. Some place the angels can see to you."

The troops raised their weapons, semi automatics primed and loaded. "Wait a minute! We're on your side. Sweet Lord Jesus –"

"Tell him I said hi," said Fitch and opened fire. The rest of the men followed suite.

The roar of the gunfire nearly drowned the screams of pain and fear. Wave upon wave of bullets ripped into the men, women and children as they tried to flee. Their bodies jerked and flailed. It put Fitch in mind of the raptures they went into at their prayer meetings. Waving their hands in the air, speaking in tongues and falling to the floor. Except there was a lot more blood and they weren't getting up again.

Fitch and his men stepped over the first lot of corpses as they advanced on the rest of the volunteers trying to escape. Their boots were sticky from all the blood. Fitch's weapon was red hot from the constant firing and his arms were sore from tensing against the recoil.

With the majority of them dead, Fitch sent five men on down the road to catch the few bastards who'd gotten away and four more into the trees to flush out any stragglers there. The rest of the men kicked their way through the bodies on the road, using their pistols to finish off the wounded.

When he was satisfied that the job was done he called out to Golding: "You got them bow and arrows to hand?" Golding pulled five bows and three quivers out the back of the jeep. He tossed a bow to Fitch who then fired an arrow into one of the corpses. Golding handed out bows to some of the other men.

"Sir, I don't understand," said one of the soldiers. "We already finished 'em off. Why turn 'em into pin cushions?"

"'Cos people have to see it was them Injuns did this. They have to know what kinda filthy savages they are."

When they were done Fitch turned to Dwight, six-foot four of red headed, red necked, good ol' Southern boy. "You got that Polaroid?"

Dwight held up an instant camera. It would have been a relic even before The Cull. "Sure have. Got it off a scav who pulled it out of an old retirement home, place was a gold mine he said."

"Does it still work?"

"Fired off a few test shots to be sure," said Dwight. "Even got spare film."

"Good," said Fitch. "I want a lot of shots of this. People are gonna see these photos and they're gonna want blood."

"Neo-Clergy's making a comeback boys," said Golding as Dwight snapped away. "Neo-Clergy's making a comeback."

CHAPTER TWELVE

They didn't look like killers, thought the Prophet. Just a lot of tired, scared Native Americans. That was the thing about evil though, it always hid in the least likely places. In the hearts of the most ordinary people. Just one of Satan's many subtleties.

As a little kid he'd always rooted for the Indians whenever he watched a western on TV. In the old movies they were always the bad guys. That's not how he'd seen them. They were noble warriors who stood up to the white man. If you saw a black man in one of those films he was usually some Stepin-Fetchit played for laughs. But the Indians terrified the white men. They had power.

All that was before he discovered they were Godless pagans. It hadn't mattered to him much back then. Church was something he went to with his momma and his brothers. It didn't affect the rest of his life. God had yet to reach down, pluck his soul from his body and carry it to Heaven. He'd seen a lot of things differently after that.

The Prophet was standing in the middle of Lame Deer on a cold and overcast day. The residents had been rounded up and marched at gunpoint into the centre of the town by the two hundred strong army of Neo-Clergy soldiers that Colt had arrived with. Many of them recent recruits, eager to see action.

They'd made the Native Americans kneel together with their hands on their heads in the middle of a vacant lot near the centre of Lame Deer. Lame Duck the soldiers had nicknamed it and the Prophet could see why. It was more of a trailer park than a real town, with a few decaying artefacts obviously erected for the benefit of tourists, back when there was such a thing as tourism.

They were a far cry from his childhood ideals of the noble savage. Ironically, what made the Prophet admire the Native American, so much as a child, their ability to terrify the white man, was what saddened him now.

It was also what had brought so many volunteers flocking to the Neo-Clergy and given Colt the new recruits he had needed to mount this occupation. It pained the Prophet to think that it was fear and not the love of Jesus that had inspired so many to rejoin the Apostolic Church of the Rediscovered Dawn. But at least they were back in the fold and could now be redeemed. As could Colt.

Colt had seemed genuinely moved when he showed the Prophet the photos. It was the first time the Prophet had seen him let his guard down and it gave him hope. It was the one tiny measure of good that he could salvage from the whole massacre, and he clung to it.

The photos had made the Prophet weep. He had known so many of the victims. Had laughed with them, prayed with them and rejoiced when their children arrived. To see them lying there, riddled with so many arrows just about tore his heart to pieces.

The photos had the same effect on thousands of others. Word of the atrocity spread throughout the Mid-West, along with copies of the pictures. Every conceivable means of reproducing the photos had been used. Any photocopier that could be hooked up to a working battery or generator, or any printing press that could be ground into life had been put to the task. The images were deemed too important by all not to be seen.

There had been a huge outcry of indignation and a demand for action. So Colt had seized the initiative. The moment had demanded a man and he had stepped forward to fill the role. Thousands had heeded Colt's call and the Prophet had never seen a time when he was so needed at Colt's side

Colt had mobilised an army and marched on the reservation in Montana. The Prophet had prayed privately with him the night before he left Colorado. He had taken Matthew 5:43-45 for his inspiration. "'Ye have heard that it hath been said, Thou shalt love thy neighbour and hate thine enemy. But I say unto you, Love your enemies, bless them that curse you, and persecute you.'"

The soldiers were muttering amongst themselves and kicking the odd Native American who complained of stiffness or arthritis. They fell silent as Colt walked into the lot with Simon Peter and several other men, one of whom placed a box on the ground so Colt could stand on it.

Colt held up a quiver he had with him and removed an arrow. It was stained brown with dried blood. "After a thorough search of your homes my men found these arrows and this explosive hidden in your meeting hall." Colt pointed to a reinforced steel box two of his men were carrying.

The Native Americans looked shocked, no doubt surprised to have been found out. Some of them shook their heads, others called out "No!' and "It's a lie!"

The chief, an old man with long silver hair woven into a plait stood up. "There has been some mistake. We are obviously as much victims here as you. I assure you, we are in no way responsible for –"

Fitch stepped forward and smashed the butt of his gun into the chief's side. The old man fell forward with a pain filled cry. Several of the other Native Americans went to help him. The soldiers stepped in and forced them to resume kneeling at gun point, including the chief, who did so with no little discomfort.

The Prophet could feel the anger and the hatred building in the men. This worried him. He hadn't realised it, but up until this minute, when Colt revealed the evidence they had discovered, he was still hoping there had been a mistake. That maybe a rogue group had committed the atrocity and that, working together with the Native Americans, they could bring them to justice. Yet even in the face of such irrefutable evidence, they tried to deny it. The Prophet feared for their lives. He was afraid he would be witness to another massacre. He said a silent prayer to God to impart His wisdom to Colt.

"It doesn't surprise me that you should continue with your lies in the face of such evidence," said Colt. "As we have seen, you tried to hide your shame and your guilt where you thought it would not be found. But lies will always be found out and evil will always be uncovered by those who have God in their hearts." There was a cheer from the troops at this. Colt raised his hands for silence.

"Those men, women and children that you brutally slaughtered had done nothing to any of you. They meant you no harm. They were good Christian people, and that's why you struck them down in such a heinous and cowardly fashion. Because the evil pagan gods you worship have filled you with such hatred for us. Hatred for our beliefs, hatred for our way of life and hatred for the freedoms we have in Jesus. Well we aren't going to sit back and take it a second longer."

There was an even bigger cheer at this and one or two of the kneeling children burst into tears. The soldiers stopped their mothers from comforting them and quieted them with the threat of violence instead.

"I want to introduce you to something," said Colt. He gave the quiver to Simon Peter and held up a Bible. "It has more power than all your hatred, all your weapons and all your explosives. It's called a Bible and it's changed the lives of millions of people around the world. Now it's going to change yours. Let me read you a section from Matthew Chapter Five, Verses thirty-eight to forty-one." The Prophet's heart leapt when he heard Colt say that. The Lord had answered his prayers after all.

"'Ye have heard that it hath been said, An eye for an eye and a tooth for a tooth: But I say unto you, That ye resist not evil... and whosoever shall compel thee to go a mile, go with him twain.'" These words were spoken by our saviour Lord Jesus Christ over two thousand years ago, yet they have never been more true. I know that many of you fear for your lives. But you needn't. We do not kill unarmed men, women and children and this is what puts us above you and your kind."

There were surprised mutters amongst the soldiers. Colt silenced them with a gesture.

"We've come to occupy your territory not only to protect our people from your murderous ways and to complete the blessed work of our Lord Jesus. We've also come to set you free. Free from your enslavement to Satan and his pagan lies. Free from your superstition and your hatred of those who would be your brothers. You've compelled us to walk many miles to come here today. Now we're going to walk those extra miles alongside you, just as our saviour commanded us. We're going to build a bigger and a better transmission tower and you're going to build it with us. In return for this and for the provisions you will share with us, we will teach of the peace and the freedom to be found in the one true God. You will be freed from Satan's grip. Freed by God's words and honest work. Work will set you free!"

The Prophet's heart leapt and sang at these words. He clapped his hands together and shouted out "Hallelujah

Brothers!" The rest of the troop followed suit, joining with the clapping and whooping. There were calls of "Praise the Lord" and a chant went round, like a call and response. "Who do we trust?"

"In Colt we trust!"

"Said who do we trust?"

"In Colt we trust!"

"Said who do trust?"

"In Colt we trust! In Colt! In Colt! In Colt we trust!"

The Prophet saw that the Native Americans looked baffled but relieved that their lives were no longer in danger. He said a silent prayer of thanks to God and realised he must start trusting the Lord more. He had, after all, never let the Prophet down before.

There was only one slight cloud of unease that refused to pass from his mind. It came in part from a look that passed between Golding and Fitch. While everyone else was caught up in the moment, they seemed to harbour a secret resentment and superiority. The rest of it came from the last thing Colt had said. Something about work and freedom. He was sure he had heard something similar somewhere else but he couldn't think where.

There you go again, he told himself. Worrying away at tiny details while the miraculous takes place right in front of your eyes.

A disaster had been averted and the souls of so many were about to be saved.

Colt stood on the spot where, just a few weeks previously, he had looked up and admired the half finished tower. Now he surveyed it's ruins.

He took Golding and Fitch to one side. "Thought you

said this Injun you had on a leash wouldn't do nothing to the site?"

"How were we to know he was going to go apeshit with a bunch of dynamite?" said Fitch. "T'aint what we told him to do."

"Don't matter what you told him to do, I put you in charge of a job and you didn't get it done proper. Next time you fuck up on a scale like this it'll be a picture of your mutilated corpses that they're passing round half of Kansas."

Colt could see that Fitch wanted to give him some backchat, but Golding caught Fitch's eye and signalled for him to keep quiet. "It's a good thing Simon Peter here worked out that I planned to use the Injuns as slave labour to replace the volunteers we lost." Simon Peter bowed his head with humility at the fleeting praise. He knew how to play this game.

"It's a good idea sir," said Golding. "That way we can work 'em twice as hard as the volunteers and feed 'em less."

"I know it's a good idea. I don't need a fuck up like you to tell me that. Now you two half-wits have got one last chance to redeem yourselves. Are you up for it?"

"Sure," said Fitch looking at the floor and grinding his teeth.

"Anything you say," said Golding, trying to get back on Colt's good side. "We're your men."

"I'll have to take your word on that. Now, this here occupation's likely to bring a reprisal from the redskins and their UTN. From what I hear their numbers are building slowly, but not enough to be a real threat to us just yet. I want you to organise sentry parties all along the borders of our current territory. Take a few experienced men and put 'em in charge of a bunch of expendable recruits. Organise a line of communication with each party that comes straight back to me here. This is where I plan to stay awhile. Tell the parties they're strictly on reconnaissance. I don't want them intervening 'less the Injuns are fucking with something of strategic importance to us. Like our transmission and broadcasting equipment."

"What if they try and attack something that ain't of importance to us?" said Fitch.

"Let 'em. The more folk are frightened of the UTN, the more they'll turn to us. It can only play to our advantage. We gotta let 'em have a few victories to keep the fear in people. It'll only strengthen us more. That was the plan in the first place."

"Sir," said Simon Peter. "Do we order any of the scouting parties to try and capture UTN members and their sympathisers? Could be good for gathering intelligence."

"Thinking what I'm thinking again? Good boy." Colt looked to Fitch. "Any of our boys experts in torture and interrogation?"

"Few. Ex-pigs and veterans mainly, plus a few psychopaths we keep on a short leash."

"Good. Post at least one with every party near a border with known UTN activity. And remember they ain't all redskins these days. Lot of race traitors sold out on their heritage and went to live like savages."

"Sir," said Simon Peter. "We've underestimated these Injuns before, there any chance they'll try a surprise attack on us here? Throw everything they got at us, like a retribution thing?"

"I doubt it. If they thought they had enough men to take us on and win they'd have left an army behind to protect the place or at least tried to attack us on the move. No, my way of thinking is that this suits their purposes just as much as it suits ours."

"Start of a beautiful relationship," said Golding with a chuckle.

"Amen to that," said Colt.

CHAPTER THIRTEEN

Cortez finished his first prayer of the day, bowed to Mecca and stood. Anna finished up her prayers and turned to smile at him. She had taken to joining him in his devotions every day. She prayed to Christ while he gave thanks to Allah most merciful and the Prophet Mohammed, peace be upon him.

It had become their little ritual. They had also begun to discuss one another's faiths, with a genuine willingness to learn from each other. Cortez's respect for the extraordinary young lady had grown tenfold.

Cortez had noticed that the fallen woman's respect for Anna had also grown, the two of them seemed quite close after their night on the mountain. This, along with her effectiveness in a fight, had made Cortez hate Linda less.

Linda was at the stove when they climbed back in the vehicle. "How do you like your rat?" she said. "Rare, medium or burnt?"

"Don't we have anything else to eat?" said Greaves. "Rat gives me indigestion."

"Don't you have a pill for that?" said Linda winking at Anna. "I'm afraid rat's the only thing on the menu. You should be thankful I managed to catch these. All we've got is those two tins of corn, which may or may not be edible. They come from that batch we scavenged in West Point, half of which weren't edible. 'Cept for that we've got some wizened apples we picked a few weeks back. Way I see it, that's lunch and dinner taken care of."

Greaves pulled a face. "We'll make Torrington in a few hours," he said. "It's just over the border in Wyoming. I'm sure we can pick up some rations there."

"What's in Torrington?" said Linda "The world's last surviving Walmart?"

"No. Beneath the City Hall and Police Department on 21st Avenue is an underground complex of offices built by military intelligence. It has an independent generator which can easily be started, and a host of cutting-edge information technology. Doubtless there will also be food stores down there somewhere."

"And stuff we can sell?" said Linda.

"Yes. There will be lots of things we can sell."

"But you've got your own particular reason for going there haven't you?" said Linda. Cortez had noticed that she could never take anything on trust. She always had to question and undermine Greaves. She probably did not like men very much, Cortez thought. Considering what she did for a living, this didn't surprise him.

"There are schematics on the memory stick we retrieved in Indiana that I have to access. They show the underground laboratories near Little Bighorn in Montana. I need to study them to find us a way in. Torrington is the only place on the way with computers that I can realistically get to work."

"What is it with you and underground buildings? Everyplace you take us is hidden deep within the bowels of the earth. Did one of your ancestors breed with a mole or something?" Greaves ignored her question. Linda finished cooking and they ate in silence.

"You know there's a few things that bother me about this whole trip," said Linda, after gnawing the last bit of flesh off her rat bones. Cortez sighed. He was just beginning to find her company bearable. "I know I was hired to take you to Montana. But I don't know if I'm happy with what's going to happen once we get there."

"What do you mean?"

"You know exactly what I mean. When we do break into this underground laboratory with Anna, what happens next?"

"Why, we save the world of course."

"You mean you infect an innocent girl with an experimental virus that's supposed to be a hundred times deadlier than the one that just wiped out most of the planet. I'm sorry, but the more I think about your story, the less I buy it."

"But I explained about the Doomsday Virus. I told you that Anna was specially bred to be its host."

"You gave us some wild science-fiction story about a virus that's going to fall in love with a girl and make her an immortal goddess. That sounds a lot more like a fairy tale than hard science to me."

"But it's true," said Greaves. "Who's the scientist here, me or you? I've seen and helped create things that are beyond the comprehension of most human beings. Who are you to start questioning me?"

"Okay then. Let's say everything you told us is true. That Anna is the special one chosen by the Doomsday Virus and that you got to her before your old buddies did. How do we know we're not playing right into their hands by bringing her to their laboratory? Come to that how do we know you're not still working for them and that all this is part of their plan to get their hands on Anna?"

"If I was still working for an organisation with the resources that they have why the hell would I put my life in constant danger travelling across the country like this?" said Greaves. "And why do you suddenly care so much? Like you said, you were hired to do a job."

"Because it's stopped being just a job. Because I care about Anna and I don't want you to put her in danger or feed her up to some killer plague germs."

Cortez couldn't keep his mouth shut any longer. "I never thought I'd say this but I agree with the whore."

"Thanks big guy, you sure know how to sweet talk a girl."

"I'm not trying to flatter you," said Cortez. "But I do share your misgivings. You've paid me well Greaves. I've earned what you've given me and it's fair to say the rewards have been good. Nonetheless a man has his limits."

"A man has his limits," said Greaves. "What the fuck does that mean?"

"It means that I too care about Anna. There is something special about her and I don't want to see her used like some lab rat in one of your experiments."

"Of course she's special," said Greaves. Cortez had never seen him so close to losing control. "I've been saying that right from the start. Don't you see what we're a part of? Don't you realise what we could do? We could change the whole world for the better. All this chaos and disorder, all this pain and death and suffering. It doesn't have to be for nothing. We could build a new world. We could bring about paradise on Earth."

"Paradise is to be found in the hereafter," said Cortez. "With Allah, the almighty."

"And what if you're wrong?" said Linda. "What if we end up wiping out what's left of humanity?"

"My friends," said Anna, joining the conversation for the first time. "I thank you both from the bottom of my heart for your concern. And I too never thought I would say this, but I agree with Mr Greaves."

"You do?" said Greaves. There were tears of gratitude in his eyes. "I mean of course you do. Obviously you do."

"I have prayed long and hard for guidance since you told me about my true origins, about this disease for which you say I'm to be a host and Mr Greaves is right, all this suffering and death doesn't have to be for nothing."

"Exactly," Greaves said, there was a trace of hysteria in his voice. Cortez had not realised quite how much this meant to him. "Of course it doesn't."

"I know what Mr Greaves has said to be true because I have felt this contagion calling to me, calling to every part of my being. As I said to you Mistress Linda it knows I am coming and it hungers for my company. Hungers like Satan himself hungers for lost souls. I have searched every part of my being and I have spoken almost constantly with my Maker and I now believe there is a reason why I alone, out of all the poor children, crafted by Satan's scientific arts, am alive. This plague is more dangerous than anyone, including you Mr Greaves, realise. Yet it is my destiny to be joined with it. God himself has willed it thus."

"Anna," said Linda. "Do you know what you're saying?"

"Yes Mistress Linda I do. I have spent all my life asking God to reveal my purpose in life. The folk of my community were good folk, gentle, honest and true. But as you have pointed out Mr Greaves, it was not easy growing up as the only Native American within the whole community. My momma and poppa never told me how I came to live with them. As you might imagine matters of birth and conception weren't spoken about much by my people. Every attempt was made to keep our minds and our bodies from sinning. What my momma did tell me was that she was sure God singled me out for a special purpose. From the moment she held me in her arms she said that she knew this to be true. She knew it with as much conviction as she knew that the sun would rise the next day, that her name was Sarah Bontraeger and the Lord Jesus Christ died so that we might be redeemed from all our sin. I was often teased as a little girl by the other children because I was so different, because no-one knew who my grandparents were. If you went back two generations, more or less everyone in the community could trace their kin back to ties with everyone else's. It was a point of pride for most of them.

"Sometimes when the teasing got too much for me, I ran and hid and cried. I would call out to Jesus to help me, to give me his comfort and to show me the special purpose he had for me. Once in a while I would feel his hand on my shoulder. I would know then, in these moments, what my Momma had always told me was true. He did have something special in store for me and when the time was right he would reveal it to me. I have been through trying times of late and I have fallen in with bad people, present company excluded. Yet my strength, my rod and my comfort still has always been my belief that I have a special purpose in God. This is my purpose to join with this evil plague and to turn it to God's will."

"No Anna," said Greaves. "It is not evil. It is just a collection of self-replicating micro-organisms. It has no purpose, no intent and no will. Not until it joins with you."

"With respect Mr Greaves," said Anna. "You have not felt its call. It is evil alright, and I must pray with all my heart for strength, so that I may do the right thing when the time comes."

"You are just full of surprises," said Linda. "You don't say nothing for days, then you come out with a big speech like that."

"Yes mistress Linda," said Anna. "I hope I have not bored you with my story. In fact my throat is dry and I would like some water if you wouldn't mind."

Cortez got up and fetched her a drink. "I was not bored at all by your story," he said. "If you don't mind. I should like to hear more."

"What would you like know Mr Cortez?"

"I am curious as to how you ended up in the house of sin where we found you?"

"Ah yes, there," said Anna and she stared into the distance.

"If it is too distressing we do not have to talk of it."

"No, no, that's alright. I think, for the sake of my own sanity, I sometimes believe that all happened to a different person. I have changed so much since I left the community. Since I met you all. I believe I have even begun to talk differently."

"Yeah," said Linda, "I'd noticed that. We'll have you cussing and spitting on the floor yet."

"That may take a while Mistress Linda," said Anna with a smile. "When The Cull came – I believe that's what you call it isn't it? – it came early to my community. Some of us took sick and died within days. It was only a few at first. We tried praying, of course, but for once God didn't seem to heed our words. Then more and more of us fell. We thought we had brought the wrath of the Lord down on our heads. There was much lamentation and self reproach, we begged God for a sign to tell us what we had done wrong, to show us how to put it right. But nothing came. There was much despair in those last days as our loved ones and all the people we had grown up with died before our eyes. We sent parties to the outside world to bring us help but none of them returned. Then there was only a handful of us left at this point, locked away in our own homes with what few provisions we had left. Momma and poppa were two of the last to go. I buried them in our back yard and I cried for days. There wasn't anyone else I could turn to for help. There were dead bodies everywhere and all our cemeteries had run out of space. I tended to the last of my brothers and sisters in the community, tried to make their last hours as comfortable as I could. Then there was just me."

Anna paused for a minute, drank some more water and took a deep breath. "You have to understand that the community was my whole world. I knew of no other life outside of it. My world had ended along with the lives of everyone I knew. The outside world was a complete mystery to me. The Amish way of life has not changed in two hundred years. Even though there was no-one left in the whole settlement I was still afraid to leave. I confess I even prayed to God to take me too, so I could join my community in heaven. "

"So what happened?" said Linda, "How did you end up leaving?"

"I was starving and delirious and suddenly I felt Jesus by my side. I knew that he wanted me to live and to leave the settlement. Only in the outside world could he reveal his purpose to me. So I collected a few possession and I set off to the nearest town. Nothing could have prepared me for what I came across."

"I imagine it would be like travelling forward two hundred years in time," said Greaves. "Or visiting another planet that was far more technologically advanced."

Anna looked at him with a puzzled expression. "Once again you must excuse me Mr Greaves but I haven't the faintest idea what you are talking about."

"Never mind. Please continue."

"I walked for days. My feet were sore and I rubbed up some awful blisters, then a man pulled up in one of them horseless buggies. The noise and the smell it made. He offered me a lift. He had heard on his... radiator, I think he called it. No, wait that's not right..."

"Radio," said Linda.

"Yes, thank you Mistress Linda. He had heard on his radio that there were people alive in the city and that there was help to be had there. He was awful kind to me, fed me and looked after me, but he died soon after we arrived in Harrisburg. The plague took him too. I was mighty sad about this. I had no idea how to fend for myself in the city. I was scared all the time and people just kept dying. The corpses were rotting by the roadsides. The smell was everywhere."

"They were bad times for us all," said Cortez.

"I was captured by a gang of men. Scavs they called themselves. They sold me and several other poor girls to the Neo-Clergy. I thought I was safe in the hands of men of God, but their faith was nothing like the faith I knew. They kept me prisoner for a long while. Then one of them said I was too old to be used for my blood, even though I was a Red Indian. I do not understand what he meant though."

"John-Paul Rohare Baptiste, the founder of the Neo-Clergy, is said to have stayed alive through transfusion," said Greaves. "That's when you take someone else's blood and put it in your body. He did this to children allegedly, thousands were taken."

"Oh," said Anna. "Anyway, eventually they sold me to Mr Edwards. I don't know how long I was there. I went inside myself. I pretended that none of it was happening to me. It was not my body that was being violated and shamed. I was somewhere else. But so was Jesus. I prayed often to him, pleaded with him. Surely this was not the purpose he had in mind for me. Then you came for me. I thought you had come to kill me. That's what happened to the girls they were done with. But I was wrong. Then, just after the night that I spent with Mistress Linda on the hillside, Jesus came to me. Though I was fallen and shamed, he came to me like he came to Mary Magdalen. And finally he revealed his purpose."

"Well we better not keep him waiting then," said Linda and jumped behind the wheel. "Next stop Torrington."

"Are you sure you know the way?' Linda said. The damnable woman could not let any opportunity to question or undermine him go by. She was worse than his mother.

Greaves told himself again, he was above things like emotions. He let it wash over him. She was simply trying to cope with the obvious inferiority she felt in his presence. Many people acted that way around him. He had learned to live with it. It didn't bother him. Was an elephant bothered by the gnats that buzzed about its hide? No. So why should he be bothered by those whose intellect was beneath his? She was there for a purpose, that was all.

They were in a corridor in the City Hall and Police Department on 21st Avenue. Thankfully the whole building was deserted. Annoyingly it did not fit the layouts he had memorised. They had obviously changed it. They had to have changed it, he was never wrong, *never.*

"No wait," he said. "We should be over by the cells. Of course, damn these ridiculous bureaucrats, they've no idea how to draw up a simple building layout." He knew that Linda and Anna were exchanging a look. Linda was trying to turn her against him, it was another one of her stupid little games. No matter though, when the time came, Anna would realise the truth and see everything he had done for her. How meticulously he had worked it all out. Then no amount of snide comments and vulgar put-downs would dampen her view of him.

She was going to save the world and he was going to make that happen. Only someone of his ability could do that. Then everyone would have to admit how exceptional he really was.

Greaves led them through the ruined offices that had once housed Torrington's finest. All that remained were the remnants of a few desks and some filing cabinets that had been wrenched open and set alight. Marvellous what humanity can do when it regresses into barbarism.

Beyond the offices and down a flight of stairs were the cells. They were dank and desolate. No-one had been near them for years, the air was stale and Greaves could see skeletons in two of them.

"I don't get it," said Linda. "If you're gonna spend billions of tax payers dollars on a super secret underground complex why would you put the entrance by a bunch of holding cells. I mean aren't you gonna be seen going in an out all the time, by the worst kind of people?"

Greaves sighed, how could he put this simply? "This isn't an entrance. We're looking for an emergency exit. One that was seldom, if ever, used. They built two of them. One comes out in a remote location some distance away and the other comes out here in case they had to evacuate quickly. They didn't want to be seen coming out, they needed complete deniability, which meant they'd have to kill whoever saw them leaving. Who would you rather have them take out, a bunch of girl guides or a bunch of junkies and rapists?"

"Why didn't they just build the whole complex miles from anywhere?" Linda said. "Then they could evacuate as much as they liked and no-one would see 'em."

"I don't know," said Greaves, he could feel himself losing control. He hated that. "Did I build the complex? No. Am I from military intelligence? No! Why are you bothering me with your questions?"

"'Cos it's fun. Wind him up and watch him go. Anyway, military intelligence, now there's a contradiction in terms."

"Now it pains me to say this," said Greaves. "But for once I agree with you."

"Steady on. Don't you have a pill for that?"

"I don't carry cyanide," said Greaves. Anna smiled and Linda smirked, conceding defeat. Now that was a snappy comeback.

They were just around the corner from the cells, standing in front of a steel security door marked 'DANGER - HIGH VOLTAGE!' This was to keep away any nosey cell guards. Greaves started tapping the wall around the jamb.

"What you doing?" asked Linda.

"I'm checking for termites. What does it look like?"

"I dunno." Linda shrugged.

Greaves found the hollow part of the wall. That's where the wires were. "Cortez, why not make yourself useful and punch a hole in the wall here?"

Cortez spun round and held a finger to his lips, listening. Everyone was quiet.

Eventually Linda whispered. "You hear something?"

"I'm not sure. Probably a rat, or some plaster falling. I better go look just to be sure."

Cortez padded off back to the cells. Linda took the butt of her shotgun and knocked a hole in the plaster for Greaves. He reached in and pulled out the wires. Hopefully they would still have residual power in them, or he would have wasted a lot of time.

"If this is the exit," said Linda. "Why didn't we just go in by the entrance?'

"Just in case there's someone still in there," said Greaves, cutting three wires and stripping the insulation. "You can never be too cautious."

Greaves twisted the copper of the three wires together in the right order, creating the feedback loop he needed. There was a sound of steel grating as the ancient door mechanism ground into life. The door moved with a jerk and swung open a couple of inches. Just wide enough to see the corridor beyond but not to squeeze through.

Linda chuckled. "Well that was handy."

Greaves lost his temper and punched the wall. He bruised two knuckles and yelped with pain. Luckily Cortez appeared and saved him from another of Linda's wisecracks.

"Couldn't see anything." He said. "What happened here?"

"The stinking door's jammed," Greaves said, shaking his hand. "We can't get through, we're going to have to force it."

They all put their shoulders against the door and strained. Nothing happened for a moment, then finally it creaked and gave just a little. Then it stopped. They pushed and grunted some more but the thing wasn't moving.

"It's no use," said Greaves. "We'll just have to wriggle through this gap."

There was a short corridor on the other side. Greaves tried the lights. They came on. Thank God there was still power. Now all they had to do was find some working PCs. Greaves was suddenly very excited. It had been so long since he'd had the pleasure of sitting in front of a computer. He hadn't realised how much he'd missed it.

Oh to stay here a few days. To comb their databases, to work out some new algorithms and just wallow in the luxury of it.

After a brief exploration they came to a room full of PCs. Greaves sat down and booted several up. To his extreme disappointment the machines weren't anywhere near as hi-tech as he'd believed they would be. In fact the most impressive models there were at least five years out of date, most of them were ten years behind and practically obsolete. Only two were able to read his memory stick, and only then after he'd done a bit of work on their operating systems.

He didn't mind too much though. It was a pleasure just to run his fingers over a keyboard again. He was lost to what was going on around him. Greaves was exploring the schematics of the lab's layout, seeing how his old colleagues had organised everything. Checking out how far they had moved on. Finding all the weak spots in their security and working out how to exploit them.

It brought back many memories. The sights and sounds of a lab, the distinctive smells. The laborious gathering of data and the sudden excitement as you approached a breakthrough, all of it came flooding back.

It was only at the last minute he noticed Cortez and Linda's agitation. They were spooked about something they'd heard. Greaves turned and saw they had their weapons at the ready. They were about to leave the room.

That's when the canister rattled across the floor. It was hissing.

"Hold your breath," Greaves shouted but it was too late.

It felt like his flesh and bones had turned to salt water taffy, his body now long and stringy.

Greaves turned to look at the computer screen. The white lines on the blue background showing the layout of the lab seemed to stretch away into infinity. Like a black hole their gravity was inescapable. He was pulled into the screen. Pulled in between the endless white lines. Down, down, down, or was it across?

Some tiny part of his brain kept screaming out to him that it was just the gas.

It must be some secret military compound, left over from before The Cull. It had hallucinogenic properties. He had to fight it. To get up and get out of there.

But the pull of the lines and the blue background between them was just too great.

So he fell.

Sound came back first. From a long way away to begin with. He could hear something slapping against skin, then he felt a tingling sensation. No, it was more like pain, pain in his cheek. Someone was slapping him across the face.

"Welcome back sleeping beauty." He heard a voice with a Mid-West accent say as he shook his head to try and clear it. His vision was blurred and he blinked to bring it back into focus. There were three figures standing in front of him. He moved his head around and saw four more figures in the room. Greaves had a throbbing headache and he felt nauseous but his sight righted itself.

He was tied to a chair, with his hands behind his back, in one of the offices in the Police Department. Two of the men in front of him were grinning – hate filled malevolent grins. The other just looked mean. Greaves was suddenly very frightened.

"Now that you're awake," said the man in the middle. "Maybe we should introduce ourselves." He had short brown hair, acne and really bad teeth, he was probably in his late twenties. The man to his left was around six-five in height with close cropped hair, a moustache and the physique of someone who worked out a lot. He was the oldest, probably in his mid-thirties. The other man in front of Greaves looked Hispanic, he had black hair and swarthy skin.

"Now we all," said Acne, "are from the Neo-Clergy. Good, honest God fearing folk, and we don't take that kindly to you UTN motherfuckers riding into our town and attempting to massacre our women and children like you did in Montana. So you got exactly five seconds to tell me what you're planning on doing here, or I can't be held responsible for what's going to happen to you."

Greaves cleared his throat. "Honestly," he said. "I haven't the faintest idea what you're talking about."

"Is the wrong answer," shouted Acne like he was some game show host. "So Jed here is going to have a little play with you. Then we'll see if you feel more like talking to us. Show him your toys Jed."

The guy with the moustache pulled out what looked like a big car battery, with a handle and two jump leads attached.

"Now Jed here," said Acne. "Used to wear a badge and work in these very offices keeping the streets clean from scum like you. So he knows a thing or two about getting pissants to talk, ain't that right Jed?"

"Sure is Billy Joe."

"How many volts," said Billy Joe. "Can you get out of that machine of yours?"

"'Bout five thousand. Maybe even ten if I work her hard."

"Maybe even ten-thousand volts. Now am I right in thinking that would hurt if you were to attach those jump leads to a part of someone's body? Say maybe their nuts?"

"It'd hurt like a motherfucker Billy Joe. Hurt like a motherfucker."

"Look," said Greaves, failing to keep the panic out of his voice. "This is ridiculous. I don't know what you want from me but you've got the wrong person. I was just passing through that's all. And the Neo-Clergy, aren't they completely defunct?"

"Completely defunct. Do you hear that Chico?" Billy Joe said to the Hispanic guy. "Completely defunct, do you like them fancy words he's using?"

Chico shook his head. "No sir."

"Me neither. And for your information the Neo-Clergy is getting stronger and stronger everyday, in spite of you and your UTN buddies trying to slaughter us all."

"I'm not from the UTN. I don't even know what the UTN is."

"Then why are you travelling with that Redskin bitch huh?" said Billy Joe. "Answer me that. What you doing in them offices underground that not even Jed here's ever heard about."

"We're just scavs. We were just passing through, thought we'd look for something we could sell. That girl, she's just someone we picked up."

"You know," said Billy Joe. "I'm liking your answers less and less. We been watching you from the moment you hit town boy. Since when do scavs drive a fancy motor home like yours, huh? Since when do scavs break into secret buildings no-one knows about and settle down to play on a computer when, to the best of my knowledge, they're as rare as hen's teeth. You're up to something. Now I've tried to find out the nice way, but you're just not playing ball. So you brought this on yourself. You remember that when you're crying and screaming for your mama."

Jed unbuckled Greaves' belt and yanked down his trousers. His genitals shrank back in on themselves.

"Well now," said Billy Joe with a filthy laugh. "They sure don't call you Moby Dick back home do they? You sure we got enough to work with Jed?"

"This'll do," Jed grunted.

"No wait," said Greaves. "Please don't do this. I'm begging you please don't do it. There's been a mistake. A terrible mistake. Please don't, please, AAAHHH!"

Jed applied the jump lead clips to Greaves' testicles. The cold metal teeth bit into his balls, sending shooting pains right up into his abdomen.

"Think that hurts do you?" said Billy Joe. "Trust me you haven't felt pain yet."

Jed connected the leads to the battery. Greaves felt the burning heat from the clips first, charring his flesh. He screamed but that wasn't the worst of it.

Seven thousand volts shot through his body. It felt like someone had punched him in the nuts. But the punch travelled right through his whole frame, pounding every molecule in his body on the way. His spine arced and his muscles went into spasm as he writhed and fought the ropes that held him to the chair.

Jed flicked a switch and Greaves slumped back down, whimpering and sobbing. His legs were jerking and twitching. He struggled for breath, but his chest wouldn't move properly, his lungs wouldn't inflate, none of his body would do what he told it.

"Oh God," he said eventually. "Oh God please, please stop this."

"Sorry partner," said Billy Joe. "But I don't think you've

had enough yet. He had enough yet Jed?"

"No sir," said Jed and fired it up again.

Another surge tore through Greaves' body. Stronger, more excruciating. The pressure was intolerable. He felt it trying to push its way out of his skull. His eyeballs strained as though they were going to pop out of his sockets. His mouth filled with blood. He'd bitten his tongue off. Oh God he had, he'd bitten it clean off. And then there was the smell, burnt flesh. His flesh.

Greaves dropped back into the chair. Had it stopped? He couldn't tell. The leads weren't connected any more. It must have stopped but it didn't feel like it had. His whole body quivered. His muscles were in knots. He wanted to scream. He wanted to vomit. He wanted his mother to put her arms around him and kiss it all better. *Oh God mother, look what they've done. Look what they've done to me.*

"You ready to talk now friend?" said Chico in a soft voice. He put his arm around Greaves. "It's the only way to make 'em stop."

Greaves nodded his head. Blood spilled out of his mouth. He tried to find his breath. What about his tongue? If he'd bitten it off he couldn't talk. If he couldn't talk they'd do it again. Oh God please not again! He'd have to tell them about his tongue. But how could he tell them without a tongue. Oh God no, oh please!

Turns out he hadn't bitten it off, just bitten a chunk out of it. It hurt like hell. Every bit of him hurt like hell. Even his eyelashes and his toenails throbbed and ached. He drew a breath and it came out like a sob. Every time he breathed out he cried harder.

"I'm sorry," he said as the snot dripped off his nose and the blood ran down his chin. "I'm sorry, I'm sorry, I'm sorry."

"That's okay," said Chico gently rubbing his back. "You take your time. Now, what were you and you're UTN buddies doing down in them offices?"

"I was... I was..." Greaves swallowed and wished he hadn't. His throat was on fire. He couldn't talk. It hurt too much. He had to talk or they'd hurt him more. "I was l-l-look... ing... at... pl-plans."

"Plans for what? Some building you want to blow up?"

Greaves shook his head. "Plans... for a... lab-lab-laboratory."

"A laboratory?" said Billy Joe. "What the fuck would you know about a laboratory?"

"I'm – I'm a... scientist. I used to work with... with the men in this laboratory, back before... back before The Cull."

"And why were you looking at these plans?" said Chico. "What's in this laboratory?"

"A virus. A special Doomsday Virus."

"And what's so special about it?"

"There's no other virus like it. You can programme it, like a computer. You can programme it so that it only kills the people you want it to kill. It's the ultimate biological weapon."

"And where is this laboratory?" said Chico. "Is it here in Torrington?"

"No. It's in Montana. Near the Little Bighorn. What used to be the river, before it dried up."

"Little Bighorn," said Billy Joe. "Ain't that where Custer killed all them redskins?"

"No," said Chico. "They killed him and all his men. It was another massacre."

"That figures," said Billy Joe. "That's why them fucking Injuns would hide it there."

"It isn't the Native Americans who've hidden it," said Greaves. He felt like a schoolboy, desperate to please his teachers with the right answers. "It's a powerful, secret organisation. They existed before The Cull and they're still around."

"And you planned to steal the virus from them," said Chico. "Is that right?"

Greaves nodded his head, then hung it in shame.

"You wanted to wipe out every white man didn't you?" said Jed. The veins were throbbing in his temples. "You wanted to kill every decent Christian man, woman and child so you could have the whole country to your stinking heathen selves. Isn't that right? Isn't it! Why you sick fucks. You make me want to puke."

Jed flew at Greaves. He swung his right arm in a powerful upper cut. It smacked into Greaves' face and he felt the chair actually leave the ground with the force of the punch. Two teeth flew out of his mouth and he landed on his back. Tiny gold stars reverberated inside his head and he lost consciousness again.

Greaves was not in a good shape when they brought him back. His face was covered in blood. His trousers were around his ankles and his loins were blackened and burned. This was not the work of men who knew what they were doing, it was the work of amateurs.

Cortez thought them beneath contempt.

"You next big guy," said the one whose face was covered in blemishes. The man with the moustache tied Greaves to bars of the cell where Linda and Anna were also bound.

There were two other men with them. They both wore

white robes with the red circle that marked them out as Neo-Clergy soldiers. They carried pump-action shotguns that they stuck in Cortez's face as the blemished one untied his hands from the bars but left them bound together.

"You need a hand there Billy Joe?" said the moustached one.

"Got it covered thanks Jed. Now big feller, up on your feet, and don't try nothing stupid. These boys here got awful itchy trigger fingers."

Cortez stood slowly. His legs tingled after sitting down for so long.

"This way," said Billy Joe and led him into the offices.

There were three other men waiting there. Billy Joe and Jed greeted one of them as Chico. Cortez assessed the situation. There was a chair in the centre of the room. That's where they had worked Greaves over and in the corner was the electrical machine they had used.

"Now sit yourself down real slow in that chair there," said Billy Joe. "Jed here's going to untie your hands and tie them behind you. If you even look as though you're going to resist, you got six armed men here who will put bullets in you."

Just as Cortez had thought, amateurs. Rank amateurs.

Cortez held his bound hands up close to his chest so Jed had to lean in to untie him. He was flanked on both sides by Neo-Clergy soldiers aiming their weapons at his head. Cortez pressed his wrists together to make them more difficult to untie and to appear more securely fastened than they actually were. His hands were free before Jed realised it. Cortez jumped on this split-second advantage.

He took hold of Jed's shirt and pulled him off balance. Then he grabbed both shotgun barrels and pulled them hard. He aimed one at the soldier on his right and one at Jed's head.

Both weapons went off as the soldier's fingers pulled against their triggers. The right shotgun unloaded both barrels into Jed's skull. The cartridges took off most of his face before tearing into the gut of the soldier on Cortez's left. That soldier's shotgun unloaded only one barrel into the chest of the soldier on Cortez's right. He was sent spinning backwards, robes on fire and a big hole in his chest.

Jed fell forward and dropped half his brains into Cortez's lap. The soldier on his left doubled over in pain clutching the back of the chair. Cortez slipped Jed's knife out of its sheath with his left hand and kicked him off. Then he stood and took hold of the gut-shot soldier's shotgun with his right hand, catching hold of the soldier from behind and putting the man between him and the other four armed men as he backed towards the door.

Finally they reacted. Most of their shots went wide as Cortez backed out of the room, Two shots thudded into the soldier he was using as a shield. The man screamed as they did, cursing his comrades.

As he got to the door Cortez fired the shotgun, winging another robed soldier. The man fell to ground screaming. Cortez jammed Jed's knife into the throat of the soldier he was holding then sliced outwards cutting through tendons, flesh and arteries. Blood spattered Chico, Billy Joe and the other soldier and they leaped backwards. This gave Cortez time to get into the corridor.

He stepped out and pressed himself flat against the wall. Billy Joe poked his head out of the room, looked up and down the passage, and Cortez drove Jed's knife right into his left eyeball. Billie Joe's face registered surprise and horror, then he fell back through the door and died from the six inches of sharpened steel that had punctured his brain. That would make the other three guys in the room think twice before leaving.

Cortez edged along the wall with the shotgun trained on the doorway. He was heading back to the cells. He kicked open a door with a broken safety glass window and stopped for a second to pick a shard of glass out of the broken wire.

Arriving back at the cells Cortez used the glass to cut through the rope that held Linda to the bars.

"I expected you sooner," she said. "You run into trouble?"

"Nothing too bad. It's strictly amateur night back there."

"You bring any weapons?"

Cortez held up the shotgun and the shard of glass. "Just these."

"Do I get to the play with the big one?" Cortez shook his head and tossed her the shard of glass. "Oh you're a cheap date." Linda said.

Cortez held his finger to his lips to silence her and motioned her to follow him. Greaves moaned in pain.

They walked up the corridor and stood either side of the door to the cells, their backs to the wall. They heard footsteps down the corridor and shouted directions, often conflicting. Linda looked wryly at Cortez. He nodded. She knew he was right.

The two robed soldiers burst into the cells first. The second was the one Cortez had winged. He was holding his shotgun in his right hand, which hung limply down at his side. He held his wounded shoulder with his left hand. Linda came up behind him, lifted his elbow with her left hand and jammed the shard of glass into his chest with her right. The man dropped to his knees and fell forward, driving the tip of the shard right through his body and out of his back.

Before his comrade had time to turn round, Cortez unloaded the remaining shotgun cartridge into the back of his head, blowing his face and brains all over the floor.

The footsteps stopped then went back up the corridor. Cortez glanced round to see Chico beating a hasty retreat.

Linda and Cortez pursued him up the corridor. When they got to the office a window was open and there was no sign of the man. They heard a motorbike start up and Cortez approached the window with care. He saw Chico speeding away.

"You were right about amateur hour," said Linda. "How'd these jokers get the drop on us in the first place?"

"One lucky punch can sometimes turn a fight. You should see how the others are doing. I'll look around for our things."

Cortez found their weapons and Greaves' great coat and carried them back to the cells.

Anna was free when he got there and Linda was helping Greaves pull his trousers back up. He was wincing and moaning from the pain. He looked like he'd been burned pretty bad.

Greaves looked up at the sound of pills rattling in his great coat. "I told them about the Doomsday Virus," he said. "I told them where to find it. I told them everything. Except about Anna. I didn't mention Anna." Then he burst into tears.

Linda put her arm around him and pulled him to her breast. "There, there. Come to mama."

Greaves put his arms around her waist and curled into her like a little boy. "Mommy, I'm sorry. I'm so, so sorry.

I just couldn't take the pain. I'm sorry. I just couldn't take it."

"That's alright. You get it all out. You're safe now. They can't hurt you anymore. You have a good cry about it."

Greaves continued to sob and Linda comforted him. Cortez had known of several men who used to cry on whores once they had come. Linda had probably comforted clients this way a hundred times before. It was obviously nothing new to her.

But for a few minutes it almost made Cortez like her.

CHAPTER FOURTEEN

"Just wanted to wish you luck Robert," said Colt stepping into the Prophet's dressing room. It had once been a classroom in Denver University's media dept. The department had a working TV studio and Colt's tech guys said that it was in a good enough condition to be adapted to their purposes.

"Why thank you Samuel," said the Prophet. "That's mighty kind of you. How's my make-up look?"

"Well I'm not much of a judge of these things. I'm just glad it's you out there instead of me. Especially if you have to wear that stuff on your face. "

"Stops the lights blanching my face. Or at least that's what I'm told."

"Is that right? Can't have that can we? Now have you had a look at the changes my men made to the script?"

"Yes I have. You know Samuel, I was hoping to concentrate more on a theme of reconciliation and forgiveness."

"I know you was Robert. But we're in the middle of an all-out war here. Don't forget how viciously they treated your followers. People'll be a lot more forgiving once we've beaten these savages. Then you can preach all the reconciliation you like. 'Sides, you got the second part of the show to concentrate on the love of Jesus. We've got to make these people realise what a threat them Injuns pose. We got to get them back into the fold. We can't save their souls 'less we do."

"Okay Samuel." The Prophet's shoulders drooped a little and his smile was forced, but Colt knew he was going to play along. "We'll do it your way."

"Atta boy." Colt slapped him on the back. "You know we got this broadcast going out to sets in twenty-three –

count 'em – twenty-three States."

"Is that right? That's a hell of a lot of ground to cover."

"Ain't it just? We tested the reception in each State. It's as clear as if you was standing there talking to the people yourself. That transmission tower we re-built helps boost the signal. We've put the word out in every one of those States. Folk's are clamouring to hear from you. People are setting up every workable TV set they can get their hands on and they're gonna draw a crowd. Trust me on this. Once folk start seeing moving pictures again they're going to be mesmerised. Mesmerised by the spectacle and mesmerised by your words. We've got so many demands from surrounding States that folks are already forming work teams to build more transmitters to get the word out. We're gonna win a lot of folks back to Jesus."

"And you Samuel. What about you?"

"Me?"

"Are we going to win you back to Jesus?"

Colt laughed again. "Will ya listen to this guy? What do you think I'm doing this for? Course you've won me back to Jesus. I never left him and he never left me."

"I hope so Samuel. I hope so."

Colt stepped out into the corridor where Simon Peter was waiting for him. "So," he said. "You checked out this 'thing' in Montana that the wetback was talking about?"

"This Doomsday Virus that you can programme to kill or spare whoever you want? Yeah we checked it out."

"Walk with me," said Colt, glancing up and down the corridor to make certain they weren't overheard. "So how's this guy's... what's his name?"

"Chico."

"Yeah Chico. How's his story check out?"

"Well, there is a secret underground lab in Montana, near the site where the Little Bighorn river used to be."

"Used to be?"

"You remember Billings got hit by those nuclear strikes that kicked off after The Cull? When everyone was blaming everyone else for starting the plague and some guys actually went ahead and pressed the button?"

"Course I remember that. How'd you live through a thing like that and forget?"

"Well this caused a lot of seismic activity, earthquakes and stuff. It's not radioactive around the Little Bighorn or nothing, but the river's dried up and there's all this molten lava in its place. Anyway there's this plateau right in the centre of all this lava. There's just one small pass onto the plateau which is only a matter of feet wide. The rest of it is surrounded by molten rock."

"And this is where the lab is? Are you sure about this?"

"We dug up two of the guys who worked on the thing. They were scared to talk to us at first, but we put the pressure on them. The lab was built by some secret government organisation, one that survived The Cull. They haven't got a lot of influence left but they still have a lot of resources. They chose this place 'cos it's so difficult to get to, and they murdered everyone who ever worked on it, to keep it quiet. Or at least they thought they did. These two guys survived by hiding under a pile of corpses. They even drew us a map of how to get there."

"And you sent men to check this out right? To see if this place exists."

"We did. There's something out there alright. In the

place they say it is. So it probably is a lab."

"And it has this Doomsday Virus there? The one you can programme?"

"Well the UTN obviously believe it does. Which is what's most important. Specially if they get to it before us."

"We can't let that happen! This virus could win us the war before it's even started."

"Right. But this place is difficult to reach, almost impossible to get into and with the resources they have, probably very well defended. We're gonna have to raise an army to get in and, if it comes to it, stop the UTN from doing the same."

"Well that oughtn't be too difficult. This weekly broadcast is gonna bring us lots of converts. Specially when we get 'em good and worried about the threat from them Injuns. They'll come flocking to us desperate for protection and ready to fight. So this Chico's story does check out then?"

"Not entirely. The stuff about a party of thirty Injuns attacking them to rescue their cohorts is probably bullshit. We had a look round the place and his story doesn't stand up. There was no UTN activity in that area around that time anyway, except for the four that the scouting party picked up. So there wouldn't have been thirty Injuns around to come to their aid."

"Is that right?" said Colt, with a knowing sneer.

"The four UTN members probably fought it out with our boys and beat 'em even though they were outnumbered. Chico probably fled and left his comrades to take the brunt."

"So what do we do with him?"

"Well he did give us some valuable information, so he has his uses. On the other hand he lied his ass off to save face. On top of that the barefaced bastard is asking for promotion."

"Is he now? Well that's what he'll get. We'll make him a lieutenant and put him on the front line of this march on Montana. If he's half the coward you say he is that's the best punishment I can think of."

"Yes sir."

"Now, how's Wyoming looking?"

"All three gangs are losing control of their territories. People are either in favour of what the Prophet is preaching, or they're scared that the gang bosses aren't doing enough to protect them from the redskin threat. There's open defiance in some places. People are refusing to pay their tributes and the men we sent in to take out lower level enforcers are doing a good job of it. The people are protecting 'em from getting caught. Even with their lives sometimes."

"And the upshot of this is?"

"All three gangs want to talk to you about joining up."

"I though they might. I ain't having anything to do with that shit-heel Benny Cooper. He was the one behind that attack on us, I know it. He's gonna be the first casualty in Wyoming. Set up a sit down with Tom Eastman and Carl Jennings. Only this time they come to my headquarters in my territory. And they come unarmed or they don't come at all."

"Yes sir."

The two of them had worked their way round to the mixing room, where the director and technical staff were preparing to send out the first *Tomorrow Show* in an age. Colt and Simon Peter stepped into the room to watch. They were greeted with hushed respect from the director and technical staff.

Colt could see the Prophet out on the studio floor. He

was standing on his mark in front of the cameras ready for his big moment. This was what they had all worked so long and hard for.

"Gentlemen," said Colt. "We're back where we should be. In control!"

CHAPTER FIFTEEN

The ground they walked was ancient ground. According to the legends of the Cheyenne, when the first people fished the land from the sea, in a net made from the promises of the gods, it was this very land that they pulled first to the surface. This very land where human beings first walked the earth. Where the grass and the corn were made to grow. Where the buffalo was brought into being to provide good hunting.

Now this ground had been prepared according to tradition, the grass burnt away and the bare earth scorched. A circle had been drawn in ash made from the burned bones of Cheyenne warriors, dead for over two centuries. Such a powder was hard to come by and only used on the most sacred of occasions. Occasions such as this.

Hiamovi sat inside the circle wearing the symbols of his totem animals as custom demanded. He wore two symbols, his headdress was made exclusively from the feathers of the golden eagle. Around his neck he wore a coyote's paw. Behind him were two braves: Abedabun, a Cheyenne scout who wore a pendant of bald eagle feathers around his neck, and Macawi, a Sioux scout who wore a rabbit's foot.

Facing Hiamovi was Ahiga, who wore a bear's claw. Behind Ahiga were Akecheta who wore a wolf's paw and Hastiin who wore a rattlesnake skin wrapped around his left arm. A single lit candle sat between the two parties.

This was a circle of truth. None who entered were to speak any falsehood. This was a sacred covenant and to break it would mean the severest punishment. In this life and all the lives that followed.

"Ahiga," said Hiamovi. "You face your accusers openly. So you can hear the charges made against you."

"I thank you," said Ahiga, "for that privilege."

"Macawi," said Hiamovi, turning to address the Sioux brave. "How did you come to hear the allegations you now make against Ahiga?"

"Great Chief, you sent us to spy on the white man's occupation of Lame Deer. We'd spent three days watching their operations, noting the harsh way they treated our brothers and sisters. Working them until they dropped. Beating them if they didn't get up again. On the evening of the third day as we were finishing our meal we were approached by two squaws. They'd risked much by coming to look for us. If their absence was discovered, they, and their family could have been beaten to death. But there were important things they had to tell the UTN, things they had to get directly to your ears."

"Abedabun," said Hiamovi. "Tell us what these important things were and why the squaws thought I needed to hear them."

"Great Chief," said Abedabun. "The squaws had been waiting on the white chief Colt, fetching his supper and doing his chores. He considered them little better than animals and so he did not watch his tongue when they were near. He was discussing word that had reached him from one of his own scouts with another white man. The scout claimed that members of the UTN knew about a virus created by white scientists. A Doomsday Virus that could be instructed to kill selectively. They said this virus is kept in an underground hideaway in Little Bighorn on the site of the Cheyenne's finest moment. Although we knew of no-one within the UTN who had heard of such a thing we thought it highly important you know of this Doomsday Virus and its existence."

"And what else Macawi," said Hiamovi, "did these brave squaws tell you?"

"They said that one of the tribe's young braves saw Hastiin planting a quiver full of bloody arrows and explosives in the council's meeting hall. They also said that one of the Elders then saw Hastiin go and inform Ahiga of what he had done. They said this evidence had been used as justification by the white man for the evil that was being done to them. They claimed that Ahiga and his men knowingly planted that evidence to give the white man reason to persecute them."

"Thank you Macawi, thank you Abedabun," said Hiamovi. "Ahiga, what have you to say about these claims?"

"I am called here when I have important work to do raising an army so that I can answer the charges of women, children and old men? Do you think this is the best use of my time Hiamovi?"

"Do you deny the charges Ahiga?"

Ahiga was silent for a long time. He held Hiamovi's gaze the whole while, without blinking.

"No," he said presently. "I do not deny them. I am bound to speak no falsehood and the claims are true."

Hiamovi continued to hold Ahiga's gaze. "When you told me of your connections among the Neo-Clergy you assured me they were superficial. Cultivated, you claimed, purely for the purpose of gathering information. Yet now you sit here and admit that you collaborated with these men to bring untold suffering to your brothers and sisters. How can this be? Why did you do this?"

"To bring you power," said Ahiga, raising his voice. "To unite all the tribes into the strong nation, that we've worked so hard to bring about. How many tribes have joined our cause? How many braves have pledged us their services now that they see what a real threat the white man is? This occupation has been the spark that lit a fire across the land. A fire in the hearts of all our people. Now they understand what true strength we will have if we all stand together. This wouldn't have happened if the white man hadn't played right into our hands. Do I regret the suffering this has caused my brothers and sisters? Of course I do. Just as I regret every casualty in every battle I have ever fought. But this is a war, we knew that from day one. Brave men and women have to fall so that their children and their children's children can reclaim the land that is theirs by right. And you call me here to discuss this matter when the most important thing these scouts learned is not being discussed."

"And that is?" Hiamovi said.

"This Doomsday Virus that the white man has created. If there is such a virus in existence, that can be told who to kill and who to spare, and if it really sits on the very spot where your people won our greatest victory against the white man then don't you think that's destiny? Don't you think that such a weapon could end this war without another shot being fired? Shouldn't we be doing everything in our power to ensure that we get hold of it before the white man does? Can we really face the consequence of it falling into his hands?"

Hiamovi was loath to admit it but Ahiga's words carried a lot of truth. The United Tribal Nations had grown on an unprecedented scale since the occupation. The tribal Elders could see the wisdom in uniting against the threat of the white man now they saw what he was capable of. As a Cheyenne chief Hiamovi had gained great stature from the fact that it was his people who were attacked by the white man. His people whom he was working so tirelessly to free from enslavement.

Hiamovi now had huge influence with every tribal council across the land. Many ways were now open to him that had previously been blocked. All this had happened as the Great Spirit had promised. The rebirth of his people was at hand. Were Ahiga's actions really evil if so great a good could spring from them? This was a circle of truth after all. No falsehoods could be spoken here. Would Ahiga dare say these things if they weren't true?

Then there was the matter of Ahiga's reputation. He was popular with the braves. His standing within the UTN was fast becoming second only to Hiamovi's. The young men and women of the tribes saw him as a virile, good-looking man of action. A leader of integrity.

He had led the most successful offensive against the white man and he had succeeded with minimal loss of life. What's more he had shown fairness and restraint to the white man, refusing to kill unarmed men, women and children. In spite of the lies the white man told about a massacre, there were too many witnesses to his actions for this to be disputed.

Ahiga was politically very useful to Hiamovi. To shame him now, to cast him out or have him killed would damage the whole UTN. It would sow discord where there had previously been harmony. It would inevitably break up the union of tribes that they had all worked so hard to build. Hiamovi would lose face by association and his standing with the tribal councils would be called into question.

Hiamovi held Ahiga's gaze again for a moment, without speaking. Eventually Ahiga blinked and lowered his eyes to show his submission to Hiamovi's authority.

"How do we know that this Doomsday Virus exists?" said Hiamovi. "How do we know this is not a trap? The squaws overheard them talking about a UTN party on their way to find this virus. Yet I know of no person within our organisation who has any knowledge of it, do you?"

"No. However I have received reports of a Native American girl travelling with three others in a motor -home who fit the description that the Neo-Clergy gave. They were picked up by some scouts in Wyoming by all accounts. Because of the occupation, the Neo-Clergy attacks any group with a Native American in it. They probably just assumed the group were with us because of the presence of the girl. This, however, only makes the story more likely."

So, Ahiga had been making enquiries about this supposed UTN party had he? This meant he probably knew in advance that Hiamovi was going to call him to a circle of truth. Hiamovi would have to watch his channels of communication in future. And watch this resourceful young Navajo even more closely.

"Most of North Montana is a wasteland now," said Hiamovi. "The nuclear strikes on Billings saw to that. Little Bighorn doesn't exist anymore, it's just molten lava. How could any white scientists be manufacturing a virus there?"

"If the scientists wanted to remain hidden," said Ahiga, "then what better place to build an underground laboratory?"

So, thought Hiamovi, Ahiga had been forewarned. This proved it. Hiamovi said nothing about an underground laboratory. Yet Ahiga dropped it into the conversation, flaunting the fact that he knew what Hiamovi hadn't told him yet. He was letting Hiamovi know he had someone passing him information. He wanted Hiamovi to be wary of even his inner circle. He knew Hiamovi would have to draw him even closer, to protect himself.

"To take such a place, and to get the white scientists to deliver such a weapon would take a great army," said Hiamovi. "We may even have to clash with the white man. If he already knows what we know he too will be raising an army. Do we have that many men?"

"We could raise them Great Chief," Ahiga said. He was calling Hiamovi by this title more and more, so were the other UTN members. Hiamovi liked it. "We must not sell the campaign to our people as a war over weaponry though. Rather let us sell it as a holy crusade."

"What do you have in mind?"

"Great Chief, my people have no love for the Hopi, this is well known. But they are seen as people of great wisdom and peace by many of our brothers and sisters in the cause. They are supposedly the record keepers. They have many prophecies, as I'm sure you're aware."

"I am. Is there one in particular that you're thinking of? One that will be useful to us in our struggle?"

"There is. They are awaiting the coming of the Fifth Age of Man. A time of great peace and spiritual rebirth. This will come after much persecution, such as your people are suffering, and involve a giant struggle, such as a clash with the white man perhaps. Then when this has come to pass a Blue Kachina will appear and the age will begin."

"This Kachina is one of their gods is it not? One that can take human form and come to earth to interact with human beings?"

"That's right Great Chief. The Blue Kachina will appear in the sky at the return of Pahana after a great struggle. She will herald the Fifth Age of Man, bring about an end to our greatest struggle and deliver us from our enemies without any bloodshed."

"I see. And you believe if we preach the coming of the

Fifth Age of Man, alongside the danger of the white man we will generate the maximum amount of support needed to raise an army? Very well, I give you my blessing."

Hiamovi stood and extinguished the candle with the skull of a coyote. This signified that the circle was now void. The men stood and kicked the ashes to the wind, wiping away the circle.

"Great Chief," said Ahiga. "May I have a private word?"

Hiamovi nodded and they moved away from the other braves. "I thank you for your wise and merciful ruling on this matter and I do not want to call your just response into question, but there may be those among us who would not appreciate the discretion you have shown in this matter. Who may use your decision against you. I would not want this to happen."

"I appreciate your concern," said Hiamovi. "But only those who sat within the circle know of this matter. I trust their discretion."

"Because you are an honourable man Great Chief. There is much at stake though. Can we afford the risk?"

"What are you suggesting Ahiga?"

"Great Chief, do you really want to know?"

Hiamovi turned away. He did not want to answer that question. Out of the corner of his eye he saw Ahiga turn and nod to his men. Akecheta and Hastiin smiled to signal their understanding. Hiamovi walked away without saying goodbye to Abedabun and Macawi. After tacitly condemning them he did not have the heart.

Ahiga had outmanoeuvred him at this turn. Hiamovi had been trapped by political expediency into a course of action he abhorred. The truth was the closer he got to achieving the power he'd been promised the further he felt from the Great Spirit who'd promised him. Yet for all that he loved the Great Spirit he could not let that power go.

"You shiver Great Chief," said Ahiga.

"Just a chill in the night air. That's all."

CHAPTER SIXTEEN

Greaves had been weird with Linda for about a week now. It wasn't anything she could put her finger on and kick his butt about. It was just the general way he treated her.

She knew he still felt uncomfortable about crying on her. He didn't have to get all pissy about it though. People acted in strange ways under the duress of battle, everyone knew that. No-one held it against you. A bit like at a swingers' party, no-one spoke about it afterwards.

That was the problem though, she had to keep her mouth shut. She couldn't confront the whole thing. So he had it both ways the little prick.

After the last guy had run from City Hall in Torrington, they'd done a thorough job of looking the place over. Greaves' instincts were good as usual and they'd made a pretty good haul. Guns, drugs, food rations, batteries and all kinds of things they could barter with. Anna had even come across a well stocked first-aid kit. They'd dressed Greaves' wounds and given him some industrial strength pain killers to get him up and running. He'd been a bit woozy for a day or two then he'd gone back to being his same irritating self.

They found bartering the stuff they'd scavenged more difficult than they'd imagined. They located a guy just outside of Casper who could get them gas. Soon as he recognised them, he was loath to do business. Seems word had already got out that the Neo-Clergy and their men were looking for them, had put out a description and everything.

What they had to offer for the gas was just too tasty for him to turn down, though it didn't stop him trying to rip them off.

After that, if they wanted anything they had to split up and go find it incognito. They drove along the back roads and stayed away from any major populated areas, trying the whole time to get to Montana while staying under the Neo-Clergy's radar.

Technically Wyoming wasn't yet under Neo-Clergy control, but their power was growing daily. The three gangs who ran the State were rapidly losing their grip and most people expected the Neo-Clergy to take over any day soon. Considering how bad she remembered things being under the Neo-Clergy, Linda was surprised to hear the majority of folk thought it would be a good thing when they did regain control.

They heard similar reports when they skipped over the border into Montana. Linda still found it kind of strange that even though the America she'd grown up in had gone, people still clung to clung to its old boundary lines and markers. Then again, she guessed that's all they had left to cling to.

In this day and age territory meant everything. It represented security, identity and a sense of order to people. Which is why, Linda supposed, the Neo-Clergy suddenly seemed so popular again. More than anything, what they offered to most people was one of those three things.

They heard a lot about the UTN in Montana as well. Greaves had brought the name up soon after they left Torrington. He said that's why the Neo-Clergy guys had jumped them. They'd seen Anna and thought they were part of this Native American army that was forming all over the country.

There was a lot of hatred for 'redskins', as the locals called them in Montana. Apparently that was because they'd carried out a massacre of over a hundred innocent men, women and children. They made sure to keep Anna out of sight whenever they passed any kind of a town or inhabited outpost. Everywhere they went people were full of fear and anger. They wanted a reckoning. But more than that, they wanted protection, and that's what the Neo-Clergy promised.

It seemed to Linda that the whole political landscape of the country was changing. The Neo-Clergy were making a big comeback on one hand. On the other the Native Americans were suddenly a force to be reckoned with. Most ordinary folk seemed to be caught in the middle, busying themselves with their daily routine while living in a climate of constant terror. A climate both sides had created to further their own ends.

The fact that they were travelling with a Native American and were wanted by the Neo-Clergy wasn't helped any by the route they had to take through Montana. Whole sectors of it were still radioactive from the bomb that had hit Billings. All the earthquakes that had happened as a result of the nuclear strike had altered the landscape too.

This meant they had to drive west and come back on themselves to get to Little Bighorn, which was where Greaves had revealed the underground lab that housed the Doomsday Virus was.

Some days they couldn't leave Bertha at all. Greaves had done some calculations about wind direction and fall-out and had determined where they'd be safe and where things weren't so good. And wouldn't you know it, he even had pills to deal with the trace radiation. He doled them out twice a day from a bottle in that stinking great coat of his.

This also meant they couldn't make quite so many

prayer stops for Cortez and Anna. They just had to do their God grovelling on the go. They seemed to have formed this little two person prayer group. Which was kind of strange considering one was a devout Christian and the other a strict Muslim.

Greaves tended to keep his nose out of their religious discussions most of the time. Probably because he was afraid of offending Anna, or that Cortez would kick his butt for being an infidel. They knew he was a sceptic anyway. He fancied himself above such simple minded superstitions. Or so he claimed. Linda couldn't help thinking his inability to accept beliefs that weren't scientific or rational made him the biggest zealot of all. At least Anna and Cortez seemed willing to listen to each others' beliefs.

The way Greaves spoke about science holding all the answers and providing the key to all man's problems made it sound like a religion in its own right. The way he spoke about Anna was kind of religious too, about her saving mankind and turning the world into a new Eden. That was practically straight out of the Bible. Even Linda knew that and it had been a long while since she'd been to Sunday school.

She guessed it was easier for Greaves to believe in paradise and saviours so long as there was a scientific explanation for them. If this Doomsday Virus was everything he claimed it was, then maybe all three of them were right. Maybe the day of judgement really was at hand. Perhaps God or Allah was about to call the world to account all thanks to a handy bit of science Greaves and his buddies had whipped up for Him.

And here Linda was, chauffeuring the key players to doomsday. She wondered if this would give her any special license with the 'Big Guy' upstairs? She wasn't even sure if she believed in Him herself. What Linda believed in was self reliance, that's why she loved Bertha so much. Bertha represented independence. There was no-one to hold her back and no-one to rely on her. It was just her and the open highway aboard her great big, beautiful bus.

"Jesus, is it me or is it getting hot in here?" she said, turning Bertha's temperature control down low. "What's the matter with your air conditioning girl?"

"Mistress Linda," said Anna. "You should not blaspheme so. You'll go to hell for it."

"Is that right? Well I'm sure getting a taste of what the temperature's gonna be like."

"We're approaching the lava flows," said Greaves. "The temperature's set to rise a lot more before we're through."

"You sure know the best spots to party don't you?"

"You know Mistress Linda," said Anna. "I think you use your humour as a way to protect yourself. To stop people from getting too close. But you should be careful what you joke about."

"Here we go. You're all set for another deep look into the dark caverns of my soul are you?"

"No Mistress Linda. I don't mean to pry into your soul, I just care about you. I know you give the appearance of being so brave and confident and I admire that, truly I do. But I think inside you're afraid to be the person you really ought to be. I believe God has a special purpose for you."

"If He has, then He's been pretty slow in telling me about it."

"Perhaps you have been slow in listening. God has created each of us with a very special purpose in mind."

"Allah says, in the Qur'an, 'Did you then think that we

had created you in jest, without any purpose, and that you would not be brought back to us – in the hereafter?'" said Cortez.

"Hey what did I do to piss you off?" said Linda. "What is this, some kind of religious pincer movement you've got me in?" She slapped Greaves leg. "C'mon science boy help me out here. Don't you believe life is just one random great interaction of particles or something? Isn't the whole universe just one wild roll of the dice?"

"Don't drag me into your pointless arguments. And for your information, it was Einstein who said 'I cannot believe that God would choose to play dice with the Universe', so you're wrong there too."

"Is Einstein one of your prophets?" said Anna.

"What?" said Greaves. "No, he wasn't a prophet. He was a man of science. Possibly the greatest theoretical thinker of his day. Although it has to be said that his general theory of relativity and his famous equation, $E=MC^2$, did not predict fundamental particle masses, however..."

"He speaks like a prophet," said Anna cutting him off.

Linda laughed. "She's got you there sport, there's no avoiding that."

"I'm not avoiding anything," said Greaves, getting a little irritable. "You're the one doing that, trying to make me the scapegoat of this conversation. And if you want to avoid that landslide up ahead you better go off-road here."

Greaves was right. The road ahead was blocked with rocks and shale.

"Left or right?" said Linda.

"Right."

For the next twenty minutes he guided them through a nightmare environment. The whole terrain had been torn apart by earthquakes and subsidence. The temperature continued to rise and Linda feared for Bertha's tires. Eventually they came to a tiny pass between two mountains.

"You expect me to take Bertha through there?" said Linda. "You gotta be kidding me."

"You want maybe we should park her up and walk then?" Greaves said. "In this terrain, in this temperature? It gets safer up ahead, I promise you."

"Okay," said Linda, slowly navigating the pass. "It better."

It didn't. The pass was bumpy going and there was little room for manoeuvre. It was only just wide enough for Bertha to fit through. The heat was becoming intolerable, it came at them in waves. There was a roaring sound up ahead.

"What is that noise?" Linda said.

"There's a major lava flow just ahead of us," said Greaves. "It's where the old river used to be. I'm afraid we've got to cross it."

"I thought you said things get better up ahead."

"They do... eventually."

Just as he said that there was a sudden earth tremor. It shook Bertha, causing all the crockery in her kitchen cupboards to shake loose and crash to the floor.

They weren't the only things shaken loose. Several large rocks came bounding down the mountain to their left. Linda swerved to avoid one of them then slammed on the brakes as another rolled right past Bertha's bonnet. Before Linda could start her up a third rock smacked right into their side.

Bertha tilted with the impact. Anna screamed as she was sent flying. Linda punched Greaves on the shoulder.

He cried out. "What was that for?"

"For hurting my baby!"

"I didn't know this was going to happen, I swear. There's a natural bridge over the lava just up ahead. It's not very wide but it's the only way across. Once we're over that we're onto a natural plateau. It will be safer there. That's where the lab is."

Linda wasn't impressed. "You've said that before, and look what happened."

She steered Bertha round the obstacles as best she could. After a little while the bridge Greaves mentioned came into view and it was even smaller than the pass, a tiny rocky outcrop that connected the pass with the plateau beyond. Bertha would only just fit across it. There wouldn't be any margin for error.

As they came to the end of the pass another tremor hit. Linda hung on to the steering wheel to keep from falling out of her seat. The rumbling stopped. It was followed by a rattling cascade. Greaves looked out of the passenger window. "Rock slide," he said. "On the other side. Drive, quickly!"

Linda kicked it up a gear and sped along the little bridge. It was like driving through an oven. Either side of them was a huge drop into a river of molten lava. The rock slide chased them along the bridge. They could hear it rattling along behind them at first, then it caught up and Bertha began to lose traction on her back tires, slowing as the rock slide engulfed her. Her underside clattered and clanged with the debris that rattled around her. They reached the front wheels and Linda lost control.

They were carried along by the movement of the rocks for a few feet as Linda fought to regain control. Bertha veered dangerously to the right. Linda twisted the wheel as far to the left as she could, but she didn't have any grip.

Bertha's front wheels left the edge of the bridge and

spun madly in mid air. The front end tilted forwards and the molten lava below swung into view. Linda's stomach turned over with sheer fright. The heat was so intense she let go of the steering wheel.

The rockslide kept on coming, it spilled over the edge of the bridge and dissolved as it hit the lava below. Linda had never seen something as solid as rock actually dissolve before. Anna started praying at the top of her voice as Bertha teetered. One more surge from the rocks and she would be gone and all of them with her.

Cortez grabbed Greaves and Anna and ran towards the back of Bertha. The vehicle rocked backwards and straightened up. Linda slammed the gear stick into reverse and hit the accelerator. The back wheels caught a tiny bit of traction and moved Bertha back a few inches. Not enough to put her front wheels back on the bridge however.

"Quick," said Linda. "You've got to get out."

Greaves tried the door but couldn't open it. "It's jammed shut. Must have been the rock that hit us."

Cortez put his shoulder to it and pushed but the door didn't move.

"Pop the back window," said Linda. "You can crawl out of that."

Another wave of rocks inched them further over the edge. Linda revved as hard as she could to stop them falling.

"Hurry," she said. "I can only buy you a few seconds, even with my foot to the floor."

"But that means you'll..." Anna couldn't finish the sentence.

"Go," said Linda as Greaves and Cortez pushed the back window out.

"I can't leave you," said Anna. "Not like this. You've

got to come."

Rocks were surging all around them pushing the vehicle further and further forward.

"We'll all die if I come. Besides, a captain always goes down with her... erm, ship."

"You can't!" said Anna, trying to wriggle free of Greaves and Cortez as they pulled her back towards the window.

"You ever think that maybe this is God's purpose for me? Don't fuck with the master plan. Go build your new Eden and build me a big statue. Git."

Greaves and Cortez manhandled Anna out of the window. Bertha lost traction on her back wheels and started to rock again as Greaves and Cortez jumped clear.

Linda took her foot off the peddle and turned to look back. For a split second she thought about running for it, but she realised she'd never make it. Time seemed to slow down as her heartbeat sped up. Everything moved in slow motion.

So much for no-one to hold me back or rely on me, she thought. What was that Cortez had quoted from the Qur'an? 'Did you then think that we had created you in jest?'

"No," Linda muttered to herself. "But you sure have a sick sense of humour you old bastard."

Bertha began to topple. Linda patted her dashboard. "Okay sweetheart. It's just you, me and the open highway to Hell."

I hope it's quick, was the last thing she was aware of thinking as Bertha went over the egde. The windscreen turned to gas. Linda's skin and lungs turned to cinders as the lava claimed Bertha and practically everything the four of them still owned.

CHAPTER SEVENTEEN

"But you don't have to burn in the fiery lakes of hell," said the Prophet. He was looking straight at the camera. It felt as though he was addressing you directly. Picking you out from the thousands of viewers across the country and looking right into your soul.

The image started to flicker. Colt rapped the top right hand corner of the ancient portable set in his office and the image fixed itself.

"Just like a woman see," he said over his shoulder to Tom and Carl.

They were sitting on the other side of his desk, looking kind of anxious. Colt had his back to them and his feet up as he watched the show.

"You gotta know how to treat it right. How to tell it what to do. Then it comes around."

"Do we have to sit through all of this?" said Tom. "I thought we came here to talk."

"You'll sit for as long as I want and watch whatever I tell you. You're on my turf now."

"The Lord said unto his disciples that he would make them fishers of men," the Prophet continued. "Well brothers and sisters, I don't pretend for a minute that I'm anywhere near as important or blessed as those first followers of Jesus. In fact, considering these are surely the last days, then it's fair to say that I'm probably among the last. But I content myself with the Lord's own words from the sermon on the mount. 'The first shall come last, and the last shall come first'. So like those twelve disciples did after the Lord God visited tongues of fire on them, I'm casting my net wide. I'm hoping to catch your soul and the souls of everyone you know.

"I'm hoping to do this because I've felt the blessed love of Jesus pluck me out of the rivers of sin and deliver me unto His Father's table. Where He was seated at the right hand. I'm hoping to net your souls for God because I have felt the blessed joy and fulfilment of His sacred love swell every ounce of my being. Swell me until there was too much to contain in just one man. Swell me until I had love to give away. Love to share. Share with everyone irrespective of creed, colour or kin.

"Because the sacred love of Jesus isn't something you can just keep all to yourself. Oh no, like the Lord told the rich man in the parable: 'You cannot store up riches for yourself in heaven.' Well I'm telling you brothers and sisters, you cannot store up God's love for yourself. You cannot salt it away for a rainy day or a comfortable retirement. You cannot hide it anywhere. You just got to keep on giving it away to everyone you meet.

"And you know what?" said the Prophet lowering his voice, coming on all intimate with his viewers. "Let me tell you the most miraculous thing about God's love. The more of it you give away – the more of it you get. That's right brothers and sisters, the more of it you get. It's like the whole flipside of the rotten economy that God tore down when he sent His plague. And that's why, when the world as we know it ends, and money disappears – we still got, and always will have, an abundance of God's love!"

The studio audience went wild at this. Clapping and stomping, cheering and whooping while the choir rattled their tambourines and crooned in harmony.

The first three shows he did, it was just the Prophet all by himself with the cameras. Then he started bothering Colt to bus in his followers to watch and to let him put together a choir.

Colt had resisted at first, he hadn't seen the point of it. But the Prophet had won him over and Colt was a big enough man to say he was glad that the Prophet had. Everybody who heard about the show was clamouring to get reception. They now broadcast as far east as Ohio and as far south as Alabama.

In every State where the show was broadcast, folk were reinstating the old chapters. They were desperate to come back to the fold. To start hanging the banners of the Apostolic Church of the Rediscovered Dawn over what was left of their towns and cities. And here were Tom and Carl, crawling back on their hands and knees, desperate to strike any kind of deal to hang on to their territories. Let 'em wait a little longer, thought Colt. He wanted to make sure the Prophet preached what he'd been told.

"Now brothers and sisters," said the Prophet. "This is a very special show. Since I last spoke to you, God has spoken to me. That's right I have had a vision direct from the Lord himself. Now I hope those of you who've been watching us from the start won't mind if I let those who may be joining us for the first time know a little about my past.

"When the Cull happened I was in a coma. I wasn't expected to ever wake up again. My brain was supposed to have been irreparably damaged. A day before they were due to switch off my life support machine, the plague took the entire hospital. It was then that God reached down and lifted my soul up to heaven. He revealed to me the shining splendour of His sacred city. He showed me the sacred purpose He had for each and every soul left on the planet and He sent me back with a mission. I was to spread His holy word to every man, woman and child left alive.

"I woke up in a hospital full of corpses. I was the only

living person in the whole building. I left that place and I began to preach the word, just as God had commanded. To be honest with you, I hadn't had much truck with religion before I fell into a coma. But as soon as I woke the words just came to me. And they've been coming ever since. So have the visions of the future.

"The past few months have been dark months for God's children. We've found ourselves under attack by a savage and heathen foe and it's taken every bit of patience and understanding we have to reach out to these people with love and forgiveness in our hearts. I have to admit I knew despair many times. I called out to the Lord to send me a vision. When none came I am ashamed to say I was angry at my Lord and I railed against Him. In my foolishness I forgot that He does things in His own time because He alone knows the right time for things to take place.

"Two days ago I was struck by the most vivid vision the Almighty has ever sent. I saw a sacred crusade. An army of God's chosen people marching towards Montana, to the site of another great massacre by the same foe who attacks us today. On the site where the Little Bighorn river used to flow, the army of God's followers will meet with an army of the godless UTN.

"I saw all this come to pass, and I saw an angel appear in the sky above the two armies. This angel had once been a woman, a good Christian woman whom the Lord had elevated above all other beings. I saw this angel turn herself into a bright and shining star, like the star that guided the Magi to Christ when He was laid in a manger. Then I saw God's people delivered from the hands of their attackers without a single drop of blood being spilled. What's more I saw a new Moses rise up to deliver them unto a new kingdom, just as the Israelites were delivered from the hands of the Pharaoh."

As the Prophet had been speaking, the choir had been singing a single quiet note in the background. Now that note rose to a crescendo as they opened their throats and sang loud. The Prophet raised his voice too. "All this will come to pass brothers and sisters," he intoned. "I promise you, as your friend and your brother in Jesus Christ I swear I speak only the truth. Don't forget to come back and join us again next week for *The Tomorrow Show*. Where we're working towards a brighter tomorrow with an eternal future in Christ."

The choir burst into one of their rousing hymns at this point and Colt clicked the set off. He'd never been one to enjoy hymns or even music too much for that matter. Well the Prophet had said what Colt had told him to say, he had to give him that. But once again, even though it was a call to arms, he'd found a way to dress it up with peace and love and Christian forgiveness. He had a way of twisting the most simple messages like that. Even still, Colt had to admit it sold. And what it was selling was an increase in Colt's power base, even if he didn't see eye to eye with the Prophet's beliefs.

Colt's God had always been the vain and jealous God who says 'vengeance is mine'. It was the God he'd been brought up to believe in and you didn't have to look too far in the Bible to see Him at work. But the Prophet had a way of taking His works, whatever they were, and putting a 'let he who is without sin cast the first stone' kind of spin on them. No matter, the Prophet could be called into line if he ever went overboard on this whole forgiveness and understanding line of his. He certainly delivered the support Colt needed. Wyoming was now Colt's for the taking.

Colt turned to the men in front of him. "Well gentlemen. What did you think? He's some preacher ain't he?"

"If you like that sort of thing," said Carl. "I prefer a bit of fire and brimstone myself, and I'm surprised to see you've gone all 'Jesus loves you' to be honest Colt."

"That's Mr Colt to you Carl. And I ain't going all 'turn the other cheek' on you, don't you worry about that. What the Prophet's peddling, that's what people want to hear these days. He's the new face of the Neo-Clergy. They want to hear about healing rifts and uniting behind a common cause against a common enemy. Good news in dark times. He's brought the people back to our fold and he's brought you back to me on your knees."

"I ain't on my knees," said Tom "I don't kneel for any man."

"I don't want you to kneel," said Colt. "I want you grovelling on your belly with your face in the shit."

"Look," said Carl, sensing a row about to flare up between Tom and Colt. "You got us in a corner Mr Colt. I admit that. But I'm a man who can do business and I believe you are too. I know the price is a little higher than when you first came to see us, but I don't want to lose what I've built up, so I'm prepared to pay it. So is Tom here. We just need to keep from getting riled so we can start talking turkey. What kind of terms are we looking at?"

Colt smiled a big fat smile. "Well now," he said, "I reckon it's time to get down to business. The price is quite simple gentlemen. I want Benny Cooper's shit-eating head on a plate. Literally on a plate. You can carve up his territories however you want. But I want that two bit fucker dead and I want you to bring me his head. I'll make certain you can start collecting your tributes again but I want half. Plus I want half of all the men under your command."

"Right," said Tom, barely concealing his sneer. "That'll

be for this holy war you're pushing. That's the real message behind the nigger's sermon. Not this peace and love you reckon everyone wants at the moment."

"Now you watch your mouth boy," said Colt. "Don't nobody use that kind of language when they're talking about my men. Way I see it, most of the world's dead and it's a bit late in the day to be digging up old racial divisions."

"Is that right? So how come you're about to go to war with the redskins? Answer me that, huh? If your war ain't about the old racial divisions then what is it about?"

"This war ain't about race," said Colt banging his desk. "It's about faith. Those redskins got all kinds of races working with 'em now, white, black, brown even Chinese. I'm at war with these heathens because they hate everything we stand for, they spit on our beliefs, they murder our women and children and they want to steal what our great, great grandfathers fought and died to leave us over two centuries ago. I don't give a shit what your colour is, you attack me and mine and you're gonna pay for it."

"Okay Mr Colt," said Carl holding up his hands to quiet everyone down. "Now ol' Tom here, he don't mean nothing by what he's saying. He's just a bit sore cos you got us by the balls is all. Now as I said, we came here to do business, but you gotta admit your terms are a bit steep. Is there room for negotiation?"

"What do you have in mind?"

"How about thirty per cent of our tributes and twenty-five per cent of our men?" said Carl. "Now I understand you're putting an army together but we got a revolt on our hands, a revolt you helped to start. We need all the men we got just to put it down."

"You play ball with me," said Colt, "and you won't need

to put the revolt down. Don't play ball and I'll just wait till this revolt's over and come in and take everything anyway."

"Now there is some truth in what you're saying," said Carl. "But if it was gonna be that easy for you I reckon you wouldn't have bothered talking to us. I'm sure you're a reasonable man. Of course you want the best deal you can get, but so do we. Way I see it, we're gonna be working quite closely together from now on, and a little bit of give and take never hurt nobody's relationship."

"Okay," said Colt. "Forty per cent of your tributes, but I still need half your men, there's no way around that. That's my final offer. Take it or get out. And don't even think about letting Cooper live."

"Well now Mr Colt," said Carl. "I reckon ol' Benny's had it coming for a long time. You can consider that side of our bargain taken care of."

"So we have a deal then?"

"I reckon we do at that." Carl leaned forward to shake the hand Colt offered him. Tom was staring down at the floor like a sulky teenager. Carl kicked him. Tom glowered at Carl and shook Colt's hand with reluctance.

"Congratulations boys," said Colt. "You just joined the winning team."

CHAPTER EIGHTEEN

This was an historic occasion. Cheveyo could not remember a time, since The Cull, that the councils of every tribe in the land had gathered for a sit down.

That they gathered in the Valley of the Chiefs on the reservation of the Apsáalooke, or the Crow tribe as they were termed by others, was also significant. Although it had suffered intense seismic disturbance following the nuking of Billings, this was still the largest Native American reservation in the country. What's more it was right in the heart of Montana, a mere twenty miles from the Neo-Clergy occupation of Lame Deer.

To meet here was not only a declaration of solidarity with their enslaved brothers and sisters, it was also a sign of just how powerful the UTN had become. They could march into a State that was seething with animosity towards them, where no Native American would be safe travelling alone, and they could set up camp mere miles away from a Neo-Clergy stronghold.

The UTN had come a long way since Cheveyo was active on the inner council. A long way in the wrong direction.

They were gathered in the meeting hall of the Crow's general council. Unlike many other tribes the council consisted of every registered tribe member over the age of eighteen. Cheveyo greatly admired the government of the Crow tribe. Although they also had executive and legislative branches, in principle every one in the tribe voted on every policy and every action that their government adopted. While the white man in his White House had boasted – before The Cull – of his 200 year old democracy, there was an older, stronger and more direct democracy being practiced right under his nose, by a nation that had lived here longer.

Cheveyo had hoped that the UTN itself would adopt a similar constitution, but it seemed that the organisation grew more autocratic with each day. Recent events couldn't have played better into the hands of Ahiga and his faction if they'd been planned. Too many things seemed to have gone wrong at once. Too many Native Americans were scared and angry.

Ahiga was respected and admired by the young members who flocked to the UTN and drove the Elders to follow suit. Just as Cheveyo said they would, but not in the way he hoped. They saw Ahiga as a wise and valorous leader, almost as exalted as Hiamovi. They didn't see the deceit and cunning in his heart. They didn't know him like Cheveyo did.

Deep in his own heart Cheveyo still believed in Hiamovi. He knew his Great Chief, as he now liked to be called, had lost his way. But he believed the Great Spirit would move his leader. Cheveyo still believed that the Fifth Age of Man was nearly upon them. He thought the way Ahiga had hijacked the prophecy was despicable. To use such a sacred pronouncement to justify their warmongering was beneath contempt and beyond despair.

There was one solitary benefit from their appropriation of Hopi prophecy however. It had made the tribes more aware of Hopi beliefs and sympathetic to Cheveyo's way of thinking. He had been gaining a groundswell of support from UTN members who were uncomfortable with the concept of all-out war with the white man; tribal Elders, braves and squaws who saw the occupation of Lame Deer as a direct result of Ahiga's militant stance and agitation.

They, like Cheveyo, believed that an escalation of

violence towards the white man would only bring further retaliation and result in an endless conflict that neither side could ever truly win. Thousands of lives would be lost to no good end. The purpose of the meeting today was to vote on whether or not they should raise an army to seize a doomsday weapon from the white man. Cheveyo and his supporters hoped to derail this motion and to bring the UTN to its senses.

Cheveyo caught Onatah's eye across the other side of the meeting hall. The Iroquois matriarch was the only other member of the UTN inner council in the hall, as the others had yet to come in. She nodded at Cheveyo and smiled. Onatah had a lot of sympathy for Cheveyo's stance and she was the closest thing he had to an ally.

Technically Cheveyo was still a member of the council himself. He had yet to be voted off, and he could have challenged Hiamovi's four month suspension if he had petitioned the other council members to vote to over rule it. He did not wish to embarrass Hiamaovi though. Challenging his ruling would only alienate Cheveyo further from his old friend. On the other hand, he did not want to apologise to Ahiga, as Hiamovi had demanded, not after the Navajo's disgraceful conduct. So he had not returned to his council duties.

Instead Cheveyo had worked at the fringes of the UTN. His status as a council member still opened doors for him. He had travelled around the country attending meetings and listening to many of his brothers and sisters' concerns, returning to the grass roots of the UTN. Now he was ready to address all the key members as they gathered to vote on going to war.

Cheveyo still believed in the basic decency and wisdom of his brothers and sisters. Any nation that could maintain such a democratic system as the Crow for so many centuries had to be responsive to reason and impassioned argument. Cheveyo had come today to win back the soul of his people. If they truly did believe in the Fifth Age of Man, as so many of them now professed to, surely they would listen to its true meaning and not commit themselves to the atrocity of war and the desecration of such a sacred ideal.

Many in the hall waited in anticipation to hear what he had to say. Cheveyo had only to wait for his moment.

Ahiga entered the hall two steps behind Hiamovi. He was shoulder to shoulder with his fellow council members, Amitola, Hinto and Huyana. As befitted their position within the UTN they had waited until everyone else was seated before they entered.

Only Onatah had already taken her place. That was typical of her. She held the respect of many UTN members with these displays of humility. Ahiga knew they were calculated to increase her standing and influence, but he was uncomfortable with the integrity they also displayed. Hiamovi had once been the same. Now he liked being called 'Great Chief' too much.

Onatah was chatting to the Crow chief Casper Yellowtail when they entered. She stopped her conversation and sat upright as Hiamovi and the other council members sat. She looked serene and full of quiet authority.

Ahiga was wary of Onatah. She was the only council member he had nothing on. He had no hold over her and she seemed unimpressed by his arguments or his actions. She expressed neither condemnation or admiration for his schemes. He found her inscrutable and therefore very dangerous. She knew this and held it over him. He had much to learn from her before he finally put her out of the way.

Ahiga wondered if that fool Hopi would try and take a seat with the council. He knew Onatah was sympathetic to Cheveyo's cowardly mewling, but she was too clever to openly endorse him. The only UTN members who actively supported Cheveyo were young weaklings and frightened old women.

Ahiga knew all about Cheveyo's pathetic attempt at uprising. He had informed Hiamovi how the cowardly little Hopi planned to foist his misguided pacifism on the UTN at this meeting. Ahiga had plans to head off Cheveyo's laughable little stand before he could even make it. Hiamovi had eventually seen sense, of course, and had given Ahiga the go ahead, but not without some reluctance. It seemed Hiamovi still had some inexplicable fondness for the Hopi. Ahiga couldn't think why, but he wondered if it was something he could use against Hiamovi at some point.

Hiamovi stood and the general murmurs of conversation died out across the hall. "Brothers and sisters. Today is a momentous day in the history of our people. We stand on the brink of a new age – the Fifth Age of Man. To see every tribe of our people gathered here today fills me with joy and great hope for our glorious future. We have many matters to discuss and voices to hear, but before all this we have another pressing matter to attend to. Ahiga, if you will."

Hiamovi sat down and Ahiga stood. "Brothers and sisters of the UTN, it pains me greatly to say it, but we have a traitor in our midst." Surprised murmurs broke out across the room and many faces turned to him in disbelief. "That's right, a traitor. One who not so long ago actually sat at the very heart of the UTN." There were more murmurs. Ahiga looked over and saw Cheveyo trying to stay calm and reassure those sitting around him who looked concerned. "Do you see what a threat the Neo-Clergy pose to us?" Ahiga continued. "When they can reach so far into our organisation and make someone of such standing turn on his own kind? You all know who I'm talking about. The Hopi chief who even now is working against the UTN from within. Trying to talk you all out of defending yourself against the Neo-Clergy aggressor. Lulling you all into a false sense of security and dividing you so that the white man can pick you off one by one. Cheveyo I accuse you of the worst form of betrayal and deceit. Do you dare to deny it?"

"Of course I deny it," said Cheveyo leaping to his feet. His face was full of righteous indignation. "This is absolutely preposterous. What proof, what evidence do you have to back these claims up?"

"I'm glad you asked," said Ahiga. "Bring in the Hopi woman"

Hastiin got up and came back with the elderly Hopi, Martha Homolovi.

"Martha," said Ahiga. "Can you tell those assembled here what you gave to a group of Neo-Clergy soldiers recently?"

Martha turned to look at Cheveyo. Her face was full of surprise and concern. "My chief, I had no idea they wanted me to speak against you."

"That's alright. Tell the truth Martha we have nothing to hide"

Martha turned back to Ahiga. "We gave them food, animal hides, fuel and... and..."

"And what else Martha?" Ahiga said. "What else?"

"... and guns. We gave them guns." Martha hung her head.

Ahiga bent towards her. "You gave guns to the enemy Martha, you and three others of your tribe. On whose orders did you do this?"

"Well my chief's. But it wasn't like you think. We were just..."

"That's enough Martha. We don't need to hear any more you can go. So," said Ahiga turning to Cheveyo. "Do you deny arming our enemy?"

"Don't be ridiculous! Those men weren't Neo-Clergy soldiers they were a band of scavs."

"Who would have taken your guns straight to the Neo-Clergy soldiers they work for."

"You don't know that. You have no way of proving it."

"And you have no way of disproving it."

"I was simply making a trade. Those men had medicine I desperately needed for several members of my tribe. The men had something we needed. They named their price and we met it. It's common practice for tribes to trade with white men when they have something the tribe needs."

"It's not common practice for Navajos," said Ahiga, banging his chest with his fist. "And it isn't common practice for the Crow tribe either. These friends of yours have declared war on all our tribes. Why would any of us give them the weapons with which to kill us?"

"They are no friends of mine. Is this the best you can do Ahiga? Because you and your warmongering faction must be desperate if this tiny transaction is all you can come up with?"

"This is just the beginning. You've already admitted to running guns to our enemies. But I can show your treasonous behaviour goes much deeper than this."

"I'd like to see you try."

"You're about to," said Ahiga and motioned to Sam Long Arrow, an Arapaho brave, to stand. "Can you tell us all where you were three moons ago?" Ahiga asked Cheveyo.

The Hopi looked unimpressed. "I attended a meeting held by the Arapaho tribe. As I'm sure you know."

"Thank you for admitting that, even though your frankness obviously comes from your arrogant belief that you're above reproach." Ahiga smiled as Cheveyo bridled at this remark. "Tell me Sam," said Ahiga. "What did Cheveyo say to you when he approached you after this meeting?"

Sam cleared his throat. He spoke with hesitation. "He, err... he told me that if I supported his attempts to sabotage the UTN's fight for freedom the Neo-Clergy would see I was well rewarded. I'm sorry to say it, but I did have a few, err... doubts about the UTN's views on the Fifth Age. He said there were lots of others like me who had accepted the Neo-Clergy's offer. He also said I needn't worry about being found out because he was a Hopi and people would believe the way he... twisted the prophecy."

"This is a lie," said Cheveyo. "It's a totally unsubstantiated accusation. I've never even seen this young brave before. There were hundreds of people at that meeting, nearly all of them can vouchsafe for me."

"Can you call any of them to speak on your behalf?" Ahiga said.

"Can you call anyone to speak on this young brave's behalf and substantiate his story?"

Ahiga turned to address the hall. "Are there any other braves here who can support Sam's story? Perhaps some of you have been approached in the same way by Cheveyo. If there are, I ask you to have the courage to be honest with your brothers and sisters. We will not condemn you for listening. We condemn only those who side with our enemy against us."

A few of those assembled shifted uneasily in their seats, then another brave stood and said: "I was approached by Cheveyo in the same way."

A further brave stood. "So was I."

Then a young squaw stood. She was nervous and managed to say only "me too", then went to sit down again, thought better of it and remained standing, biting her thumb and looking at the floor.

Cheveyo looked like he had been totally blindsided. "This is preposterous," he said. There was a shrill note in his voice. "I've never spoken to any of these people. This is all your doing." Cheveyo pointed at Ahiga. "You told them to say these things to discredit me."

"Come now Cheveyo. I thought you could do a little better than that."

"Can't you see what he's trying to do?" said Cheveyo, addressing the hall. "Don't you see his little game? He's trying to discredit me so he can silence everyone who's against this war he's trying to peddle. This is all lies. All of it." Cheveyo turned to Hiamovi. "Great Chief, surely you can see that none of this is true. In all the years you've known me and counted me as your friend have you ever known me to turn on my own people? I helped you build the UTN from nothing. Why would I suddenly turn on it and try to tear it down? You can't honestly believe these fabrications can you?"

Hiamovi stood. He wore a solemn expression. "Cheveyo can you bring forward anyone to speak for you now and defend your name?"

"Well no. But why should I need to? This is so obviously a fabrication."

"So you say. But you can produce no-one to verify your side of the story. It pains me to say this, because we are old friends, but it seems the case against you is irrefutable. You've admitted to giving guns to the Neo-Clergy. You claim this was a trade in return for medicine. Yet, according to the testimony of others, you've been shown to have collaborated with the Neo-Clergy to sabotage and subvert our movement. This calls your claims of simply trading with scavs into question. And you can't produce even one person to verify your story."

"Not at such short notice no. But give me time and I can tear this preposterous accusation apart."

"With witnesses bought for you by the Neo-Clergy no doubt," said Ahiga.

Cheveyo looked about the hall trying to find someone on his side. "Great Chief, Onatah, brothers and sisters of the UTN, don't you realise what's at stake here? The Fifth Age of Man isn't some excuse to go to war to steal a weapon off the white man. It's a sacred becoming. A radical new development of our consciousness, a whole new way of being. You can't let this man and his accomplices silence me with their lies."

"Enough," said Hiamovi raising his arm for silence. "Cheveyo we've heard plenty of testimony claiming you're a Neo-Clergy collaborator. But we haven't heard anything from you that disproves it. All you've done is accuse your brother's and sisters of lying at the encouragement of a fellow inner council member. I find your behaviour dishonourable. You've done nothing to prove your innocence. I have to declare your guilt and make certain you're punished."

"Great Chief don't do this, I implore you," said Cheveyo. "For the sake of our friendship, of everything we wanted the UTN to be. For the coming of the Fifth Age of Man."

"It's for the sake of all those things that I pass judgement Cheveyo," said Hiamovi, with genuine sadness. "You're a proven traitor to your own people. I'm going to expel you from the UTN for life. You're to be taken from this hall and confined under armed guard until the Neo-Clergy is no longer a threat to our people."

Ahiga nodded and Hastiin and Akecheta seized Cheveyo. Cheveyo glared at Ahiga as they dragged him from the hall. Ahiga met the Hopi's gaze. He acted as though he was unmoved, bored even by the Hopi's reaction. Inside though, he was choking on his anger.

"Brothers and sisters," said Hiamovi once Cheveyo was gone. "I know some of you were taken in by Cheveyo's promise of a Neo-Clergy reward. I know you were going to speak out with him. I don't approve of your actions but I won't have you hunted down and expelled. Now is not the time to turn against each other. That is what the white man wants. Now is the time for lenience and unity. To show we can come together in a common purpose. For this reason I give a full pardon to all of Cheveyo's conspirators as long as they give up their attempts to sabotage us, and start to work with us again."

There was a huge cheer at Hiamovi's magnanimity. Everyone clapped, stamped and whooped victory cries. Ahiga was impressed. He would have rooted out all of Cheveyo's sympathisers and put them down with brutality. Instead Hiamovi had effectively silenced them. No-one would dare speak out against the war now, or they'd be branded a traitor. Yet he'd still managed to look merciful and just while he did it. He'd forced everyone to side with him and made it look as though he'd restored unity where there'd been dissent and division.

The rest of the meeting went exactly as Ahiga had planned. He couldn't have hoped for a better outcome. He didn't feel victorious though. He just felt an uncontrollable anger growing inside him. At first he tried to ignore this, it made no sense. Then he realised where it came from.

It was the Hopi's glare as he was dragged out. Ahiga had seen that self same look before. From the most beautiful pair of brown eyes he'd ever seen. Eyes that had looked up at him along the barrel of a pistol. A barrel he'd pushed between two tender lips. Lips that could have sealed Ahiga's fate if they'd chosen to.

Instead they were wrapped silently around his gun. Ahiga still felt the recoil as he squeezed the trigger and silenced those lips forever. He still heard Fitch and Golding's laughter. "That's the end of that little faggot!" Fitch had said.

"He ain't gonna fuck with any of the 57th Street bangers no more," Golding had said. "Ain't that right Tom?"

Ahiga had dropped the gun and left the room. He vowed right then he'd make them pay. Now he was about to make good on that.

CHAPTER NINETEEN

Cortez was tired and hungry. He hadn't eaten since the previous night and he hadn't slept since the night before. All their provisions had gone down with the whore. The brave, dead whore that Cortez couldn't find it in himself to hate anymore.

He said nothing about his hunger and fatigue and neither did Anna or Greaves. He could see they weren't taking it well. Anna was quiet and withdrawn. She walked with her head down and her shoulders slumped, hugging herself. She shivered whenever she stood still.

Anna had taken the whore's death very badly, screaming and kicking as the vehicle went over the edge. Greaves and Cortez had to pull her back to avoid the lava that splashed back up onto the bridge, sizzling as it cooled to form part of the surface. Cortez had noted, with the air of detachment he got in those situations, that this is how the bridge must have formed in the first place.

Anna had cried for several hours after that and there was little Greaves or Cortez could say to console her. They were dealing with the loss themselves. Once she'd cried the whole thing out she had just sunk into herself. Cortez couldn't think of anything to say to comfort her and not even the words of Jesus or Mohammed, peace be upon them, sprang to his lips.

Greaves was not in a good way either, he was nearly out of painkillers. Cortez could see that he was trying to ration his remaining supplies and was still walking bow legged on account of the burns on his thighs. Whenever he stood up, the scent of rotting flesh wafted off him.

Greaves had taken them around the edge of the plateau in order to come back on themselves towards the opening of a ventilation shaft in the centre. This was apparently to avoid being picked up by the lab's security. It was a favourite tactic of Greaves. Cortez was beginning to recognise them now. He no longer thought of the little guy as his employer. Cortez instinctively knew the haul that went down with the whore and her vehicle was the last payout Greaves was ever going to make and Cortez hung around now out of a sense of obligation.

He felt a little like he'd let Greaves down by getting him tortured, even if he had saved his life after that. Now he wanted to make sure the little guy stayed out of trouble in the final stages of the mission. Cortez felt he owed him that at least.

He also felt responsible towards Anna. There were few women in his life he had thought of as friends and there were even fewer Christians, especially since his conversion. But Cortez thought Anna a very dear friend, no matter what either of them believed in. He felt there was something holy about her intentions to find the virus in the complex below. He wanted to make certain that she saw this through to the end.

They sat for hours by the ventilation shaft, watching the sun go down as Greaves had been insistent they only attempt to enter in the dead of night. They said very little as they sat together. There was very little any of them had to say. Greaves had a pocket watch that he kept consulting every half hour. Timing was everything in this operation he told them.

Cortez was about to stand to get the blood flowing in his legs when Anna cried out. She clutched her stomach and writhed as though in pain. Cortez bent over her to see if she was alright and Anna, forgetting herself, clasped hold of his robes and pulled herself close.

"It knows I'm here," she said, choking out the words

between spasms of pain. "Merciful father, so many of them. So hungry for me." She clung on to Cortez who did not know how to respond. He did not wish to be disrespectful of Anna, to compromise her modesty. He felt uncomfortable being so close to her, but he was the only person to whom she could be close.

To Cortez being physically close to another human being meant he was going to hurt them. He was very good at causing pain. He knew little about giving comfort. He cast his mind to the Qu'ran and remembered Muhammad himself, peace be upon him, had said, "I commend you to be good to women." While Allah had been explicit in saying: "Whether male or female; you are of one another."

She felt tiny next to him, whimpering in pain. Cortez placed his large, scarred arms around her. This felt strange to him, but not unpleasant. He didn't believe it was wrong. He was honouring the teachings of the prophets, and helping his friend.

"It's your biogenic field," said Greaves. "It can sense your proximity. I imagine if you were to examine the virus under an electron microscope you would see an increased level of activity. Something akin to excitement, no doubt. It senses in you the potential of what it might become. It feels the hunger of all life to evolve, to improve its condition and to grow more powerful."

Greaves words didn't help Anna any, but after a while the pain died down and she was herself again. She pulled away from Cortez, suddenly embarrassed by their closeness. Cortez, for his part, didn't know where to put himself either and they turned away from each other. Greaves saved them any further uneasiness by glancing at his watch and deciding it was time to crawl down the ventilation shaft.

Taking a Swiss army knife from his pocket, Greaves undid the screws on the grill. The shaft was a sheer drop, so they proceeded by pressing their palms and their feet against opposite sides and shuffling down. Cortez could see Greaves was having trouble with this. He was weak from pain and lack of food and the effort probably wasn't good for his wounds.

Fortunately the vent changed direction, slanting off at an angle about twenty feet down. Greaves let go of the sides with gratitude and slid down the smooth metal of the shaft. Cortez and Anna followed suit. They crawled along the last few feet of the shaft as it became horizontal.

The shaft ended in a grill, six feet off the ground, that looked onto a corridor. Greaves snipped a hole in each corner of the grill's wire and reached through to undo the screws holding it in place. They lifted the grill off but Greaves made them wait before climbing out of the shaft.

"As part of an energy efficiency drive, the security system only ever uses a third of it's cameras at any one time," said Greaves without looking up from his watch. "They're programmed to go on and off in a predetermined sequence. If you know the sequence you can pass through the building without once being caught on camera. There's only a skeleton security crew posted this time of night, so if we're lucky, we won't run into any of them on the way there." Greaves looked up from his watch. "Right. Time to go."

Cortez helped Greaves out of the shaft then lowered Anna down without making a noise. They crept along a labyrinth of corridors, each one looked identical to the last with only the numbers on the doors varying. Greaves would stop them occasionally, look at his watch for a moment, then tell them to continue.

The whole place felt like a morgue or a hospice to Cortez. It wasn't anything specific he could put his finger on. It just felt like somewhere that people came to die.

They followed Greaves around a corner and walked straight into a wall. No doors, just a dead end. Greaves looked confused. He put his hands on the wall to see if it was real, then he looked back round the corner to check where they were. "This can't be right," he said. "This should lead to a flight of stairs. I memorised the whole map. I've got a photographic memory and perfect recall."

Anna turned and walked back down the corridor. "It's this way," she said. She was as confident and nonchalant as Greaves was flustered and confused.

"Wait," Greaves said. "Where are you going? You'll get us caught. You can't possibly know where we are."

Anna spoke in a calm voice. "I know exactly where to go. It's calling me. You might not understand this Mister Greaves, but every molecule in my body is alive with the sound of its need."

"Err, well... yes. Of course I understand. I've just never heard you talk this way before. We have to wait for this camera to go off then you better lead the way."

Cortez smiled. Greaves was not used to someone knowing more than him. Knowledge was how he kept control of things. Now they were in Anna's hands. They followed her back along the corridors and down two flights of stairs.

As they rounded a corner they heard footsteps coming towards them. Anna, Greaves and Cortez froze. Greaves glanced at his watch and then at the camera mounted just above them. He signaled that they had ten seconds until the camera came on.

The footsteps moved away and Cortez realised he had

been holding his breath. Anna led them to a set of double doors. They looked impregnable. Beside them was a keypad.

Greaves inspected the keypad and nodded. "They never change," he said, smiling. "Doesn't matter what happens to the world, they use the same old security tricks. The code is a basic algorithm, with two variables determined by the number of the floor and the department. Now let's see..." Greaves started to tap away. He looked happier than Cortez had seen him in a while.

The double doors clicked then opened with a pneumatic hiss. Anna strode through them as if she was being pulled by some invisible force. Greaves was still tapping at the keypad which was now making a high pitched whining noise. Cortez was not certain if he should stay and look after Greaves or go and accompany Anna.

Greaves waved him on. "It's okay. You go after Anna. I just have to override and re-set all the codes. It's just a precaution. I won't be long." Cortez left him and hurried after Anna. She was marching past cages of rabbits, rats and mice.

The doors hissed shut behind him. Cortez hoped Greaves wouldn't need pulling out of the shit anytime soon. Right now he had to look out for Anna.

Greaves was going to do a number on their internal coding. They'd always underestimated him. That's how he'd gotten away and stayed one step ahead of them.

Using the keypad to access the whole complex's CPU, Greaves sent a counter command worming its way back through the system, changing the codes for every electronic lock in the place. It would take them three or four hours to isolate and countermand the code he'd set up, once they'd noticed. Until that time he was in control of every security door in the complex. That would hopefully give them the edge they needed to get out of the place with the virus.

Greaves punched in the new code and the doors hissed open once again. The code would change every two minutes, based on a cunning variation of the geometric theta progression. At the moment only Greaves knew what the code would be at any one time.

As Greaves stepped into the lab, he remembered a novel from a summer school he had attended in American Literature when he was thirteen. He was home from MIT and had no-one to play with. He didn't have any friends his own age and his fellow students were college kids, at best they thought him cute, at worst a victim for pranks. So his parents sent him on courses at the Massachusetts College of Liberal Arts during the vacation.

The novel was by Thomas Wolfe, its title was *You Can't go Home Again*, which always had a special significance for Greaves, it seemed to sum up his own life. Up until this moment, when standing in the lab Greaves found suddenly he was 'home again'.

It all came flooding back to him. It was the sterile smells that did it, evoking a host of memories. His heart beat faster as he remembered the thrill of discovery. The methodical application of process and the intuitive teasing of a theorem from a growing set of results. Oh God he'd missed it.

For a second he thought he'd give anything to be back there. Making things happen, proving his theories, all of them. Proving to his father that he was more intelligent and he did have more ambition.

But that life was gone now. They'd stolen it from him,

stolen his last chance to live out that dream. Now he was going to steal their prize discovery in return. Steal it and use it properly. This was his real destiny.

He hadn't realised it when he first joined their project. He was just glad to be back in research. But from the moment they employed him he was fated to take the virus and rebuild humanity.

Greaves was impressed by how well equipped the new labs were. Beyond the room with the caged creatures there were many fascinating bits of apparatus and technology. He was sorely tempted to take a quick tour of the whole facility but he didn't have time.

Anna would have gone straight to the virus. The biological imperative that now impelled her would override everything else in her brain. He had to find her and Cortez. They would need to be told how to remove the virus from containment and how to transport it out of the complex.

To his left Greaves saw a sign for a virology farm. There had been talk of creating such a facility when he had worked at the previous lab. An artificial environment in which the natural evolution of viral strains could be hot-housed and accelerated. Greaves couldn't resist taking a look, after all, it was on one of three routes to where the Doomsday Virus was contained.

He tapped the entrance code into a keypad and the door slid open. The temperature was much lower inside and there was a thin vapour of condensation in the air. Greaves peered through the mist and tried to make out the contents of the lab. Then, out of the corner of his eye, he saw a movement.

Greaves peered over to the other side of the room and was shocked to see a figure wearing a bio-hazard suit. He didn't realise he was at risk of infection. He hadn't expected the labs to be manned at this hour.

"What the hell are you doing here?" the figure demanded. "How did you get clearance? What's your command sector?" Greaves had been so confident the place would be empty that he didn't know how to respond. "Tell me your rank and centre number. Who sent you here?"

Greaves suddenly recognised the voice. It was Joe Black Feather, the Native American virologist. He'd never worked directly with the man, but he'd seen his work. He'd been through the man's results several times on audio file. Greaves just had to hold Joe where he was long enough to get through the other exit, then he could lock him in. The man didn't have the new codes to get out, so he could be contained.

"It's just a routine check," said Greaves. "Sinnot was surprised to see you working late and sent me to check if you were taking the customary precautions." Sinnot had been project leader when Greaves last worked for them. He dropped the name, hoping that would be enough to keep Joe quiet.

"Sinnot detailed me to this shift," said Joe. "Why would he be surprised to see me working late? Who are you and why would he send you? You're not even properly suited up. Don't you know there are live specimens in this room?"

Greaves had backed up to the other door. There wasn't a keypad next to it. There were no other visible means of opening it. He would have to get quickly back out the way he had entered. Joe was walking towards him and was now directly between Greaves and the exit.

"You're right of course," said Greaves. "I didn't realise you were handling live specimens. I'll go suit up."

"How could you not realise I was handling live specimens? That's what we do in the farm. Who are you anyway?"

Joe was right in front of him now. Greaves stepped to his left and Joe moved to block him. Greaves tried to walk around him and Joe stepped back in front of him. He wasn't going to let him out until he had answers. Greaves could think of nothing to say.

He pointed behind Joe to the door. "Look here he is. Now we'll get this sorted."

Joe turned around to look and Greaves rushed him. He pushed Joe hard and he fell, taking Greaves down with him. The pain from his wounds was so great that Greaves had white flashes before his eyes. He was less steady on his feet than he realised but he was the first back on them and he bolted for the door. Joe grabbed his ankle and Greaves tried to kick him off but it was too painful. Joe started to pull him over again. Greaves cast about for something to grab hold of and his hand landed on a metal stool.

He swung the stool and smashed it into the side of Joe's head. Joe yelped with pain and let go.

Greaves rushed from the lab and closed the door behind him. Joe didn't attempt to follow, instead he lunged for a button under a bench top. An alarm began to blare.

No, this couldn't be happening. Not now. Not after everything he'd been through. Not when he was so close to saving the world. He was cleverer than them, he'd proved that.

Wait, all this could be turned to his advantage. He wasn't beaten yet. He still had the whole place on lock down.

Cortez charged into the room with the caged animals as three armed guards ran up to the door and began banging on the glass. "What happened? Why are their guards here?"

Greaves pointed to the virology farm. "We had company. I only saw him at the last minute and I managed to lock him in that room. Unfortunately he set off the alarm."

"Do you want me to kill him?"

"No. We can use him as a hostage. In fact, I've just had a better idea." Greaves hobbled past the cages and out into the rest of the lab. Beyond the far door six glass walled rooms were laid out in a hexagonal grid. In the centre was a long thin booth with six walls.

Anna was pressed up against the glass of one wall. She looked like a starving child gazing through a window onto a feast. Inside the booth were six titanium containers. They looked like huge metal eggs with LCD displays monitoring their temperature and large tubes pumping liquid nitrogen into each.

Even at sub-zero temperatures, when most other organic matter would have no energy to move, Greaves knew that inside the containers the Doomsday Virus would be frenetic with excitement. Bursting with longing for its last surviving host, a longing that was about to be fulfilled.

Greaves shuffled past Anna into a room filled with consoles and keyboards. He booted up a mainframe and hacked straight into the complex's intranet. He was home again. There was nothing he couldn't do in this space. It didn't matter how many guards the complex had, or how well armed they were, all the hi-tech equipment they'd managed to maintain wouldn't help them. Greaves was untouchable.

As Cortez joined him in the room the polymer coating on one of the glass walls became a large screen. Doctor Joseph Sinnot stared down at them. He wore a stern expression and looked like he had just had just woken and dressed hastily.

Sinnot hadn't changed much since Greaves had last seen him. The chestnut hair that fringed his bald pate was flecked with more grey and the furrows on his brow were deeper, aside from that he was the same old smug asshole.

Smug, but shocked enough by the sight of Greaves to lose his composure for a second. "Matthew Greaves! We thought you were dead."

"Very much alive I'm afraid Sinnot."

"Not from the look of you and not for much longer when we get to you. What are you doing in my complex?"

"I'm concluding our research. Putting our discoveries to the correct use."

Sinnot laughed with derision. "Our research? I think you flatter yourself. I seem to recall you worked as a lab assistant on the project. It was your job to wash the flasks, tidy the draws and sweep the floor. I imagine you told your cohorts you were an important scientist. But the truth is you were paid less than the janitors and your duties were practically the same."

"I was responsible for more breakthroughs in the development of the virus than any other person you employed," said Greaves, who hadn't stopped typing throughout the whole conversation. "You couldn't even have started without the papers I published in the first place."

"Ah yes. The papers you published when you were only twenty-three. The last time you did anything of merit. Six months after gaining your third PHD and less than a year before you were institutionalised. It was your father who had you sectioned wasn't it? Just after your mother died. As I recall, the judge agreed you were a danger to yourself. Sad little Matthew Greaves, such a promising start you had, such a pathetic waste of potential your life has been ever since."

Greaves knew what Sinnot was trying to do. He wasn't going to be distracted though. He wouldn't rise to the taunts. He was under pressure to turn this situation to his advantage. He wouldn't buckle this time. He was stronger now.

Things had been different back then. There had been so much expectation about his work. So many job offers. His peers were envious and in awe of him. Everyone was waiting to see when he was going to trip and fall. The tension was too great. Rather than trip he dived head first over the edge. His mother died, then his nerve went and for a short while so did his mind.

"A whole decade and nothing to show for it," said Sinnot. "Three PHDs and you couldn't even get a job flipping burgers. Then one of my colleagues recognised your name on a job application. She took pity on you and convinced me to take you on. We threw you a few tiny crumbs of research to occupy you while you did your menial chores and suddenly you think you're leading the project. Such pathetic delusions of grandeur."

Sinnot was twisting the truth. But then he always had. They'd thrown him more than a few crumbs of research. They were getting nowhere when they hired him as a lab assistant. The researchers had all read his papers, so they began discussing theories and problems with him in the canteen.

After a while he was attending weekly debriefings. He went over their findings with meticulous care and suggested new lines of enquiry. Suggestions that led to breakthroughs and the project's first real successes. He hadn't done this alone, but they had been struggling until he joined the project.

The whole time this was happening Sinnot had been

promising Greaves a full time research fellowship. Dangling it in front of him like a carrot. But the fellowship never materialised and they kept paying him the tiny pittance he got as a lab assistant.

Sinnot never ran out of excuses as to why Greaves hadn't been made a fellow on the project. It was always just around the corner, it was only a matter of funding, or bureaucratic procedure, or a company policy hurdle that needed to be overcome.

Finally Sinnot realised that Greaves knew far too much about a project his shadowy pay masters wanted to keep secret. He probably figured it was cheaper to get rid of Greaves than to buy him off with a fellowship and tie him into the project. Whatever the case, Greaves narrowly escaped with his life and went underground.

He'd spent the year leading up to The Cull hiding under an assumed identity, learning as much as he could about the shadow government funding the Doomsday Virus. The hidden cabal of power brokers who make all the real decisions about how the world is run. Most of them were ultra-right wing trillionaires who'd gotten rich raiding the funds of the world's military industrial complex. There wasn't a scrap of information about them in the public domain. But no political ruling was made without their sanction.

"Don't think your amateurish attempt to disable our locks will buy you any time," said Sinnot. "And your inadequate effort to hack into our intranet has already failed."

"That's what I want you to think," said Greaves. He was now seconds from finishing. This would wipe the smug look off Sinnot's face. "The second you realised I was hacking the intranet, you naturally attempted to isolate the mainframe I was working on and disable it. The first thing I did was install a programme that would make you think you had done just that. It was simply a matter of distracting you while I finished what I was actually doing. Which, in case you're wondering, is this." Greaves typed in the last bit of executive sub-coding and pressed the Enter key.

"What have you done Greaves?" said Sinnot. He suddenly looked worried.

"It's a rather superior bit of viral software I've been working on," said Greaves. "It compresses every bit of information in your whole system by half every sixty seconds. Every single bit of research, every equation, every memo, folded in half and half again, every minute on an infinite cycle. The longer you leave it working the longer it will take to decompress and retrieve the information. Any attempt to stop this happening will result in every bit of information you have, years and years of research, being wiped without trace. If you try and retrieve the information from back up sources this will simply activate the virus all over again. The only way to reverse this is by inputting a variable code."

"What do you want for the code?" Sinnot said.

"I and my colleagues are going to leave here with the Doomsday virus. You are going to give us safe passage to the edge of the plateau. We've taken a hostage, Joe Black Feather, who was working in the Virology Farm. He will accompany us across the plateau to prevent you attacking us. When we're far enough away, we'll send Joe back with the code."

"How do we know you won't just kill him?"

"You don't. You'll just have to trust us."

Sinnot leaned to one side, talking to someone off-screen. He leaned back into shot and smiled. "I've got a better idea. How about you give yourselves up right now and we'll let you live long enough to give us the code to retrieve all our files?"

"And what makes you think we'd do that?"

"Well, our little conversation has been somewhat diverting, if a tad tedious, but then you always had that failing I'm afraid Greaves. You see I'm also capable of distracting you while I finish what I'm actually doing. Which, in case you might be wondering is this."

A high pitched cacophony of screams came from the room full of caged animals. Greaves rushed into the room. All the creatures in the cages were writhing and twitching with pain. Blood was running from the eyeballs and noses of those who weren't shrieking with agony. Giant welts and blisters were appearing on the skin of others.

"What have you done?" Greaves shouted.

"It's a fast-acting mutant strain of the Ebola virus, designed to be airborne. We introduced it into the air supply of those labs, right after we hermetically sealed them. We'll have to sterilise the area afterwards, but you'll be dead by then. Unless of course you surrender this instant and give us the code to decompress all our files. Oh and you only have a few minutes to decide. After that the virus will start to take effect on you and the antidote won't work. You'll die a death a thousand times worse than these vermin."

Many of the animals lay dead now, their insides eaten away by the virus.

"What about Joe?" said Greaves. "You're not going to let him die. He's too useful to the project."

"Joe is sealed in the virology farm, in a bio-hazard suit. You saw to that for us."

"What about Anna then? You must know who she is. Surely she's too valuable to allow her to die?"

"We know exactly who she is. Thank you for finding her for us. Though she's not as valuable as you think. We have been growing new hosts in her absence. Her DNA will be useful to our studies, but we can extract that from her corpse." Sinnot was lying, Greaves could tell. It didn't help him any though.

Nearly all the animals were dead now. Greaves coughed and put his hand to his mouth. It was flecked with blood and phlegm. He didn't have much time. None of them did. Suddenly he was a million miles from being 'home again' and Thomas Wolfe was right after all.

He hung his head. "Alright. You win."

CHAPTER TWENTY

It was the largest army of Native Americans that had ever marched. There were braves and squaws from every tribe in the land. Never had Hiamovi seen his people so united.

Since the motion to raise an army and march on Little Bighorn had been passed, growing bands of warriors had made the perilous journey to Montana from every part of the country.

The fact that they were marching to a showdown with the white man at the site of the greatest Native American victory was seen as an incredible omen by most of those assembled. There was a high sense of purpose among all the volunteers who had gathered to fight. A spiritual fervour was in the air. The Fifth Age of Man was nearly upon them.

For some it was a fight to ensure the freedom and autonomy of everyone left alive in the former United States, while for others it was a chance to settle old scores after so many years of oppression.

The Neo-Clergy were building their own army in Colorado. Their crazed leader Colt had used his lies and propaganda to terrify his own people into forming an army to strike at the Native Americans, although he was going to find them ready and waiting for him.

Hiamovi's standing as a spiritual and political leader was now greater than ever. Many in the UTN spoke of him as a saviour of the Native American race. Everything was coming to pass, just as the Great Spirit had shown him in the vision he'd recounted to so many of his people.

What the Great Spirit hadn't told him was how empty it would leave him and how far he would feel from the source of all his inspiration – the Great Spirit himself. He hadn't felt the Great Spirit's presence for more moons than he cared to admit. Not since he'd promoted Ahiga to the inner council. Ahiga who brought him so much power but put his soul in such jeopardy.

As Hiamovi sat brooding in his saddle, Ahiga rode over as though he could read his leader's thoughts. They rode at the front of around two hundred and fifty braves and squaws all mounted on horseback. Behind them in excess of two thousand more volunteers marched on foot. Most of them were armed with whatever weapons they had scavenged or made along the way.

The journey had been harsh but their Crow guides knew the best routes through the devastated terrain. Now they approached the plateau. It was about half a mile in the distance. Hiamovi could see it through the heat haze that came off the lava.

The horses did not like the heat or the uneven ground. They were whinnying and difficult to control. Ahiga dismounted, as did Hiamovi.

"Great Chief," said Ahiga. "The way ahead is hazardous but that could be used to our advantage."

"Go on."

"There is a narrow pass between two steep hills. Beyond that is a small bridge over the lava to the plateau. The bridge is only big enough for a few people to cross at a time. We could take the pass and defend it against Colt's whole army with five or six hundred braves."

"Okay. And what about our horses?"

"I don't think the horses will be able to cross to the plateau. The heat from the lava is too great and they're likely to panic. It would probably take too long to lead them all across anyway. We'd have to take them one at a time because of the size of the bridge."

"Very well. We'll corral the horses out of sight behind the hills. Detail six hundred braves to hold the pass. Make certain we have at least a hundred of our best sharp shooters among them. I'll lead the rest of the troops across the bridge and onto the plateau. I want you to take up the rear to oversee the fortification of the pass and the safe passage of the troops."

"As you wish."

Hiamovi knew Ahiga was displeased with this order. The Navajo saw himself leading the whole army to victory while Hiamovi remained a remote figurehead, watching the battle from a safe position. Hiamovi needed his expertise in the rearguard action though. He also wanted to keep the young buck in his place. Hiamovi was coming to trust Ahiga less and less. He suspected the Navajo of working to his own agenda and wanted to diminish his growing influence within the UTN. If Ahiga was to fall victim to his own heroism in the coming bloodshed then Hiamovi would not be too upset. He would make a useful martyr.

As he handed his steed over to another brave and led the army on foot towards the pass, Hiamovi realised, to his shame, that he was thinking just like Ahiga. Perhaps that was the Navajo's great legacy to the UTN.

"We've just had some more news," said Bennet. He pushed his horn rimmed glasses back up his beak of a nose in a way that never failed to irritate Sinnot. "It gets worse."

"We've got over two thousand Native Americans camped outside our complex looking for a way to break in," said Sinnot. "How could it possibly get any worse?"

Sinnot hadn't slept in twenty-four hours. Not since he had been woken with the news that the complex's security had been breached. Since then he'd been forced to initiate a complete overhaul of the security protocols. He'd had to instigate the retrieval and reclassification of every bit of data stored in the complex, and personally oversee the detainment of Greaves and the two other intruders. He was in no mood for one of Bennet's reports. He wanted Bennet and Roth out of his office and the debriefing finished as quickly as possible so he could go and grovel to his masters in the patron's suite.

"Reports have confirmed that the Apostolic Church of the Rediscovered Dawn have also raised an army," said Bennet. "They're marching here and will arrive in less than twenty-four hours."

"The Apostolic...?" said Sinnot. "You mean the Neo-Clergy. I thought they'd disbanded."

"They've been undergoing a bit of a resurgence of late," said Roth, his pudgy moon face always wore an 'eager to please' expression.

"Why on earth are they marching out here?" said Sinnot. "Why don't they choose somewhere else to have their big showdown?"

"I would have thought that was rather obvious," said Bennet. "Like the intruders we just captured, they want to get their hands on all the biological weaponry we've been developing. Just like our patrons, they probably think it will allow them to take over what's left of the world."

"Quite," said Sinnot. "Frankly, I'm still more afraid of our patrons than an army of Native Americans or mad born-again Christians. Still this is something we're going to have to overcome, or we'll be in serious trouble."

Sinnot and all his colleagues referred to their paymasters as 'patrons', but they all knew it was a euphemism. They were their masters plain and simple. Men who were used to wielding untold power and using unlimited resources to do so. They'd been raised to do it since birth. It was bred into their bones. Even though Sinnot and his colleagues had once faced them down back before The Cull, had taken the Doomsday virus and bartered for their lives, the patrons still terrified him.

Sinnot knew it was only the plague that had killed so many that had paradoxically saved him and his associates. It hadn't taken them long to determine that the plague killed according to blood group. So Sinnot and his colleagues had developed a way to change their blood group. This was how over half of them had survived The Cull.

It was also their key bargaining tool with their masters, when they wanted to come in out of the cold. The ability to produce new strains of the Doomsday Virus had helped. If they'd been able to find out where the six hosts were hidden they'd have been in an even better position. Unfortunately when they fled their masters, Sinnot and his colleagues had split up into cells. The cell who had hidden the hosts did not survive The Cull.

Even still the secret of changing their blood group was enough to bring them back into the fold. For all their power, their masters could not isolate themselves enough to prevent infection. So Sinnot and his associates had come slinking back with their tails between their legs, but at least they were alive. They'd started work on guaranteeing their masters complete biological domination of their whole species once again.

They'd built this complex in Little Bighorn to start over. It was supposed to be impregnable and it was supposed to be totally secret. In the last twenty-four hours it had proved to be neither. He daren't go and tell that to his masters without a solution. They wouldn't like the idea of being the spoils of some war of faith.

"Why can't we just release something into the atmosphere on the surface?" said Bennet. "Something we can immunise ourselves against and let that take care of them?"

"We don't have anything that'll spread fast enough," said Sinnot. "Nothing for which we've got a fool proof antidote. We can't protect ourselves fully against any virus we have that's virulent enough to do the job."

"Haven't we got a workable strain of the Doomsday Virus?" said Roth.

"No," said Sinnot. "And there's no way we could release it without the proper controls in place."

"What about something from the armoury? There's those prototype sub-sonic bombs."

"And how would we launch them?" said Bennet with his customary sneer.

"We could use the micro gliders," said Roth. "We could send the guards up and get them to drop the bombs."

"The micro gliders are for aerial reconnaissance only," said Bennet. "You can't use them to go dropping bombs on people. They're not equipped for that."

"Also, we can't control the detonation or the blast radius enough to be safe," Sinnot said. "The sub-sonic bomb shreds all matter, organic and non-organic. We'd have to detonate it high above the ground so we didn't do as much damage to the complex as we would to the armies."

"What are we going to do then?" said Roth, there was more than a hint of panic in his voice. "We've only got forty armed guards in the place. There's over two thousand out there already and more coming. We can't possibly fight them all off and it's only a matter of time until they break in."

"Maybe," said Sinnot. "Maybe not."

"What do you have in mind?" said Bennet.

Sinnot smiled. "Stealth."

"Stealth? Can you elaborate?"

"We offer both sides exactly what they came here for. Or at least that's what we'll lead them to believe."

CHAPTER TWENTY-ONE

Colt looked out of his tent at the makeshift camp they'd erected in the parking lot of a half-built mall just off Highway 87. Earthquakes, plagues and nuclear strikes had ensured that this temple to consumerism had never been finished. All that remained was concrete and girders. When God didn't want a thing built, He didn't want it built. Even still, Colt couldn't help thinking that an earthquake or a plague or even an A-bomb by itself would have been enough. All three, now that was overkill.

They were a day's march from Little Bighorn. By all accounts the Injuns had got there already. Colt was waiting for Simon Peter to return with the scout's full report. The smells of roasted rodents wafted through the camp as the bodies of rats, possums, rabbits and hares were turned on spits.

To stop the men from fighting or getting drunk to relieve their boredom, Fitch and Golding were leading them in song. A special hymn they'd concocted for the occasion:

Mine eyes have see the glory of a million red skins dead,
They thought they'd fight our wives and kids but got our men instead.
To victory we march just as our saviour Colt has said
His truth goes marching on...

Colt should have smiled as they burst into their ' Glory Gorey Hallelujahs', but he wasn't in the mood. He was a day or so away from the biggest and most crucial fight of his whole career, leading an army against the most Godless people left in America. He faced the opportunity "to correct history and make certain the right side wins this time," as he had put it in his speech to the troops.

Only his heart wasn't in it, thanks to the Prophet. The man had insisted on accompanying the troops despite Colt telling him it was not the place for a man of peace. The Prophet was convinced his prophecy would be fulfilled and that they would win without a drop of blood being spilled. Personally, Colt thought they had more chance of finding an intact hymen in a cathouse, but the Prophet wouldn't be told.

Colt was still dwelling on this when he heard Simon Peter's cough at the opening of his tent. "C'mon in," he said.

Simon Peter stepped inside.

"So what's the news son?"

"Well sir, it's just as we feared. The Injuns have taken the pass which leads to the plateau. There's about five or six hundred of them holding it at the moment. The rest of them, about maybe one and a half thousand, are all camped out on the south side of the plateau."

"Any chance we can storm the pass? Maybe catch 'em napping?"

"Sir, it's too narrow for that and they're too well fortified. They'd pick us off one by one if we came down the middle and if we tried a pincer movement we'd still be fighting up hill. They could potentially hold us off for days. Even if we took the pass they could still fall back onto the plateau. There's only a tiny bridge leading to that so they could pick us off as we came."

"So that's it then? Game over, let's all go home and let them take over the country. Is that what you're saying?"

"Sir, no sir. Over on the north side the chasm between the mainland and the plateau is not as great. There's one spot where the distance to cross is only nine or so feet. What's more it's behind a rocky outcrop. So you can't see it from the south side of the plateau or the pass where the Injuns are."

"Is that right?" said Colt, as though he was only half listening. He had his back to Simon Peter and was staring up at a wooden crucifix that was hanging from the central pole of his tent.

"Sir, I don't want to speak out of turn but I think I might have guessed what you're planning to do."

"Have you now?"

"Well sir, as you're no doubt aware I sent some of our men to explore the construction site behind us and they've found some working rivet guns and welding torches. There's also a lot of girders in perfectly good condition. We've got enough men and vehicles to carry them over to the plateau to put together a bridge long enough to cross over without the Injuns seeing us. We've also got more than a few men in our command with construction experience. So I imagine you're going to order several squads to transport the materials to Little Bighorn, in advance of the main body of troops, with enough time to build them a bridge for when they arrive. Am I right sir?"

Colt didn't answer.

"Sir am I right?"

Colt turned from the crucifix and faced Simon Peter. "Are you right?"

"About your plans sir."

"Yes I think you must be."

"Do you want me to pass your orders on to the men sir? I could get them started straight away."

"Yes I think that would be a good idea."

"Sir, I hope I'm not out of line in asking this, but is everything alright?"

Colt looked directly at Simon Peter and spoke sharply. He didn't like being asked such a direct question. "You have your orders soldier. Dismissed."

The truth was that everything wasn't alright. Everything hadn't been alright since he'd met with the Prophet for their prayer meeting the night before last. From the Prophet's point of view the purpose of the meetings were to win Colt's soul back to the path of righteousness. From Colt's perspective he was trying to keep the Prophet on a tight leash.

Colt was concerned about the Prophet preaching his prophecy concerning a bloodless victory. He didn't want his men getting too complacent. They were about to face an army of two and a half thousand redskins. He didn't want them walking into battle with just a Bible and a belief in divine intervention.

Colt had challenged the Prophet about the truth of his vision. "Come on Robert," he'd said. "Now I ain't questioning every vision you've ever had. I'm sure some of 'em did come direct from God. Hell, I'll even believe He's got some express courier service between Him and you using angels, if you want me to but you gotta admit this whole business with the bloodless victory, well it's mighty convenient wouldn't you say? I mean it was great when we were on a recruitment drive. But now we need the men to face up to the hard realities of armed combat."

The Prophet had smiled. "I can only preach what my conscience dictates and what the Lord himself tells me."

This had not convinced Colt. "Don't you see how it could endanger the men's lives? Why it's plain irresponsible to preach those things. What are they going to do when they walk into battle and real bullets start flying?"

"Pray."

"Prayer don't stop bullets Robert."

"It can move mountains."

"Really? Well I ain't never seen a mountain moved that way."

"That's because you haven't been looking in the right places. And because you haven't been praying right."

"And what have I been doing wrong?"

"Pray with me Samuel and I'll pray to the Lord to send you a vision. For Christ himself to remove the scales from your eyes."

So Colt had knelt with the Prophet in prayer. Mainly just to prove to him how wrong he was. The Prophet spoke to the Lord and Colt joined him. Only this time it seemed the Lord was listening.

Colt had his eyes closed and he had the definite feeling there was someone else there in the room with them. Not right next to him, like one of his men, but hovering just above his head.

Colt opened his eyes and he wasn't in the tent anymore. He was on a hillside just outside an ancient city. In front of him there was a post in the ground. No, there were three posts. Only they weren't quite posts. Colt began to look up.

Then he stopped himself. He closed his eyes and shook his head. This wasn't real. He was inside a tent in Montana. The Prophet must have slipped him something.

He opened his eyes again and the hillside was still there, only it was starting to get indistinct. He looked through it and saw the Prophet in the tent with him, still praying.

The Prophet looked over at him and smiled and pointed upwards. Colt turned to look and he was back on the hill. Slotted into the top of the post in the ground was a crossbeam. Hanging from that crossbeam by the nails in his hands was a man, with two other men hanging from the crosses either side of him.

No, it wasn't just a man. Colt took one look into his eyes and he knew who it was. In those eyes there was more suffering and more love than Colt knew existed in the world.

It was all true. He really had suffered all those centuries ago and He had gone on suffering ever since. He would continue to suffer for as long as there were men and women who needed to atone for their actions.

He did this because of love. The love of a creator who gives life to the universe as a sacred gift and asks for nothing in return. The love that compels Him to put on human form and come down and suffer with His creations for as long as there is human suffering. To show them that no matter how low they sink, no matter how great their despair and how terrible their degradation, He is always there with them and always will be.

"No!" Colt shouted and jumped to his feet. It was all too much for him to take. The vision evaporated and he was back in the tent next to the Prophet. The vision was gone but the meaning wasn't. They were responsible for that perfect, sacred man's suffering. Everyone alive was. Colt was, in everything he did. Yet He suffered willingly. He submitted to those agonies because He loved us all.

Colt could hardly bring himself to speak the man's name. A name he had been raised with, fought and killed for. A name he was going to go to war for, and thereby cause the man even more suffering. Christ, his saviour.

"No!" Colt shouted and knocked the wooden crucifix off the tent pole.

The Prophet got off his knees and took hold of Colt's shoulders. "Samuel. Did you see it? Did you see it?"

"Get off of me!" yelled Colt and he pushed the Prophet to the ground.

The Prophet stood again. "But don't you see what this means? Samuel, don't you grasp its meaning?"

"Get out of here," Colt pushed the Prophet out of his tent. Of course he grasped the meaning. That's what he couldn't take. Every time he closed his eyes the vision was there. Challenging everything he had ever fought for, was the very thing he thought he was fighting for.

"Go on get out," Colt shouted as the Prophet stumbled backwards into the camp, looking hurt and confused. "You stay away from me, you hear? Don't you come anywhere near me again!"

The Prophet pulled himself up to his full height and left with as much dignity as he could muster.

"Looks like someone had a lover's quarrel," said a voice from around one of the campfires.

Colt went apoplectic. "Who said that? Which one of you lousy, stinking cowards said that?"

A hush fell across the whole camp.

Colt bore down on the fire from where he'd heard the comment. Around fifteen men sat huddled there. "Which one of you was it? Come on tell me or I'll have the lot of you shot."

Three of the men pointed to one bearded individual. He was shaking with fear. He patently regretted what he'd said. "I'm sorry Mr Colt sir. Truly I am. I didn't mean nothing by it. Just a dumb quip was all."

Colt saw the man was wounded. His shoulder was crudely bandaged.

He remembered that an advance party had traded shots with a group of Injuns two days before. They'd killed two of the redskins but suffered the first casualties of the war. This man must have been among them. He sat in front of the fire with a filthy coat draped around his bandaged shoulders and shivered from the night air and his fear of Colt. Colt could see the man was suffering and he was reminded of the endless suffering of the man on the cross.

One of his sergeants stepped up next to Colt. "I'll have the man disciplined right away sir."

He nodded to two men around the fire who leapt to their feet and hauled the bandaged man to his.

Colt's every instinct told him he should punish the man. Such insubordination should never be tolerated in the ranks. He had to maintain his own standing in front of the other men. But his instincts were stifled by an untapped well of compassion that suddenly rose inside him. He knew its source. It was the vision. Like a creeping weakness it seemed to sap all his strength and anger.

Cot turned his back on the man. "Don't bother," he muttered to the sergeant. "He's suffered enough." Then he walked back to the tent and under his breath he said. "He'll never stop suffering."

The morning after Simon Peter had outlined the plan about the bridge, Colt stood looking at it. It wasn't entirely complete but it was an impressive sight. Put together with steel girders the bridge spanned the chasm at its narrowest point. It was just wide enough for three men to cross it side by side.

Simon Peter and his team had worked through the night to build it. They hadn't been seen by the UTN, they'd have been shot if they had. Colt was impressed by their bravery and their industry. By late afternoon it would be ready.

Colt had arrived in advance of the other troops. The whole army was proceeding along a special route that would allow them to arrive at the north side of the plateau without the redskins seeing them. The plan was to get the main force to march straight across the bridge the moment they arrived and get as many as possible onto the plateau before the Injuns noticed.

Colt was gambling on sending a tight phalanx of soldiers into the centre of the Injun's ranks to catch them by surprise and rout them. Then the rest of his troops would advance as they arrived on two outward fronts like the horns of a bull.

It was a risky manoeuvre that until a few days ago would have had Colt's adrenalin pumping. Now his heart wasn't entirely in it. It was taking all the mental energy he had to repress the memory of the vision. And to stop himself thinking about the futility of bloodshed and the families of all the men he was sending to their deaths. Damn that fool Prophet.

"Err, sir," said Simon Peter breaking Colt's stream of thought. "There's a man on the other side of the bridge who wants to see you. He's asking to speak to our leader."

"What," said Colt. "Who the hell is he?"

"He says he from the complex. He wants to make a deal with us."

"A deal. What kind of a deal?"

CHAPTER TWENTY-TWO

"It's quite simple really," said Joe Black Feather. "We have two armies camped out on our doorstep. We think we know what you're after. We can't keep both of you out so our best bet for survival is to strike a deal with the side most likely to win."

"And you think that's us?" said Hiamovi.

The Iroquois smiled. "Well, I hope it is. You got here first and you've got the best tactical position. So it's a safe bet to say you've got the upper hand. As project leader it's my call as to which side to pick and, well to be fair, I'd rather fall in with my own people."

"And what about your associates?" said Hiamovi pointing to the man and woman with Joe. "They don't look like our people."

"No but with respect, I see a lot of white faces among your ranks too."

"Fair point. So what are you offering?"

"Am I right in assuming that you're here for the Doomsday Virus?"

"If that's the virus that you can tell who to kill and who to spare then, yes, that's what we're here for. We won't leave without it and we're prepared to fight."

"Yes," said Joe. "We assumed you were. You have far too many men to hold off for long and we have the additional problem of an army of happy-clappy rednecks bearing down on us. So here's the deal. You agree to protect us from the Neo-Clergy and to spare us when you unleash the virus and we'll show you how to use it. We'll even throw in a guided tour of the complex for you and your retinue, to show you that everything's above board."

"Wait here," said Hiamovi. He left Joe and the other two from the complex and went to consult with Onatah and Ahiga, who had been listening at a distance. "What do you think?"

"It makes sense I suppose," said Onatah. "We have them backed into a corner. They're trying to find some room to manoeuvre."

"I don't know," said Ahiga. "It all seems a little too easy to me. They're rolling over really quickly without any fight. I would have thought they'd put up more resistance."

"As the man said though," said Onatah. "There's more than two thousand of us. There's no way they can keep us out. Maybe they'd have put up more of a fight if the Neo-Clergy weren't on their way too."

"Do you think that could have swayed them?" said Hiamovi.

"If you look at it from their point of view, they have to pick one side in order to survive. Who would you choose, us or a bunch of Darwin-hating Christians who believe that if it isn't mentioned in their Bible then it's the work of Satan?"

"Good point. But can we trust them?"

"Probably not. But we have an army and they don't. What are they going do? The way I see it, this could be a way to win the war against the Neo-Clergy without endangering the lives of any of our young braves or squaws. Isn't that at least worth exploring"

Hiamovi was silent for a moment, weighing up what his comrades had said. "Very well," he said, at length. "You're right Onatah. This offer deserves to be explored. I shall check out the complex. It will also give us some idea of their defences if things don't work out and we do need to attack."

"Great Chief," said Ahiga. "I'm concerned for your safety. Let me and my best men go with you."

Hiamovi looked into Ahiga's eyes. Ahiga looked straight back. He seemed to be in earnest, but you could never tell with this Navajo. Ahiga had done more to increase Hiamovi's power base than anyone else in the UTN, yet he always seemed to have a private agenda. This made it difficult to judge if he was a friend or enemy. Hiamovi decided this was the best reason to keep him close. He could keep an eye on Ahiga inside the complex. This way he wouldn't be left in charge of the troops.

Hiamovi put a hand on Ahiga's shoulder. "I would be glad to have you at my side. Detail two other braves to accompany us."

"Braves Great Chief?" said Onatah raising an eyebrow. "Are no women allowed to accompany you?"

"Onatah," said Hiamovi. "I need your wisdom and the fury of my sisters out here on the plateau. Colt's army will be here any day and I need someone I can trust to hold them at the pass if I'm not here."

"Very well," said Onatah. "You can trust us to protect you while you check out your new toys."

"The entrance is hidden just around here Mr Colt," said the moon faced man who called himself Roth. "If you and your associates would like to accompany me." Roth led them to a shaded alcove in the rocky outcrop.

Colt was surprised when Roth tapped a portion of the alcove's wall and the rock sprang back to reveal a keypad.

Roth noticed their wariness and smiled. "This is just a security precaution. We don't want just anyone getting in now do we?"

Colt determined to ignore his smug and patronising manner until he had the virus in his grasp. Then he'd kick the man's teeth down his throat.

A door slid back to reveal an elevator. Roth bowed and motioned for them to enter like some sarcastic bus boy. His manner angered Colt. That was good. Anger made him feel in control, more like his old self.

At the bottom Colt and his men stepped out of the lift to be greeted by more patronising smiles from guys in white coats. Something didn't smell right to Colt. He couldn't put his finger on it but there was something about the place that felt wrong. It wasn't just that they were acting like they were trying to pull a fast one. There was something kind of eerie about the whole facility.

If they thought they were going to get an easy ride siding with him to protect them from the Injuns, they had another think coming. He'd play along for a little while till he got his hands on what he wanted, then he'd set them straight. And he could guarantee they wouldn't like it when he did. They might be scared of the redskins, but they were going to be a lot more frightened of him when he was done.

Roth showed them around the complex. Colt and his men saw the barracks where the guards were housed as well as the scientist's living quarters and recreation areas. Their rather extensive armoury was filled with all sorts of gadgets. By the time Roth showed Colt the kitchens and macrobiotic food vats, Colt was getting bored and ready to wring the podgy goon's neck. "When are you gonna show us what we came here for?" he said.

"Any moment now. But first we have a little surprise for you. Call it a peace offering." They turned a corner and behind an open glass door, lying on stainless steel tables, were the unconscious bodies of five redskins. Colt even recognised a couple of them. The big one was Hiamovi, the UTN's head guy. The Neo-Clergy's biggest enemy.

"Are these for real?" said Colt.

"Why don't you touch them and see?"

Colt and the other three walked into the room.

"That's Tom," said Fitch, pointing at the man sprawled next to Hiamovi. "The Navajo we told you about. Calls himself Ahiga now."

They stood over the bodies and prodded them.

"What's this powder they're covered with?" said Colt rubbing it between his fingers. It smelled musky but it felt squishy when he touched it.

"I'm glad you asked that," Roth said and the glass door slid shut behind them.

"Hey what is this?" shouted Colt.

"It's a trap Mr Colt," said Roth through the intercom. "I would have thought that even your basic intelligence would have grasped that. The powder you mentioned is a genetically amplified pollen. It's derived from a plant similar to the Venus flytrap, but it's effect is over a hundred times more potent. It's what incapacitated the Native Americans in there with you. You only have touch it for it to take effect. Pleasant dreams Mr Colt."

Colt felt a torrent of righteous fury well up inside him, drowning out any compassion that he might have felt before. He went to throw himself at the glass door but his legs wouldn't move. They were numb. He couldn't feel his feet or his fingers. Out of the corner of his eye he saw Golding topple to the floor.

A huge wave of drowsiness overcame him. He heard Simon Peter and Fitch hit the ground. He wanted to fight it but even his massive anger wasn't strong enough to keep him conscious.

Colt fell to the floor.

Cortez's fever broke on the second day of captivity. He was lying on the floor of his holding pen with his knees up in the air. It was too small for him to lie stretched out and it wasn't big enough to be called a cell. The pen felt like somewhere you'd keep an animal.

They'd given Cortez the antidote to the virus soon after he and Greaves had surrendered. He'd taken real sick but when he thought about what happened to the rats he'd probably gotten off lightly. Cortez propped himself up on his elbows and breathed deeply. He stank of sweat but he had that slight euphoria that comes when your body has fought off a serious infection and returns to its old self.

In the distance he could hear the squeak of wheels and the clatter of metal plates. Twice a day someone opened a hatch in the door and stuck a metal bowl of slops through it. The slops were cold and tasted like baby food, although Cortez had been too sick to eat more than a mouthful or two up until now.

He was ravenous, but he suppressed his hunger and listened carefully to the trolley. The last two days had been a haze of fevered sensations but he tried to recollect what he could about the usual routine of mealtimes. The trolley sounded as though it was making more stops than usual. He was also fairly certain it sounded a lot more laden with slop bowls.

Cortez searched his memories for approximate times. Each time the trolley called the bowl was dropped off, then collected ten minutes later. When the hatch in the door was unlocked it fell forward to provide a surface to rest the bowl on. Cortez couldn't remember any other regular visits by anyone else. All this was important to what he was going to do.

As he heard the key turn in the lock of his hatch Cortez put his foot against it to stop it dropping properly. This annoyed the orderly who cursed the stupid mechanism and reached down to try and force it with his hand.

Cortez moved his foot and sprang forward. He grabbed the orderly's wrist and caught the man off balance, pulling him forward with some force. The man's arm came all the way through the hatch and Cortez heard his head smash into the door.

Leaning forward he pulled even harder on the man's arm. There was a louder thump as the man's head collided with the door again. Cortez saw blood trickling down the man's shoulder. He felt for a pulse in the wrist. There was none.

Cortez slowly let go of the arm and pushed it back out of the hatch. Then he peered into the corridor. Cortez could just about manage to reach out of the hatch with his right arm. He pulled the orderly closer and began to feel through his pockets.

There were no keys. He pressed his face up against the opening and peered up and down the corridor. The keys had fallen out of the orderly's hand and landed about two feet away. Too far away to grab. *Damn!*

Cortez pulled the orderly closer and, using his right hand, he felt for the man's belt. He undid it and tried to flick the belt down the corridor to catch the keys with the buckle. It didn't work. He couldn't see where he was aiming the belt and it wasn't long enough.

Changing tactics, he searched the body again with his right hand, going through all the orderly's pockets. He struck lucky when he came to the man's back pocket. There was a penknife.

Cortez dropped the knife in his lap and reached out of the hatch to feel for the door lock. He was lucky it was only a simple bolt with a padlock on it. As Cortez suspected, this wasn't a proper holding area. It was a place in the complex where they locked up things they were experimenting on.

The bolt was held to the door with four screws. Cortez reached around and began to unscrew them with the penknife. He nearly dislocated his shoulder, but after twenty minutes the first screw came out. Cortez dropped the knife. It hit the ground out of reach. Using the orderly's arm he knocked the knife back into his reach, picked it up and started on the second screw, ignoring the shooting pains in his shoulder.

Onatah was sitting with Huyana and Amitola when the aircraft appeared. One flew north, while the other flew south towards them. They looked like planes but as the southbound one flew low Onatah could see it was too small to be piloted and must be flown by remote control.

About a hundred braves reached for their rifles as it swooped over their heads. Onatah raised her hand to stop them firing. Doors opened in the plane's under carriage and a grey object parachuted down.

Everyone rushed back from the spot where the small square object landed. Onatah walked into the space the warriors had cleared around it. She bent down and picked it up.

"It's a bomb," someone called out.

"Don't touch it!" another cried, "you could set it off."

Onatah smiled. She hadn't seen one of these in years. It was rare to find one that worked. "It's alright," she said to everyone. "It's a laptop." She flipped up the screen. Four green words were flashing in the centre.

PRESS THE SPACE BAR

Huyana and Amitola peered over her shoulder. "What should we do?" said Huyana.

"For the time being," said Onatah. "We play along."

She pressed the space bar.

The screen showed web cam footage of a bald white man in a lab coat. "My name is Sinnot," said the man. "I am in charge of the complex I assume you are trying to conquer."

The camera moved from Sinnot's face to show two unconscious bodies tied and bound to chairs. It was Ahiga and Hiamovi. Three armed men stood behind them. "We have taken your leaders captive. If you try to break into the complex we will not hesitate to kill them. As you are probably aware we have a lot of biological weapons. I'm guessing that's why you're trying to attack us. If your entire army does not vacate this plateau and leave the surrounding area we will unleash them all on you. Do not think you will survive such an onslaught. You have twenty-four hours to comply with our demands. That is all."

The web cam footage came to an end and the screen went blank. Onatah felt sick. This was the last thing she wanted to hear. Their leaders were captured by the men they came to conquer and their enemy was about to attack them.

"What shall we do?" said Huyana. "They've got our

chiefs."

"Hush," said Onatah. "Not so loud. We've got to choose our moment to tell this to the troops. We must proceed with caution."

"We've got to get off the plateau," said Amitola. "You heard them. They're going to wage biological warfare on us."

"I don't think so. They're scared of us. That's why they've done this. If they really had those capabilities they'd have used them already. I think they're trying to face us down with a bluff."

"But they have our leaders," said Huyana in a quiet but desperate voice. "You saw the footage. I mean they went into the complex with that scientist, how are we going to handle this?"

"Order most of the troops to fall back to the pass," said Onatah. "I want every scout we have out combing the plateau. Tell them to keep hidden though. We need to find a way into this complex. We also need to find out where the Neo-Clergy are camped."

"Do you think they're already here?" said Amitola.

"Two planes left the complex," said Onatah. "The other headed north. It's a safe bet that it was headed towards the Neo-Clergy army. Tell the scouts to look for their location. Sinnot may even have pulled the same trick on them as well."

"You think they might have Colt and the other Neo-Clergy leaders?" said Amitola.

"It's possible. There's no reason they wouldn't try the same tactic on both sides. If it worked on us, it might have worked on them. In the meantime we need to gather as much intelligence as possible about our enemy and the people holding our leaders. I'm guessing the Neo-Clergy will be doing the same thing so send out patrols to look for their scouts and any spies."

"What do we do about Hiamovi and the others?" said Huyana. "How will we free them?"

"We need to find the weaknesses of the people holding them," said Onatah. "And we must pray to the Great Spirit for their safe return.

CHAPTER TWENTY-THREE

The last screw wasn't budging. Cortez felt his shoulder pop. The pain was too great and he couldn't move his fingers. He pulled his arm back through the hatch and clicked his shoulder back into its socket.

He'd have to kick the lock off from inside. One screw wouldn't hold it. He shifted his bulk round in the pen, wadded his coat up against the door to muffle the sound, and rammed his heel into the metal. The bolt was stubborn but it gave on the fourth kick and the door swung open.

Cortez climbed out, stretched his back and dragged the orderly's body into the pen. He picked up the keys and grabbed a couple of bowls off the trolley. His stomach growled in anticipation as he drained both bowls in a couple of gulps.

Looking down the corridor at the pens on either side Cortez could see that at least ten were occupied. They hadn't been when he first arrived. This meant the complex had been forced to adapt its facilities to take prisoners in the last day or so.

It must be under siege. Someone else had found out about the virus. The only other people Greaves had told were the Neo-Clergy soldiers who tortured him. The coward who ran must have got word back to his superiors. This might complicate matters a little. Cortez had to get Greaves and Anna out.

First he walked past each of the doors to the pens and listened to see if he could identify the occupants. He recognised Greaves straight away from the smell. Cortez unlocked the pen and helped him to his feet.

"Good work," Greaves said. "Now we need to get Anna."

"Do you know where she is?"

"They didn't lock her up with us. They took her somewhere else. She's far too valuable to them. They'll want to study her for a while then dissect her most probably."

Cortez unlocked the food hatches on the other pen doors and peered in.

"What are you doing?" said Greaves.

"They have a lot of armed men. We may need to fight our way out and it won't hurt to have a bit of back up."

"Is that a good idea? How do we know we can trust any of them?"

"We have a common enemy. That comes before any other loyalties. They need to get out of here as much as we do."

On the right hand side of the corridor were five Native American prisoners. On the other side were four dressed in Neo-Clergy uniforms. They all looked groggy as though they were just coming round. Cortez unlocked the pens on the right hand wall and helped the prisoners to their feet.

"Who are you?" said the tallest Native American. "Where are you taking us?"

"It's alright, we're prisoners too. We've just escaped." Greaves pointed to the dead orderly in Cortez's pen as proof of this. "My name is Greaves and this is Cortez."

"We need to find our friend and get out of here," said Cortez. "Will you work with us?"

The tall Native American said: "I am Hiamovi, Great Chief of the UTN. I have an army waiting outside. If you can get us out of here, when I take the complex I will guarantee your friend's safe return."

"There isn't time for that," said Greaves. "She's too important and she's in grave danger."

Hiamovi and his comrades bristled at the way Greaves spoke to them. Cortez recognised the response. It was the way all powerful men react when not addressed with enough respect.

"Our friend is the key to getting us all out," said Cortez. "That is why we need to locate her. My friend meant no disrespect."

"We need weapons to fight our way out," said a shorter, stockier Native American, who appeared to be second in command. "Do you know where we can get some?"

"Well now," said a deep, Mid-Western voice from one of the pens. "I believe I can help you there."

Colt had his face pressed up against the hatch. Two men he'd never seen before had let the redskins loose. They were talking about escape and he wanted in.

"See while they put you fellers under they had to distract us," said Colt. "They was so cocksure they actually gave us a tour of the place. I know exactly where we can get all the weapons we need."

"We?" said Hiamovi, looking at Colt. "There is no 'we' here Mr Colt. Why would I release my greatest enemy?"

"Way I see it," said Colt. "You ain't got no choice. The seven of you aren't gonna fight your way outta here with your dicks in your hand. You're gonna need fire-power and you're gonna need more muscle. I can supply you with both."

"Tom?" Fitch called out from a pen next to Colt's. "Hey is that you Tom. C'mon Tom, for old time's sake let us loose."

"You know these men?" said Hiamovi to the brave next to him.

"My name is Ahiga. Be sure and use it."

"Sure To... I mean Ahiga," said Fitch. "Anything you say. Just get us out of these cages. We can help each other, right?"

"Great Chief," said Ahiga to Hiamovi. "This is one of the men I spoke to you about. The ones I used to run with."

"These are your contacts in the Neo-Clergy, the ones you colluded with?"

"These men have been of some service to you. I'm not saying I can vouch for them, but I have worked with them. Maybe they can be of some use."

The sneaky Injun was planning something, Colt could tell.

So could Hiamovi. "We are about to go to war with these people. They have already murdered and enslaved hundreds of our brothers and sisters. Why would I want to set him free to lead his army against ours when I have him safely locked away?"

"Because we've been in this together since day one," said Colt. "We've been working with each other every step of the way. You've needed a bogeyman to scare your people into submission and so have I. We've played that part to perfection for each other. We've been playing the same tune and dancing the same steps, right down the line. You wouldn't have come to power without the threat I pose your people. And hey, I'm a big enough man to admit you've helped put me where I am. Like it or not, we need each other. We're perfect together."

Colt was finally putting his newfound compassion to good use. It wasn't choking him, it was helping get what he wanted, allowing him to feel and think like his enemy, so he could use it to his own benefit. "Now I want to get back to my troops as much as you do. I want to make sure they're safe and ready to fight just like you. The best way for us to do that is to help each other, just like we been doing from the start. Doesn't mean I want to get all lovey-dovey and start burying the hatchet. But we've got a common enemy and that means we've got a common goal. Like they say, 'you keep your friends close but you keep your enemies closer.' Are you sure you want to leave me all the way down here where you've got no idea what I'm up to?"

The big wetback called Cortez pulled the keys out of his pocket. "This is the situation," he said. "I need to free my friend. She holds the key to controlling the Doomsday Virus. She's the only person that does. That's why our common enemy, the scientists, have her. My friend with the glasses here has memorised the blue prints to every floor in the complex..."

"There are nine," said Greaves. "Ten if you count the generator's sub basement."

"Thank you," said Cortez. "There's nearly forty armed men in the place..."

"Forty-two to be exact."

Cortez placed a hand on Greaves shoulder to stop him interrupting again. "If we're going to have to shoot our way out we're going to need as many men as we can get." Cortez turned to Colt. He was a powerful looking man, Colt would give him that. "I need to know that if I freed you and your men you'd fight alongside us, not go off on your own or try and attack us while we're in here."

"I'm not going to let you free these men," said Hiamovi. "I thought I already made that clear."

"With respect Great Chief," said Cortez. "I may not control an army but we're holding the keys to the cells, no-one else here knows how to get around the place and we're the only people who know how to get the

Doomsday Virus out of here. We're the ones who set the terms of this escape."

"How do I know you're not planning to double cross us once you get the virus?" said Hiamovi.

"Of course we're planning to double cross you," said Greaves. "Just as you're already thinking of ways to double cross both Colt and us, and Colt here is dreaming up ways to get one over the rest of us. That doesn't matter. What's important is that none of those plans will come to anything unless we all agree to work together right now to get out of here."

"He's got a point Hiamovi," said Colt. "I don't like him anymore than you do, but you can't argue with the little runt."

Cortez looked Hiamovi in the eye. "Agreed?"

Hiamovi nodded.

Cortez met Colt's gaze.

"I got no argument," said Colt. "I want to get out of here and get some payback."

His anger had fused with his compassion turning it into a fierce protectiveness. He felt protective of the men in his command and of his faith. He was ready to kill to see they came to no harm.

Cortez unlocked Colt's pen and offered Colt his hand to help him up. The two sized each other up as Colt got to his feet. *Be careful of this man*, Colt thought. *Better to have him on your side when it counted.*

As Cortez freed Colt's men they squared off against Hiamovi and his braves. Neither side took their eye off the other for a second. Hiamovi and Colt had been bitter enemies since each began their rise to power. This was the first time they'd met face to face. Not as opponents, but allies in a desperate bid for freedom. Fighting side by side to escape and go back to their war.

CHAPTER TWENTY-FOUR

Fitch still had a stinking headache when he reached the bottom of the stairs. The little faggot with the glasses was seriously pissing him off and as soon as Fitch got a gun, that little fucker better not turn his back on him.

He'd led them all over the complex, hiding round corners waiting for cameras to go off. Then they doubled back on themselves and headed for a stairwell they'd already passed. And the faggot Greaves comes on all superior like that's what he'd planned the whole time. Acting like his college education meant the rest of them ought to kneel and kiss his heiny. Fitch was going to put his fist up it in a minute.

He was still groggy from that pollen shit that had knocked him out. His head throbbed and his guts wanted to puke, only he wasn't going to let them. Fitch hoped they'd get into this armoury soon, because someone had to die for the way he was feeling.

At the top of the stairs Greaves started whining about the door to the armoury being an exit only door with the lock on the inside. "I didn't anticipate this from the blueprints," he said. "What we need to do is punch a hole..."

Fitch stepped up to the door and pushed him aside. "One side Einstein," he said, then he caught a whiff of the runt. "Jesus you stink!"

When the big, bearded wetback started to get up in his face, Fitch knew he was outclassed. He held his hands up. "Listen. I got no beef with you. But while Joe College here was getting his ass kicked by frat boys, I was getting my education in jacking Seven-Elevens. This is my area of speciality."

Fitch took in the door. It was heavy and there were no locks, or handles showing. "We need to jimmy it," he said. He looked around and saw the metal spindles on the stairwell. One good kick and they'd come free. He nodded to Golding to join him and they tore three loose.

"You wanna give us a hand Tom?" Fitch said, then realised his mistake. "I mean Ahiga. This is a three man operation you know that?"

Tom looked over at his Chief, who nodded and them helped them ram the spindles into the door jamb between the hinges. They leant on the spindles and popped the hinges out of the jamb.

The three of them busting a back door to jack some stuff was just like back in the day with 57th Street bangers. Everyone in Boulder knew about them. They ran Lomont. Tom joined them straight out of reform school where he'd met Golding. Golding and Fitch grew up on the same block. The three of them were the meanest mother-fuckers their age and they were on their way up in the gang.

At one point Tom had looked to take over as leader. Fitch and Golding had put a stop to that after they'd discovered Tom's little secret. He'd have been dead if word got out. But instead of slipping a noose round his neck they put a leash on him. Turned him into their bitch. The Cull came down pretty soon after that and Tom had drifted back to his own folks and became Ahiga. Fitch and Golding went into the Neo-Clergy.

Cortez was first through the door. Fitch and Golding followed. They entered a side room filled with metal shelves and boxes. There were pegs all over the walls with stuff like flak jackets, gas masks and bullet proof vests hanging from them.

Fitch walked past a shelf and saw a guard with a clipboard. He had earphones in so he wouldn't have heard them come in, but he looked up and saw Fitch. Before either of them reacted Cortez was right behind the man, grabbing his head and wrenching it round. Fitch heard the man's spinal column snap with a crunch of vertebrae. He was blown away. Cortez was quick and lethal.

Greaves bent down and picked up the clipboard. "It's an inventory. The guns are in the next room."

Cortez was careful to make no sound as he stepped into the room. A huge cache of firearms were on display. He heard the sound of voices coming from behind one of the racks.

Cortez signalled to Fitch and Golding to be quiet and get out of sight.

"So Burns tells him if he's late again he'll be on permanent latrine duty," said a guard, stepping into sight.

"He's such a jerk off," said the guard next to him. "They should clean the latrines with his face. Have we done grenades yet?"

"I don't think so."

Cortez found a row of belts, each with a knife and a sheath on it. He took one knife and tossed it to Fitch then removed another for himself. He signalled to Fitch and Golding to go down to the far end of the racks and to come up on the left hand guard from behind.

Cortez went the opposite way and came around the other end of the racks. As he glanced into the aisle where the guards were he heard a clatter from the other end of the room. Fitch or Golding must have knocked something over. The two guards turned to see and Cortez took advantage of their distraction.

He came up on the second guard from behind, placing a hand over the man's mouth Then he brought the knife round and rammed it into his heart. Blood gushed out in warm spurts, spilling down Cortez's hand as he gripped the knife.

The first guard dropped his clipboard and backed away down the aisle, fumbling for his weapon. Golding grabbed him from behind and held his arms while Fitch stuck his knife into the man's guts. He pulled it out and stabbed him twice more.

The guard broke free from Golding screaming in pain as blood poured from his wounds. Catching hold of the guard again Golding put a hand over the man's mouth as Fitch stuck him repeatedly with his knife.

Cortez heard footsteps approaching on the opposite side of the room and, as another guard entered, he brought the knife down on the top of the man's head, ramming it through his skull.

The guard stepped back staring at Cortez with anger and shock. His eyes rolled back into his skull and a thin trickle of blood ran down his face.

Cortez was about to step over the body when a bullet whistled past his ear and clipped the wall next to him. He dived out of sight and dragged the body of the guard towards him. Cortez pulled the man's pistol out of his holster. He leaned round the doorway and let off a shot into the office beyond.

Several more shots tore through the doorway hitting the walls and the floor and, from what Cortez could see, there were two more guards in what looked like a front office.

Cortez turned to see Fitch and Golding loading three pump-action shotguns. Colt and Hiamovi were coming up the centre aisle. Cortez raised a hand to caution them and they stopped.

Fitch threw Cortez a shotgun. Cortez lifted the dead guard's body into the doorway to use as cover and draw the other guards' fire. Four or five bullets thudded into the corpse. Cortez could see that one guard was using a desk as cover. He got a bead on the man's position and squeezed the trigger.

The round blew a huge hole in the desk. There was a scream of pain. Fitch, Golding and Cortez counted silently down from three before entering the room and letting off a barrage of gunfire.

The desk was blown apart along with the body of the guard behind it. The last guard made a bolt for the exit. Fitch caught him with a blast to the shoulder that threw him against the door. Cortez and Golding opened up, tearing chunks out of him.

Cortez checked the front office. There were no more guards, but the gun shots would surely have alerted the others. He needed Greaves and his smarts to lock the place the down and get them a way out.

Greaves was out in the main armoury watching the escapees drool over the weaponry on display. They were helping themselves to whatever they could carry, discarding one weapon as soon as they saw a better one.

His heart sank as soon as shots were traded. The noise was deafening. It would bring half the guards in the complex down on them. They had to secure the armoury, then find a way out.

Greaves moved to the exit at the other end of the room. It was electronically activated and it opened onto stairs leading to the officer's quarters. The keypad was on the other side of the door. There was no way Greaves could disable it.

He turned and called to one of the Native Americans who was helping himself to ammunition. "Quick. You've got to shoot at this wall. Right there where I'm pointing." The brave did nothing but stare at him suspiciously.

"There's an electronic lock on the other side of this wall. This leads to the officer's quarters. Any minute now guards are going to be swarming out of it. We have to take out the lock."

The brave turned to look at Hiamovi who nodded and the brave fired three shots into the wall.

Greaves jumped out of the way as chunks of plaster and dust flew. The third shot hit its target and sparks leapt out of the hole.

Cortez put a hand on Greaves' shoulder. "We need to secure the entrance to the front office."

Once in the office Greaves found the control console and activated the security shutters. Reinforced steel slammed down over the doors.

There were shots from the stairwell outside. When they got there they saw that Colt and his henchman, Simon Peter, were at the door. "They tried to get in by the stairs," Colt said. "We put a stop to that."

"Is there another exit out of here?" Cortez asked Greaves.

"Yes. There's another door on the opposite side that leads to a different stairwell, but they'll be trying that one as well now. We've got to barricade both doors."

"No shit," said Colt. "But that won't hold 'em long. I thought you were the one that who had everything planned out. Least ways that's how you act. Now it's all falling apart, where's this brilliant plan of yours?"

Greaves didn't have an answer. He always had an answer.

Something always came to him. But nothing came now. He felt himself start to buckle under the pressure. He was close to physical collapse from illness and infection. He hadn't eaten or slept properly in weeks. He was starting to get palpitations. It was just like his breakdown. He felt events spiralling out of his control. They were looming over and threatening to crush him. No, he was stronger than last time, older and wiser. He thought of Cortez who overcame everything that was put in his way. *Be like that*, Greaves told himself. *Be like Cortez.*

It was all Sinnot's fault that he was feeling this way. He was the one who had dragged up Greaves' past. There had been so much pressure on him from such an early age, so many expectations and so many great things he was supposed to have done by now. As Sinnot had said, so much wasted potential.

Greaves could have been anything but he ended up a lab assistant. And Sinnot had cheated him out of his last chance to be something worthwhile, to live up to all that incredible early potential. To redeem himself.

That's what he was in search of when he found Anna – redemption. To make up for all that lost promise he would rescue the remnants of humanity from their own stupidity.

Sinnot and his idiot colleagues had no idea what they actually had in the Doomsday Virus. They hadn't the foresight or the imagination to see. All they wanted was to hand it over to their paymasters so they could go on running the world in the same stupid and brutal way they always had.

Greaves was so close, but it was all getting too difficult. Too many things kept going wrong. He started to hyperventilate. He reached into one of his pockets for a paper bag to breath into. He could see the men around him smirk. They were no better than the jocks from high school who laughed at the prepubescent maths whiz who had to do gym with them along with his other lessons.

As they moved one of the shelves in front of the doorway, a box of night-vision goggles fell off it.

"I've got it," Greaves said. "We kill the lights and use these goggles. They won't see us but we'll be able to see them."

"How are we going to do that?" Colt said.

"We'll take out the fuse box on this floor to begin with."

"That's no good," said Fitch. "They'll just wait till we go up to the next floor where there is light."

"That's just to buy us enough time to get out of here before the explosion," Greaves said.

"What explosion?" Colt said.

"Here's the clever bit. In the far room is where they keep all the high explosive. This room and the main one are right over the generator in the sub-basement. If we set enough explosive in these two rooms, we'll take out the floors above and below. We'll also destroy the generator and kill the power to the whole complex, while taking out the guards in the barracks above us at the same time. Those that are left won't be able to see and they won't be able to re-arm themselves because we'll have totalled the armoury. What's more, once power is down all the freezing equipment that's keeping the biological weaponry safe won't work. We'll have just enough time to get out before the place becomes infected. Everyone else will be too busy evacuating to avoid infection, to stop us taking the Doomsday Virus."

The looks on all the men's faces changed. They couldn't see a flaw in the plan. They stopped sneering at Greaves and in spite of themselves they all looked impressed.

"Now you see why I keep him around," said Cortez.

CHAPTER TWENTY-FIVE

Anna had given them every kind of bodily fluid. They'd taken her blood, urine, saliva and they'd even done something called a smear test. The man called Sinnot and his scientists buzzed around her with so much excitement they reminded her of the clients at the Pleasuredrome. Only they seemed more cowardly than those men and a lot more dangerous.

Now they were subjecting her to something they called a CAT scan. She was strapped to a padded metal table that moved in and out of a revolving tunnel. In the next room she heard them discussing the images of her brain that appeared on a computer screen.

"She's too old," Anna heard Sinnot say. "She's got too many defined neural pathways, we couldn't counteract them all. Besides the micro-circuitry is to small to fit an adult brain."

"We can shut down any part of her brain that resists processing," said the man called Bennet. "Any vital functions that effects can be controlled by our CPU. We've already proven that."

"Besides," said another man who she thought was called Roth. "We don't need to rebuild the micro-circuitry, just the bio-connector, which is the easiest part of the apparatus to replicate."

"But we've never done this with a subject of her age," said Sinnot. "She's not pliable enough for our requirements."

"She's the only hope we've got." Bennet said. "Our masters aren't taking our failure well, and we've got nothing else to bargain with."

Anna could feel the Doomsday Virus elsewhere in

the complex. It was writhing inside the super-cooled containers. It already felt like another part of her body. When she was back at the community Anna had once heard a woman who had lost two babies talking. She had said she could still feel both of them at her nipple a month after they'd gone.

And there was Old Eli, a farm worker who lost a hand in a shooting accident. He told Anna once that the back of his hand still itched from time to time even though he couldn't scratch it.

That's what the Doomsday Virus felt like to Anna. Like some kind of phantom limb that had been cut off at birth and kept in jar. Now she was here in the complex it had come to life. She could feel its excitement, its hunger to be joined with her again.

Anna heard the doors to the lab hiss open and she craned her neck to see four guards burst in. "Sir," Anna heard a guard say. "You've to come with us straight away."

"What the hell are you doing in here?" Sinnot said. "You've absolutely no clearance. We're conducting important work."

"Sir we have orders to get you and your team to safety."

"Safety? What on earth are you talking about? You're about to place our whole work in jeopardy!"

"It's you and the other doctors who are in jeopardy. The prisoners have escaped and they're armed."

"Armed?" said Bennet. "How did that happen? "

"I can't tell you that now sir."

"One minute," said Sinnot. "I'll get the girl and we'll leave. "

"Sir, our orders said nothing about the girl. Only you three doctors."

"Don't be ridiculous man," said Sinnot. "Don't you know how important she is to our whole work here?"

"I am authorised to use force if necessary, sir."

Off in the distance Anna heard gunfire. Elsewhere she felt the virus thrash with a wild longing.

Ahiga was on point when the lights went out. The little guy disabled the fuse box and everything went dark. Ahiga switched on his goggles in time to see the rest of the group charging up the stairwell.

Only Fitch and Golding were left. They were moving their heads from side to side in panic and bewilderment, with their hands stretched out in front of them. They couldn't see a thing, their goggles weren't functioning. Ahiga had removed the battery packs before handing them their equipment.

"Wait!" Golding called out.

Ahiga placed a hand on his shoulder.

"Quiet. There are soldiers nearby, you don't want to give away our position."

"Who's that?" said Fitch.

"It's Tom. I've been sent back to get you."

"I thought you were on point." Golding said.

"I was. Until you two got left behind"

"Our fucking goggles aren't working."

"That's okay," said Ahiga putting his hands on both their shoulders. "I can probably fix them in a minute. We've got to get you to safety first."

Ahiga led them back into the main room of the armoury where the high explosive had been primed.

"Hold on a minute," said Fitch. "This feels like the wrong direction."

"You're just disoriented by the dark. It'll pass in a second."

"Aren't we supposed to be going up some stairs?"

"Not the first set we just passed," said Ahiga. "We need the next set at the end of this corridor."

There was a burst of gunfire in the distance. Ahiga used the opportunity to steer Golding and Fitch into the front office. "We have to duck into here for a second. You can't see to shoot and we're pinned down."

"Can you fix our goggles now?" Golding said.

"That explosive is going to go off any second." Fitch said. "Are you sure we're far enough away to be safe?"

"Trust me. We're in the perfect spot."

Ahiga took Fitch and Golding to the far end of the office and positioned them so they were facing towards the door.

"What's going on?"

"Quiet!" Ahiga hissed. He moved the body of the guard that was up against the door and shifted a filing cabinet around to create a little nook in which he could shelter.

"Now," Ahiga said. "Let's do something about those goggles of yours." He clipped both their battery packs back in and dived into the nook he'd made for himself.

A second later the explosive went off.

Ahiga was thrown forward by the force of the blast. It lifted him off the ground and rattled him around in his hidey-hole like a dried pea in a rain-shaker.

The noise was like a bitch slap from a thunderclap. He didn't just hear it, his whole body felt the impact.

The blaze was fierce, white and iridescent. It burned bright images on the back of Ahiga's eyes, even though he had them tight shut. He contented himself by thinking what the blaze would do to two sets of eyes made more light sensitive by night vision.

Ahiga was too stunned for a while to realise it had stopped. The first thing he was aware of was that the walls and the ground had stopped shaking. He caught his breath and slipped his goggles on. He was pinned in by the filing cabinet he'd moved.

Lying on his back Ahiga pushed the cabinet with his feet. It toppled back then disappeared from sight. There was a crash as it hit the ground twenty feet below.

Ahiga stood and looked down. Where, seconds ago, there'd been a series of large rooms, there was now just a crater. No ceilings, no floor, just a gigantic pit filled with rubble. Half dead bodies writhed amid arcs of electricity that leapt between severed cables and shattered generators.

He wasn't out of hell yet. He was just on a different level.

All that was left of the office was a two foot wide ledge that had once been the floor, and the wall behind Ahiga. He realised his hearing was coming back when he started to make out the groans. Dying men calling for their mothers with their last breath, or cursing their God for letting this happen.

There were groans right next to Ahiga. He turned and saw Golding and Fitch under a pile of dust and rocks. The blast from the explosion must have knocked them into the back wall and stopped them being crushed in the pit.

Thank the Great Spirit they were alive. He wanted them to suffer so much more.

Anna had gotten her arms free of the straps when the lights went out. The whole room shook. All the windows cracked and Anna heard several panes crash to the ground. There was no sound and no light. As she tried to find a way to undo the straps her eyes got used to the dark. She began to hear voices off in the distance.

Though her arms were free, Anna's chest and legs were still bound. Anna had hardly any room for manoeuvre and she couldn't find any way to release the remaining restraints.

The voices from the corridor outside started to get closer. She saw the flicker of torch beams.

"Wait, it's over here."

"See I told you."

"Shit. I never knew there was medical equipment on this floor. You think there's drugs?"

"One way to find out man."

Two men entered the room. Anna blinked as torch beams found her.

"This must be her then. All trussed up and ready for us."

"Our orders were to take her to quarters and lock her up. Sooner we get that done, sooner we can sneak out of here."

"Fuck our orders! I ain't got me none for months. Might be months before I get my next chance. We don't even have to pay for this. She's tied down and everything."

"What if she's just a kid though? Or one of those things they make out of the kids?"

"Don't matter. She can be anyone you like in the dark."

It was just like being back in the Pleasuredrome. Pathetic men and their disgusting appetites. Only this time Anna didn't feel violated, or victimised. She felt mad as hell. Her anger became eager movement in the vats of the Doomsday Virus. Like she was flexing a huge muscle.

One that was waiting to be a part of her.

The man undid the strap that was holding Anna's legs down. She tried to kick out at him but he grabbed her surgical smock and yanked. "Hey quit pushing," the man said. "You'll get your turn..."

His words trailed off in a choking gurgle. The man put his hands to his throat. He was still holding his torch. For a brief moment his face was caught in the beam. A knife was sticking out of the front of his neck.

He dropped and Anna heard more footsteps enter the room.

"Hey wait! It's okay man, we got orders we're supposed..."

The voice was cut short by the sound of a jaw fracturing. The man's cries were soon muffled by the sounds of boot leather colliding with flesh.

"Anna, are you hurt?" It was Cortez's voice.

"I can't find the release for these straps. I'll have to cut them." Anna felt the knife touch her as Cortez hacked through her restraint. It was sticky with the blood of the man who'd tried to rape her.

"How is she?" said Greaves. "Did they hurt her?"

"I'm fine," said Anna without hiding her annoyance. "Thanks for asking me."

"I'm sorry. I just didn't know if you were conscious or not. We've got to get you out of here. The virus is up on the next floor."

Anna's emotions were in conflict as they helped her down from the table and out of the room. Greaves handed her a pair of goggles that helped her see in the dark. Outlines appeared, drawn in a ghostly, green half-light.

She wasn't angry at Greaves specifically. He just reminded her of the scientists who had pawed her then left her strapped to that table. He'd spoken over her as though she wasn't there, just as they had. Now he was desperate to get her to the Doomsday Virus so he could finally finish this little experiment of theirs. In many ways Anna was more of a piece of meat to this man than she was to the men who had tried to rape her.

Maybe it was unfair to say that of Greaves. He had tried to connect with her. He just wasn't any good at it. Uniting her with the Doomsday Virus was like an article of faith to him. As though it was going to save his and humanity's soul.

He didn't even seem to realise that about himself. For a man who had amassed such an incredible amount of knowledge on so many things, Greaves was totally lacking in self knowledge. You didn't find the sort of redemption he wanted in a test tube.

"Damn it," Anna heard the man called Colt say. "Where are Fitch and Golding?"

"Great Chief, Ahiga is not with us either."

"Do not worry," she heard the Chief say. "Ahiga is a resourceful man. I am sure he knows exactly what he's doing."

Ahiga had opened the shutters on the front office and led Fitch and Golding out into the empty corridors beyond. Golding's face was badly burned from the explosion and both men were now totally blind.

Ahiga stood behind them, steering them with a hand on each of their shoulders. He guided them into a dead end and up to a wall. "That's far enough. Now I want both of you on your knees."

"Hey, what is this?" said Fitch. "I thought you were gonna get us out of here."

Ahiga put a pistol against each of their temples. "I said on your knees."

Both men did as they were told.

"Do you remember a guy called Frankie McKenzie?" said Ahiga. "Used to run with us back in Lomont. Good man to have in a fight but lacking in smarts. Which is why he always got pinched. Guy became a three time loser thanks to a man called Robert."

"Robert! Is this about that faggot fucking parole officer?" said Fitch. "What, you're finally gonna get sore with us?"

"I'm not getting sore. I'm getting even. Why else do you think I led you down here and got your eyes burned out?"

"C'mon Tom," said Golding. "I mean what did you expect us to do when we found you was carrying on with another man like that? You're lucky we let you live. You practically forced us to do it."

"Way I recall it," said Ahiga. "You forced me."

"You were getting above yourself," said Fitch. "What else was I going to do when I found out? You had to be brought back to earth."

"Put on a leash you mean."

"If you like, yeah." said Fitch. "Like Golding said, what do you expect? You get turned out in prison fine. You do what you gotta do to get by inside. You don't carry that sort of thing on when you get out though."

"I didn't get turned out when I was inside. I didn't let a single man in there lay a finger on me."

"So what, you suddenly develop a taste for it when you get out? That's sick."

"I fell in love. I didn't want to. I fought it for a long time. It started after my parole finished. Robert was my officer. He dropped by to check up on me a few times and it went from there. I knew what it meant if we were found out. Robert would lose his job and I'd end up in some alley with a knife in my back.

"Except what happened when you found out was a lot worse. See, Frankie went away for the last time on a parole violation. So you got the 57th St bangers all good and stoked on crack and bourbon and told us you knew where the parole officer who sent Frankie away lived. Told us we should go down there and sort him out, as payback for what he did to Frankie. Wasn't till I got there that I realised where I was. Then it was too late, I wasn't going to say anything.

"So I went along. We broke in, we dragged Robert out of bed and we knocked him about. He recognised me straight away. He knew that if he gave anything away it would be the death of me. So he kept his mouth shut and took everything you gave him. Then you put the gun in my hand. Told me to put it in his mouth and kill the only person I ever loved. I did it too. Because I was a coward.

"Not an hour goes by when I don't regret it. Right up until the very end Robert kept his mouth shut. To save my life, even when I took his. I killed Robert to prove my manhood and my bravery to the rest of you. But in dying the way he did, Robert proved he was far braver and far more of a man."

"Enough with the speeches already," said Fitch. "If you're gonna kill us just get on with it. Don't expect us to beg."

"I'm not going to kill you. Not unless you force me to. Now lie down. You this way, and Golding like that."

Ahiga arranged them so that both men were lying on their sides facing each other with their feet in opposite directions. Fitch's face was right up against Golding's crotch and Golding's was in Fitch's. Ahiga pressed a pistol to each of their temples. "Now I want you to get each other's weapons out and you can guess where I want you to put them. Just think of that pistol and how Robert took it."

"Go fuck yourself," said Fitch. "Not even a bullet in the head will make me do that."

"I'm not gonna put a bullet in your head. I'm gonna fire one up your ass if you don't do what I tell you. Now this is a small calibre pistol. That bullet's gonna bounce around quite a lot before it stops. Do a lot of damage. Even still it's gonna take a long time before you die. Hours and hours of unending agony. Blind and trapped all the way down here, with the rats gnawing on your face as you shit out your own innards. I reckon there's nothing you won't do to avoid that. You ain't brave enough.

"So now, in order to survive, you're both gonna do something that you'll have to live with for the rest of your lives. Something you'll never escape and never live down. Something I'll always have hanging over your heads. Just like you did with me. Now quit stalling and open wide."

CHAPTER TWENTY-SIX

"Tell me child," Hiamovi said to Anna. "What tribe are you from?"

Anna had been quite shocked to see Native Americans and Neo-Clergy fighting together to help Greaves and Cortez rescue her. She was still getting used to the idea.

"I'm very sorry, erm... Great Chief," Anna said. "But I don't know. I have no memory of it but I was conceived and grown in a test tube, in a hellish place like this. I've hardly ever met any of your... our people. I was raised in a Christian community. I suppose you could say my tribe are, were, the Amish."

"Hear that Hiamovi?" said Mr Colt. "Girl's a Christian. Don't hold with your pagan superstitions."

Hiamovi glowered back at him but didn't answer.

He was a strange man this Native American chief. The hard emotional front men of power hide behind did not sit comfortably with him. He seemed to Anna like a good man who was learning to be bad. The duplicity and ruthlessness of wielding power did not come naturally to him.

Colt on the other hand appeared to be a man whose conscience had just caught up with him. Like the gold cross he wore around his neck it had grown heavier with every vicious thing he had done in its name. Anna noted that they were both wrestling with the same dilemma, but in opposite ways.

Anna also felt as though, in their own perverse manner, they were courting her. Like she was the only child of a wealthy land owner. Both men wanted to wed her to their cause. Both craved the power they thought she could give them. Once again it came down to men and their insatiable appetites.

The doors of the lab were wide open when they arrived.

"Oh," said Greaves in surprise. "How convenient, a flaw in their security even I didn't foresee." He stood in the doorway to block everyone's path. "There's a lot of deadly and infectious material in there that's about to get loose. Wait here a moment."

Greaves appeared a moment later with his arms full of bio-hazard suits. "You're going to need these." He handed a suit to everyone but Anna declined hers.

"I won't be needing that," she said.

"No, of course not," Greaves replied.

The doors to every room in the lab were wide open as they walked through. Only the hexagonal booth with the titanium containers remained shut. Anna felt a hole open up inside her, one that longed to be filled by the virus. She wanted to cradle it with her body and let it grow inside her.

Anna, who had been leading the small war party through the lab, turned to stop them now. "I can take it from here."

"Wait," said Greaves. "You have to check the thermostat before you release the container's lid. Otherwise the pressure could..."

Anna held up her hand to hush him. "That's alright. Like I said, I can take it from here."

The door to the booth slid open as Anna approached and slipped inside. The air was still and cold but it also felt somehow turbulent. The lids to the containers popped open by themselves.

The virus itself was doing this. Anna could suddenly sense it crawling on every surface.

There is always a point of no return when we commit

ourselves to a course of action, Anna thought. This is mine.

As in all those moments, Anna felt a sense of dread for every unknown thing this might mean. And a sense of loss for everything it wouldn't.

She opened herself up to the virus, took it inside her as though she was drawing breath through every orifice and every pore of her body. A million unseen microbes fell on her, hungry to feed. And like a mother suckling her young, she nourished them.

Tears ran down Greaves' face as he watched through the visor of the suit. It was happening. Everything he had planned over so many years was coming to pass. Humanity's salvation, he had really made it happen.

The moment was broken by the noise of footfall getting closer. It sounded like there were lots and lots of men heading their way.

"They're on to us," said Colt. "They knew the first place we were gonna head would be straight for the Doomsday Virus."

"You didn't think they'd give it us without a fight did you?" Hiamovi said.

"No-one gives up a weapon like this without a fight."

Greaves saw Anna fall to the floor. She was entering the transitional phase of symbiosis. The virus was attacking every single function of her body and mind. Breaking it all down so it could rebuild and replicate it. She would come close to a state of total death before it brought her back to eternal life.

Anna was incredibly vulnerable. If anything happened to her in this state it could jeopardise the whole process.

"We have to get them away from here," said Greaves. "We need to draw their fire to protect Anna. She needs time to recover. If anything happens to her now it could mean her life. Then everything we've fought for will be pointless."

"What're you suggesting?" said Colt.

"If we cut across the main corridor they're coming down, we can double back and attack them at the rear. They'll be caught off-guard and we can draw them back the way they came."

"Is the position defensible?" said Colt's henchman Simon Peter. "More importantly is there somewhere to retreat to if it's not?"

"There's a staircase just around the corner," said Greaves. "If we make it a quick hit-and-run operation, we could cut along the floor above to throw them off our scent and head back down another staircase to pick Anna up again. But we have to go now!"

Cortez looked at Colt and Hiamovi, who both nodded. Then he motioned with his head for everyone to follow him.

As they ran out of the lab Greaves took a last look over his shoulder at Anna, writhing on the floor. He hadn't told her about all the pain. He hadn't know it would be so great.

Hiamovi ran shoulder to shoulder with Colt and a step behind Cortez. He was an intriguing man this Latin American. A fearsome warrior who quickly took control of a situation. Yet he reinforced Hiamovi's authority with his men. Unlike Colt who tried to undermine it.

Hiamovi would make sure Cortez fought with the UTN

when they got back up top. Cortez would make a great general and he would bring the girl and the Doomsday Virus with him. Whatever they had planned for the virus Hiamovi would make sure the UTN was a part of it.

They turned the corner and saw a line of about thirty guards heading away from them. They fell into formation in the corridor. Hiamovi and Colt stood either side of Cortez and aimed their semi-automatics. Akecheta, Hastiin and Simon Peter knelt beside them, weapons levelled.

They opened fire. Four guards fell in the first volley. The men jerked and threw themselves into a crazy war dance, spraying blood from multiple wounds as the bullets smacked into them.

The guards in front froze at the sound of gunfire. They spun round and tried to find cover as they groped for their rifles. Three more of them fell in another salvo as they turned. Two of them to body shots. The last to a spectacular and bloody head shot.

Before the guards had a chance to return fire Hiamovi and the others took off round the corner. At the edge of his vision Hiamovi saw Hastiin collide with Greaves. The little guy was having trouble keeping up. Cortez dragged Greaves to his feet and pulled him along with them.

Hiamovi's heart was racing. Killing was something new to him. He'd fought in one way or another most of his life, but only now was he learning to kill. To his alarm he found it addictive. Like political power, once tasted it was hard to put down.

The stairs slowed them down and their pursuers gained ground on them. Shots rattled around the stairwell as they ran through the door onto the next level.

"The... canteen and the... kitchens are this way..." Greaves said, trying to catch his breath. He looked ready to drop. Cortez grabbed the little man's collar and dragged him in the direction he'd pointed.

The next few minutes were a blur. Hiamovi heard the guards coming up the stairs. He remembered racing into the kitchen when three figures jumped out at them. Everyone pointed their weapons but the middle figure called out.

"Wait Great Chief it's me."

It was Ahiga with Colt's men.

"We have to get to the staircase just the other side of the kitchen," said Hiamovi.

"No, Great Chief." Ahiga said. "We've just checked, there's about twenty guards on their way up it."

"We're trapped," said Greaves.

"No. You can take the elevator." Ahiga said.

"Elevator?" said Greaves. "What are you talking about. There's no power, or haven't you noticed? How could we take the elevator?"

"We did dickwad," said Fitch. "And something's powering it. I dunno, maybe they got a back-up generator."

"What in hell's happened to your eyes?" Colt said. "And where have you been?"

"We're blind," said Golding. "Bomb did it."

"They came back for me," said Ahiga. "We didn't get out in time. The bomb caught us all. Guess I just got lucky."

"You got that right," said Fitch.

"Wait, it's *their* elevator," said Greaves. "It stands to reason they'd have a secret one installed, powered by a secret source. You must have stumbled on it."

"Hold on there Einstein," said Colt. "Who the fuck are 'they'?"

"The masters of this place. The men who bankrolled

the whole operation. The twisted old men who've been hiding down here waiting to regain control of a world their families have run for generations."

"Great Chief," said Ahiga. "There isn't much time, you have to leave now."

Ahiga took them through a hidden door to a small alcove where an elevator waited. It was tiny. There was room for only four or five of them at best.

"We'll have to take two trips." said Hiamovi

"There isn't time Great Chief. There is room enough for the seven of you at a push."

"What are you saying?"

"Someone has to stay behind and take care of all these men on your tail. I think that job falls to us three." Ahiga cocked his thumb at Fitch and Golding. "These two would only slow you down."

They reminded Hiamovi of hunting hounds brought to heel.

"Now hold on boy," said Colt. "Ain't nobody tells my men what to do apart from me."

"Mr Colt sir," said Golding. "It's okay, the redskin's right."

"And what about you Fitch? What do you have to say?"

"Ain't shit for me up top. Not as a fucking blind cripple. Time's running out for you though sir. You better get along."

Hiamovi and Colt stepped into the lift first. Cortez and Greaves followed. Fitch had been right, Greaves didn't smell good, as Akecheta, Hastiin and Simon Peter noted when they squeezed in.

"Great Chief," said Ahiga. "The UTN and the Fifth Age of Man are noble causes, no matter what sort of deeds they are built on. Don't waste this moment. Don't let everything we've done be in vain."

"I won't," said Hiamovi as the doors slid shut.

As Ahiga watched Hiamovi go for the last time, he wondered if he was leaving everything he'd built up in safe hands. Then he realised he had little time for such thoughts, these were the last minutes of his life. A time for action.

He pushed Fitch and Golding back into the kitchen. They'd stopped bitching about being pushed around and just accepted it now. Ahiga turned on all the ovens and every gas ring without lighting them.

"Hey what's that smell?" Golding said as the appliances hissed away.

"That," said Ahiga. "Is the smell of our coming victory."

A minute later both squadrons of guards converged on the kitchens. By the time the torch beams had landed on Ahiga, Fitch and Golding standing in the middle of the room it was too late to mention the smell of gas.

Ahiga's right arm was raised. In his hand he held a Zippo lighter. Fitch and Golding both had hold of Ahiga's wrist.

"You're not getting away from me mother-fucker," said Fitch. "I'm gonna follow you all the way to hell, just to see you suffer."

"Race you," said Ahiga and struck the wheel.

CHAPTER TWENTY-SEVEN

Anna came to with sound of the explosion. The ceiling outside the lab had come down and shaken her awake.

She stood slowly, limbs shaky. She drew a deep breath and let it out again. She was light headed and more than a little euphoric.

Anna felt as though she had just pulled through a thousand major illnesses all at once. She had walked in the valley of the shadow of death and climbed out to bask in the sun. She wanted to burst into laughter and tears at the same time.

The virus had shown her death and transformed her body. She heard a ringing in her ears. No, not in her ears, in her whole body. So much sensory information was suddenly flowing into her. Things that she would never normally know about.

She could taste and smell every surface in the lab, all at once. Feel the bodies of every rat, spider and fly in the complex. Anna heard the bacteria in the guts of every person and felt the chemical electricity crackle through their brains.

She was no longer human.

The virus's millions of endlessly replicating microbes were spreading throughout the complex. Each one sending back information along a complex chain to the nexus of their activity. No wonder they had to rebuild her normal human physique. If, in fact, her physique had ever really been human.

Anna reached out with her mind in a hundred different directions to find a way out of the laboratory. The way she'd come in was blocked but there was a further series of rooms beyond these, that led to a staircase.

Anna found the doorway. She didn't need to see in the dark. She had thousands of extra senses now. The door was locked. She felt the static hum of electricity coming off it. Strange, Anna had thought all the electricity to be down. She reached out in search of another source and found a smaller back-up generator, channelling energy to only a few parts of the complex.

Anna concentrated and was able to cluster a whole culture of microbes around the wiring of the lock, eating it away until it shorted and the door slid open. The minute she stepped inside the room she knew she didn't want to see what it held.

This was where the thick blanket of sorrow, the air of death and clinical cruelty that pervaded the whole complex originated.

The rooms were full of corpses. Deep frozen corpses, dissected corpses, disease ridden and putrefying corpses and, in the ovens out the back, the ashes of burned corpses. It was the age of the corpses that troubled Anna. She could tell from all the information she was receiving what they were. But she did not want to admit it.

In the last of the connecting rooms Anna felt life of a kind. Sickened by so much dead flesh she instinctively moved towards it.

The room was filled with preserved body parts, limbs, internal organs and bones. Many of them had been sliced open for inspection. All of them belonged to children no older than eight years old. Many came from unborn foetuses.

At the far end, beyond a series of midsections sliced from infant brains and placed between perspex, were three incubators. Anna came closer, hardly wanting to see what they contained. She was not pleased when she did.

Inside all three incubators were four month old babies. Their expressions were entirely vacant. Their limbs twitched one at a time in an ongoing pattern, like they were puppets or automata. Over two thirds of each child's skull was missing. Their brains were exposed and a complex array of micro-circuitry was fused to them. Wires ran from the circuitry out of the incubators and into a series of monitors and displays.

A door hissed open behind her and Anna turned to see four figures enter in bio-hazard suits. She had been so engrossed and repulsed by the children in the incubators she had not noticed their approach, although she was now aware that her microbes had been alerting her for some time. She just hadn't acknowledged them.

The figures removed their head gear. It was Sinnot and his cronies Roth, Bennet and Joe Blackfeather.

"I see you've been admiring our handiwork," said Sinnot. "Impressive aren't they?"

"What in God's name are you doing to them?" said Anna, barely able to control her anger. "What is this place?"

"Ah, I believe it's time to admit our guilty little secret. You see Anna, everything you see around you is a testament to our failure and your uniqueness."

"I don't understand."

"And neither do we. We don't understand you. How your biological composition works and, more importantly, how to replicate it. You see we're missing the original research team that created you, not to mention all their research. For a brief while, just before The Cull, it was necessary for us to hide from our employers. We hid in splinter cells to avoid detection and we took everything we had done with us. That was when we left you with the Amish.

"Or rather when our colleagues did. They left you to

grow up there. Monitoring you and the five others like you from afar. Then The Cull hit and we lost contact with our colleagues. Lost everything they knew. Our old employers took us back, we began working on the project again. But try as we might we could never create another host for the virus. Not without the original research.

"We tried of course. We've been trying for years. At times we've come close but never close enough. All our efforts have ended in failure. The subjects have always died, often quite painfully."

"You mean," said Anna. "All these children..."

"Complete failures everyone. It's quite tragic when you think about it. We've created the perfect biological weapon. The single most effective way of dominating a global population that has ever been conceived. And yet we just can't seem to find the last piece of the puzzle."

Anna could feel her anger at these cold little men rising. The offhand way they discussed their atrocities enraged her. Her fury spilled out like a wave across every interconnected micro-organism in the complex.

"And what," Anna said, pointing to the incubators. "Are you doing here?'

"Ah yes, those," said Sinnot. "Now that's a little project we are rather proud of, something that hasn't ended in failure and frustration. You see, when they came to understand our project fully, our employers wanted more than a host for the Doomsday Virus. They wanted something they could dominate entirely. It wasn't enough to condition the child from birth to obey them without question. They had to have complete control over it. To make it something that would answer their every whim.

"So we began to experiment with mind control. Every mental process of the creatures you see behind you is controlled by our equipment. There is no function of their brains that we don't control."

"When you were scanning my brain, this is what you were planning to do to me wasn't it?" Anna said.

"I'm afraid you're right. But it wouldn't have worked anyway. Besides, that's all rather academic now, wouldn't you say?"

"You admit all this to me without any regrets?"

"Oh I have plenty of regrets. Years wasted following fruitless paths of research. It would make you weep if only you knew."

"Don't you know what I could do to you? Don't you know what I've become?"

"Oh yes Anna. More than anyone left alive we know what you've become. That's why you won't do anything to us. You need us. No-one left alive knows more about the virus, certainly not that pathetic fool Greaves, You see Anna we four are the closest thing you have to a real father."

That was what sent Anna over the edge. That was what made her unleash a fury she'd been bottling for years. That they could liken themselves to a man as gentle, wise and compassionate as her poppa. These evil little men who had murdered and tortured so many children and animals. All to satisfy their appetites for forbidden knowledge.

Now they were going to pay.

Greaves fired his last shot and yelped as he burned his hand on the muzzle. He dropped the pistol and dived behind the bureau they were using as a barricade. Bullets thudded into it.

The others were nearly out of ammo too. The elite

bodyguard firing on them weren't. And those men outnumbered them nearly three to one. Everything was falling apart.

Greaves had begged them to go back down for Anna in the lift, but Colt and Hiamovi had over-ruled him. Especially after the gas went up. So they'd ridden to the top and come out in the luxury accommodation of the shadowy figures who ran the whole operation.

For all the fear they had instilled in Greaves and his colleagues over the years, they weren't very impressive close up. They were just fragile old men whose wizened faces had twisted themselves into permanently evil expressions, like gargoyles carved out of flesh. Looking at them made you shudder, but not with fear, with revulsion. Like looking at a famine victim or a dying animal that's clinging on to life out of sheer cussedness.

Their bodyguards were another matter. They were impressive, terrifyingly so. After an initial exchange of fire they were now pinned down by about ten of them. They were in an oak lined study and were firing from behind a mound of priceless old European furniture.

One of the Native Americans next to Greaves, tried to make a break for the door behind them. What was his name? Hasty something. Hastiin, that was it. He got halfway before catching a bullet in the throat.

He dropped the two shotguns he'd been carrying and put his hands up to the wound. Around ten more bullets hit him and he fell face first to the floor.

Simon Peter tried two crawl over to Hastiin's body to retrieve the weapons the brave had dropped. A bullet to the shoulder put a stop to that plan. It spun him round and he caught another two in the face.

The other Native American, Akecheta, seemed to snap under the pressure. He let out a scream like a war cry and unsheathed two mammoth hunting knives. Leaping over the barricade he charged the guards. He only got half way to their position before a hail of bullets slammed into his torso, pushing him back. His body lay slumped in a thick red pool while the echo of his cry reverberated around the room.

It was desperate. They were all going to die. Greaves never thought it would come like this. After everything he'd survived. He'd been so close to seeing the new dawn of mankind. He could only hope Anna would know how to use the virus properly.

CHAPTER TWENTY-EIGHT

Anna unleashed the virus. She also let go of her anger. Every bit she'd been carrying around since her whole community had died. All of it was channelled into the virus. Every tiny microbe in the complex was alive with her rage.

Like a billion tiny teeth sinking into Sinnot and the other three, the microbes tore and rent their flesh. Sinnot held out his hands to stop her, imploring her. "N-no..." was as far as he got before he vomited his own spleen. It covered Bennet's back. Bennet hardly noticed. He was too busy bent double trying to stem the tears of blood running from his empty eye sockets.

Anna was intoxicated by it. Wave upon wave of pleasure shot through her body, running up her spine and down the inside of her thighs, leaving the front of her trousers wet.

What's happening to me?

Then like an adolescent waking from a wet dream she realised.

Oh my God, I'm having my first orgasm.

But it wasn't enough, the power she felt was incredible, undeniable. She couldn't stop herself. She had to use more. To punish every living thing in this vile, Godforsaken place. Like an angel of the Lord's wrath wielding a flaming sword.

She sent her anger out to find every human being in the place. She tore the life out of each one she found, working her way through every floor above and below her. Putting an end to the misery of the dying and the living alike.

Until finally she found the last four human organisms

cowering behind a mound of furniture. These she recognised. They had helped her in what now seemed like a former life. These she spared.

It wasn't easy to reign-in the virus. It hurt. It took all her strength to do it. Like wrestling a prize bull to the ground by its horns. The virus was made primarily to kill and it didn't like being stopped.

Exhausted, Anna fell to the ground.

The bullets stopped. There was no more firing, just silence. Greaves wondered if this was some tactic, or whether they were going to finish the job hand to hand, but nothing happened.

"They're dead," said Colt, sticking his head out. "All of them, they just dropped dead."

Greaves looked up to see that he was right. The guards lay slumped on the ground.

"It's Anna. She's done it. She used the Doomsday Virus to kill them all and rescue us." He couldn't believe he was still alive. He stood up and went to examine the bodies of the dead guards.

"How do we know this is her?" said Colt. "And not some other thing that got loose?"

"Look how quickly it killed them all. We wouldn't be alive now if there wasn't some human intelligence behind it."

The other three came from around the barricade to see. Colt and Hiamovi retrieved some of the guards' weapons. Neither one of them taking their eye off the other.

"Time to leave I reckon," said Colt. "After you Hiamovi."

"What, and show you my back? I don't think so. No,

we'll leave here shoulder to shoulder all the way."

And that's how they left, with Greaves and Cortez following.

Anna propped herself up on her elbows then got carefully to her feet. Her strength and vitality seemed to come back to her in a big wave. So did her remorse.

Her clarity returned and she realised what she had done. How she had sinned and trespassed upon everything she'd been raised to believe in. All those lives she had taken. All of them sacred, no matter how they'd been spent.

She was worse than all of them, scientist and soldier alike. She'd committed mass murder and she'd enjoyed it. It had given her more pleasure than anything she had ever done in her life. She was a monster.

Looking back over the last few months it was easy for Anna to see how she could have arrived at this point. The people she'd travelled with, and had come to see as her friends, all of them had killed without compunction, as a matter of course. She'd come to see it as necessary to survive, if not natural.

Then there was all the anger she had stored away inside herself. An anger she had never faced or acknowledged. An anger that had grown in strength exponentially until nothing could hold it in check. Anger that cut her off from the still quiet voice of God.

There was also the laboratory that triggered her response. All of the hideous secrets it kept. All the suffering it displayed. And the men who caused it, regretting only what it hadn't brought them.

This was the sort of place in which Anna was created, along with the virus that surged thorough her. Her origins lay in suffering and torture. In spite of what Greaves believed, nothing born in this way could ever bring a brighter future for mankind.

No matter how pure and bright the vision that might have inspired it, no new world could be created like this.

Anna discovered she had more knowledge at her disposal. It seemed the virus was able to digest and recall every bit of knowledge from its victims' brains. Every guilty secret, each childhood memory and all the disparate bits of information that her victims had hung on to was now at Anna's fingertips.

She picked through it all, like turning the pages of an encyclopaedia, until she had gathered the bits she needed.

The secret route to the surface.

The location of the micro-glider stationed in the hangar along with something called a sub-sonic bomb.

The whereabouts of the public address system that could be worn around the neck.

Where a working rocket launcher could be found.

And the exact spot on which the Neo-Clergy had built their metal bridge across the lava.

Then she went to find them all.

CHAPTER TWENTY-NINE

As he walked out of the complex alongside Hiamovi, Colt knew that he was being watched. He'd detailed men to find and monitor every exit and he was pretty sure Hiamovi would have done the same.

They were both wearing their bio-hazard suits and the first thing they did was take off the head gear and shout to their men, while walking cautiously away from each other.

Colt scanned the surrounding area for any sign of his boys. He saw that Cortez and the runt Greaves were hanging back, trying to remain neutral and not pick sides. Colt would see they weren't harmed until he'd gotten the virus.

Two redskins popped out from behind a rock close by, and two more followed them. Colt reached for his weapons and called for his men again.

Eventually as the redskins ran to surround their leader, Carl Jennings appeared with three other men.

"You took your time," Colt snarled at them. "Where in hell were you?"

"Sorry Mr Colt sir. We just wanted to make certain it was really you, and not some redskin trick. We were sent word that you were held prisoner."

"I was but I got myself out. And now we've got a war to finish."

A signal flare went up. Colt wasn't certain who had fired it, but it set a stampede in motion. From the north side of the plateau Colt's troops advanced at a jog. Hiamovi's warriors advanced to meet them from the south.

Colt, Carl and the other men pointed their weapons at the redskin party, who also had them in their sights. Both armies gradually fell into formation behind their leaders. There was a tense expectancy in the air. Thousands of men and women faced each other down. All of them eager to spill blood.

Cortez stood by the entrance to the complex. He was weighing up the situation.

"Come on," said Greaves, tugging at his arm. "Let's go and get Anna."

"Wait a moment," said Cortez. "I have a feeling about this."

In the distance, coming towards them, Cortez heard the *put-put-put* of a small engine. He looked up and saw an aircraft come into view. It was a micro-glider.

The pilot hanging beneath it was carrying a rocket launcher. Aiming it towards the north she fired. This caught the attention of everyone on the plateau. The rocket found its target. There was a giant burst of flame and smoke followed by the sound of falling, rending metal. The pilot dropped the rocket launcher. It landed mere feet away from Cortez.

"Now there is only one way off this plateau," said the pilot. It was Anna. She addressed everyone through some speaker strapped to her chest that carried her voice across the whole area.

"You've come here to seize the world's deadliest biological weapon," Anna said. "As your leaders will tell you, I am that weapon. But I am not going to be the prize in any battle. I have the power to kill everyone left on the planet. Sparing only those whom I choose. That power does not belong to any one set of people, nor any creed or faith. It would not bring hope or salvation to them. It would simply be the death of their faith.

"The one thing that can bring a war of faith to an end, is the one thing it's fought over: faith itself. It is through my faith that I have come to this decision. I should never have been created. I was born out of evil intentions to do the bidding of evil men. If I continue to live I will only create more evil intentions. So I am going to put a stop to that.

"I also hope to put a stop to this conflict. Strapped to my body is a sub-sonic bomb powerful enough to blow me into tiny little shreds. The blast will send these tiny fragments raining down over every part of the plateau. The Doomsday Virus that flows through my body is so infectious that if the tiniest bit of my flesh touches you, or someone near you, you will die painfully within seconds.

"The bomb is set to go off just before I run out of fuel three hours from now. Three hours is just long enough for every man and woman to leave this plateau by the pass to the south, but only if everyone works together. If you get cannot put aside your petty conflicts, you will all die.

"Only the river of lava that flows around this area will keep the Doomsday Virus from spreading. But if anyone returns within your lifetime they will certainly become infected. If they leave they will take the virus with them and wipe out all life forever. Once you have left this plateau, you can never return.

"The future of the earth is now in your hands. Your decision will affect all life on the planet. Choose wisely."

Greaves ran right down the middle of the two armies. "No Anna stop," he cried out. "Don't you realise what you're doing?"

"Of course. I know exactly what I'm doing."

"But it doesn't have to be this way. You can fly over the lava and drop the bomb into it. You don't have to die. You can live and you can save the world. Why do you want to throw away everything we've worked for?"

"It wasn't anything I ever worked for," said Anna. "It's what I've been working to stop.

Colt signalled to Hiamovi that he wanted to talk. The two of them broke ranks and, surrounded by a party of their men, met in the middle of the two armies. Colt's men measured themselves against the redskins, who stood their ground and stared right back. Both sides trying to psych the other out.

"Do you think she means it?" said Colt. "What if that bomb ain't for real?"

"Can we afford to take that chance?" said Hiamovi. "You saw what she did to everyone in that complex. Why wouldn't she mean it?"

Colt looked up at Anna. Her arms were stretched out at her side, her hands were just a little above her head with the palms turned out, and her legs were together.

For the rest of his life, when he thought back on that moment he was never entirely sure why he made the decision he did. Maybe it was the fact that he knew their armies were too evenly matched for either to strike a decisive victory. They would only suffer losses that neither side could ultimately afford.

Perhaps it was the realisation that they needed each other. To remain in power Colt had to keep his people scared of Hiamovi, who in turn needed him to terrify his own people. It was a mutually beneficial arrangement. If either side were to fall, the other would not be far behind.

But then again, it was possible that it was because, hanging there, Anna reminded him of his vision of the Lord in all its intensity. And that meant it was impossible to deny the compassion that arose within him.

"Okay," said Colt. "But my people get to leave first. You wait till we're all off and then you follow."

"Oh no," said Hiamovi. "That won't work. We leave this plateau like we left the complex. Shoulder to shoulder, everyone of my people and yours."

"Alright," said Colt offering his hand. "That ain't gonna be easy, but you got yourself a deal."

Hiamovi had accepted Colt's hand. He had made only one provision to the deal. That he and Colt be the last to leave the plateau. Only when both their armies were safely across would they leave, side by side.

Now he stood with Onatah, watching his people march along the tiny causeway, right alongside Colt's men. A scuffle broke out in the centre of the line between one of Hiamovi's braves and another of Colt's mob.

"You two either side," Hiamovi bellowed at the line. "Grab that brave." The men in the line did as they were told. "Now throw him over the side."

"And I want you to do the same with that son of a bitch," Colt hollered from his side. Both captive men tried to plead with their leaders. But to no avail, their comrades pushed them over the side into the burning lava below.

"I want you to understand," shouted Hiamovi to his people. "That there are no sides at this moment in our struggle. We all have to work together or we all die."

The lines settled down into silent animosity, marching

along next to each other. There were no further incidents.

"Not quite the outcome that we envisaged is it?" Onatah said. "And yet, maybe it is."

"How do you mean?" asked Hiamovi. "I can't believe any among us foresaw this."

"Perhaps we all did. We came here to bring about the Fifth Age of Man, didn't we? At least that's what I thought we were fighting for. Didn't the prophecy say that a Kachina would arise from one among us. I saw that girl as clearly as everyone else. She is one of our people. Yet she has the power to kill everyone on the planet, sparing only those she chooses. That would make her a god in human form or, as the Hopi would have it, a Kachina."

"Go on." Hiamovi said.

"She's supposed to appear in the sky at the return of Pahana and herald the coming of the Fifth Age of Man. She will bring about an end to our greatest struggle and deliver us from our enemies without any bloodshed. Forgive me if I'm wrong Great Chief, but isn't that exactly what we've just seen?"

"I suppose you could see it that way."

"Great Chief, we staked a lot on coming back with the Doomsday Virus and striking a decisive blow against the Neo-Clergy. The UTN is not a single rock solid alliance, it's a series of very tenuous ones. We need something the tribes can unite behind to keep them together as a nation. What better than the arrival of the Fifth Age of Man, the fulfilment of the prophecy? A fulfilment to which we have over two thousand witnesses."

"And what about Pahana?" said Hiamovi. "The brother who returns with the lost tablet to lead his people?"

"You might not know this Great Chief," said Onatah.

"But Cheveyo always believed you were the harbinger of Pahana's coming returned to his people. That's why he supported the UTN so fervently."

"Ah yes, Cheveyo." A great regret welled up within Hiamovi.

"You know Great Chief, an act of mercy towards one of our most prominent Hopi chiefs might just be what the tribes would expect from the returned Pahana. It might signal a new direction for the UTN. Especially if you were to restore his position on the inner council, wouldn't you agree?"

"You are a wise woman Onatah," said Hiamovi. "And you know how to plead a cause. I am glad we are friends, from now on, please call me Hiamovi and not Great Chief." Off in the distance, for the first time in what felt like an age, Hiamovi heard Coyote howl.

"And she was raised in a Christian community," said the Prophet. "That's what she told you?"

"Enough with the questions," said Colt. "I've been through this with you already."

"But don't you see what this means? The prophecy, the one I've been preaching for months. The one I told you would come to pass. It has. You saw it. Didn't I tell you it was going to happen?"

"I didn't see nothing. 'Cept a wasted opportunity."

"Oh no Samuel. You don't get away that easily. Didn't I tell you an angel who had once been a woman would appear in the sky above the two armies and turn herself into a bright and shining star."

"What?" said Colt in disbelief. "That squaw who just fouled up months of planning? She ain't no angel. She's just some medical freak show is all. 'Sides, I didn't see her turn into no star."

"She said three hours didn't she?" said the Prophet. "It's dusk already. In another hour it's going to be night and that's when she detonates. Lighting up the sky like a star."

"Now you're just straining to fit the facts to your story."

"No I'm not. Didn't I also tell you she would deliver us from the hands of our enemies without a single drop of blood being spilled? Look what's happening now Samuel. We're walking side by side with our enemy off the battlefield without a single casualty. This is a genuine miracle we're witnessing here. And you know what that means. You know why God sent you that vision of our Lord Jesus Christ?"

"No Robert. But I don't think anything's going to stop you from telling me."

"Why you're the new Moses I saw. Come to deliver his people unto a new kingdom, just like the Israelites. This was your testing ground Samuel. God sent you here to cleanse you, to make you a better ruler. This was your time in the wilderness, and you've come through. What's more you've got a genuine miracle, as witnessed by thousands of the faithful to legitimise your rule. There aren't many rulers who can say that."

"You're a wily old buzzard aren't you Robert. I should always keep a close eye on you."

"Why Samuel, coming from you, I'd swear that's a compliment."

As the sky darkened Cortez stood at the mouth of the pass and watched the explosion. He did this in honour of his friend and her great bravery.

Once over the bridge, the two armies had parted and

gone their separate ways without incident. Perhaps this was because the area was about to become contaminated or because they had nothing left to fight over. Maybe it was simply the will of Allah.

Hiamovi had offered Cortez a place in the UTN before he left. Cortez had neither accepted nor declined. He wasn't certain what his options were just yet. Hiamovi had understood and had given Cortez a location where he could meet up with the UTN later if he chose.

He thought it a little ironic that Anna had indeed become a saviour, of a kind, to these two causes. Not at all the sort of saviour that Greaves had foreseen.

Greaves had refused to leave the plateau when the others did. Cortez had tried at first to persuade him to come with them, then he had simply attempted to drag him away. But Greaves fought too hard and, in the end, Cortez had honoured his wishes and left him there. He was no longer in Greaves' employ and the two no longer had any obligation to each other.

As the explosion faded from the night sky, Cortez said a prayer to Allah for the safe conduct of Anna's soul. He also asked for guidance on what he should do next and where he should go.

A verse from the Qu'ran came into his mind, as if from nowhere.

'Allah guides whom He wills to His light... Allah is knower of all things.'

Cortez smiled to himself. "Well that," he said aloud to the empty landscape around him, "is as good an answer as I'm likely to get."

CHAPTER THIRTY

Greaves cackled with delight as he found another tiny fragment of Anna's flesh. This one contained a trace of cartilage. He carried it over to the container that he'd found inside the complex and added it to the small pile of fragments he'd already collected. He brushed a tiny bit of grit off it before he dropped it in.

Then he washed his hands in the plastic tub of water he'd also brought from the complex. He had to keep himself clean. He didn't want to contaminate the samples.

Greaves knew that if he collected every single scrap of her body into one place, the Doomsday Virus would reassemble it and bring her back to life. He just had to find every tiny piece of her. Her near immortality would do the rest. She would be resurrected and they could start again.

It wasn't going to be an easy task. She had rained down in tiny blood red fragments across the whole plateau. He only had a short space of time before the extreme heat dried the pieces rendering them useless.

Finding her in the first place hadn't been an easy task. And he'd managed that. He'd proven how brilliant he was. He hadn't wasted all his early potential. He hadn't. He would redeem himself yet. All he needed was a little faith in himself. Isn't that what Anna herself had said? Faith would redeem them all.

Greaves had pleaded with Anna not to do it. When all the others had run in fear of their lives, he alone had stayed with her to the end. She had stopped answering him in the last hour. She had just prayed quietly to herself.

Greaves had seen the fear of death on her face. She was so young. She had so much life ahead of her. The virus was also working away inside her. Trying to change her mind.

Desperate to live.

Anna had shown incredible determination in defying it. If only she could have used that determination properly. But there was time for that yet. He would bring her back. He would convince her of her destiny. He wouldn't fail this time.

Greaves saw something else at his feet. Was that a piece of her? He touched it to his tongue. It tasted raw. Only then did he realise his mistake. He could have contaminated it.

"It's alright," he told himself. "Calm down, just add it to the pile. The virus will sort out everything else" He coughed and more blood came. He was dying and he knew it. The only reason the Doomsday Virus hadn't taken him yet was because it had been told to spare him in the complex.

It didn't matter though. It simply gave him a deadline. He could still find every piece of her in time. He could. He wouldn't lose her again.

He had lost so much, first his mother and then his mind. Then he had lost his bright future and later any hope of regaining it. Then he had lost nine tenths of the world. So many people taken from him. And finally he had lost Anna.

There was still time though. There was still a chance. He could bring her back to life. He really could. Then he wouldn't have to face up to all the loss. Wouldn't even have to admit to it. He wouldn't.

He would redeem himself. He really would.

If only he could find all the pieces...

THE END

JASPRE BARK is a novelist, children's author and comics writer. He has written two previous novels *A Fistful of Strontium* and *Sniper Elite: Spear of Destiny* (also for Abaddon). His children's books have been translated into five different languages and are used in schools throughout the UK to improve literacy. Jaspre has written comics for just about everyone in the British comics industry, from *The Beano* to *2000 AD*, and an increasing number of American and international publishers. Prior to this he worked as a film journalist and cable TV presenter by day and a stand-up poet and playwright by night. In 1999 he was awarded a Fringe First at the Edinburgh International Festival.

coming
September
2008...

Now read the first chapter in the next exciting novel
in *The Afterblight Chronicles* series...

THE AFTERBLIGHT CHRONICLES

ARROWHEAD

Paul Kane

COMING SEPTEMBER 2008

NOVEMBER 2008 (US)

ISBN: 978-1-905437-76-4

£6.99 (UK)/ $7.99 (US)

WWW.ABADDONBOOKS.COM

CHAPTER ONE

The arrowhead embedded itself in the wall just millimetres from his left temple.

Thomas Hinckerman had screwed up his eyes as the crossbow was raised, flinching only slightly when he heard the impact; in one way relieved to still be alive, in another wishing this ordeal could be over soon. The apple on top of his head wobbled slightly. There was a wetness running down his face. He assumed it was sweat. But when he opened his eyes and looked down – carefully, so as not to dislodge the fruit he was balancing – he saw the spots of red on the floor. The bolt had nicked his skin...

And seconds later there was pain.

Not that he could feel it much – this latest wound paled into insignificance compared with his others: the bullet-hole in his shoulder, for example, the fingernails dangling off, pulled with pliers, the missing teeth, or how about the cigar burns on his stomach? Still, he'd fared better than his friends, Gary and Dan. Their bodies were still cooling on the floor near the entrance to the station.

It had been his idea initially, taken from those stories of refugees trying to enter Britain simply by walking, long before the virus came and took its toll. Before The Cull. Back then those people had wanted in, but now it seemed like a much better idea to get out of the country before things grew even worse.

Thomas suggested it to Gary, a former scrap metal dealer, and Dan, who used to be a butcher, because they felt the same. He'd met them at the local impromptu meetings just before The Cull had finished decimating the worlds' population, when everyone was still trying to figure out what could be done about their loved ones, their neighbours, those who were dying all around them. They weren't the kind of folk Thomas would have mixed with before all this, not the sort of men you'd see hanging out at the library where Thomas had worked. But fate had thrown them together, and they'd stuck like glue through all the madness that had followed.

Now they were dead. Just like he would be soon. Thomas was under no illusions about that, not after he'd seen them murdered in cold blood. His last memories of the men he'd trekked thirty-one miles with, sharing adversities he never would have thought possible, were Dan's brains exploding all over his own shirt, feet still twitching as he hit the ground, and Gary dancing like a puppet as he was riddled with bullets from a machine gun.

They'd all emerged from the tunnel and into the station at Calais that morning, their torches almost out of batteries, supplies exhausted a day ago, glad to be free, glad to be back above ground. They'd passed dormant trains, their yellow noses rusting, glass at the front smashed. They'd seen no-one, not until they reached the station. There Gary spotted a lone figure sitting on one of the benches inside the foyer.

They must have been watching from the start, though; because as the trio walked over to make contact, Dan was already dropping, a bullet coming out of nowhere to blow half his head away. And then the other men emerged – a half dozen or more, heavily-armed; one with silver hair carrying what looked like a sniper's rifle. That's when they'd pulled Gary's strings...

They'd been waiting, too, he found out. Waiting for someone like him to come. Thomas had been left alive, just clipped with a bullet, to tell them what he knew.

He was dragged to his feet by two men, one with a

slight paunch, the other smoking a cigar. Their leader wasn't a huge man, but carried himself well. He had the air of someone much larger. He was dressed in grey and black combats, and was wearing sunglasses. When he took these off and stared into Thomas's face, he saw that the man's eyes were just as black as his glasses. There were jewelled rings on most of his fingers. He spoke with a French accent and his first question was: "Are you in pain, Englishman?" When Thomas nodded, the man smiled with teeth as yellow as the noses of those trains. Then he stuck two of his ringed fingers into the hole in Thomas's shoulder. His whole body jerked, but he was held tightly by the men on either side.

When Thomas had recovered enough to speak, he whispered: "What... what do you want from me...?"

"Information," said the man.

"A... about what? I don't know anything."

He smiled again. "We will see."

Thomas was introduced to a broader man with olive skin and short-cropped hair. Thomas was told that his name was Tanek. "When Tanek was in the army," the man in combats told him, "his speciality was making people talk." The Frenchman nodded firmly, and that's when the pliers had come out. Tanek had gone to work on his fingernails first, grasping the little one on his right hand firmly, then yanking it off, the nail splitting and cracking as it went.

Thomas let out the loudest scream of his life. Even getting shot hadn't hurt like that. Through the tears, he saw the outline of the Frenchman's face again. "I need to know about the place you've come from," he told Thomas.

"W-What...?"

Another nail was pulled. "Yaaaaaahhhh"

The Frenchman slapped his face. "What is the situation in England? Do you understand me?"

Thomas shook his head.

"How organised are the people over there, are there communities? Are the defence forces still operational?"

Thomas laughed at that one, which earned him another lost nail. "Everything's gone to shit," he shouted back at the man. "It's chaos. Fucking chaos. Why do you think we came through the tunnel? It's like being back in the dark ages."

The Frenchman chuckled. "I see."

They continued to question him for at least a couple more hours, asking him everything he knew about Dover, where they'd entered, about the surrounding areas of Kent, what he'd heard about London and other areas of England – which was very little since The Cull. Thomas had no idea why they were putting the questions to him, but he answered as honestly as he could, especially when Tanek pulled out his molars, then snatched the cigar from one of the men holding him and used that as well. He'd co-operated as well as he was able and his reward was to be handcuffed to a notice board, ruined fingers dangling limply, while some of the men took it in turn to play 'William Tell' with a crossbow Tanek handed around, and an apple – a fresh golden apple that would have made Thomas's mouth water had it not already filled with blood. And had his mouth not been taped over because they were sick of hearing his cries.

As he opened his eyes now, he saw that motorcycles were being wheeled into the station, six or seven in total. He also heard one of the men call out their leader's name: De Falaise.

The man came to join Tanek, just as another bolt was clumsily fired from the crossbow. It wound up in Thomas's right thigh. His muffled grunt caused much amusement amongst the group.

De Falaise raised a hand to stop the game for a moment, walking towards Thomas. "I thank you for your help, it was fortuitous that our paths should cross. From what you have told us, it would appear there is much in the way of opportunity for people like us in your land. Unlike the situation we leave behind... Your people are weak, we are not."

It was then that Thomas knew what he had in mind. De Falaise and his men were going to use the bikes to make the same trip he'd done, but in reverse, shooting up the tunnel and into England just like one of the bolts from Tanek's crossbow. And they would probably do just as much damage.

"In return, my gift to you, Englishman," said De Falaise. Thomas looked into those black eyes, and thought for just a moment he might let him live, let him go. Then he saw that smile on De Falaise's face, and struggled against his bonds, the apple falling from his head. De Falaise stepped aside and there was Tanek, with his weapon loaded again – aimed at his head. Unlike the others, he would not miss.

In seconds it was over, and De Falaise was already giving the order to move out, to take the bikes down to the tunnel so they could be on their way. Tanek paused before leaving, to pick up the apple and take a bite.

"Come," said De Falaise. Laughing again as he led the way. "There is much to do, much to see. And a country just as ripe for the taking."

For more information on this
and other titles visit...

**Abaddon
Books**

THE AFTERBLIGHT CHRONICLES

The CULLED

Simon Spurrier

Price: £6.99 ★ ISBN: 978-1-905437-01-6

Price: $7.99 ★ ISBN: 978-1-905437-01-6

THE AFTERBLIGHT CHRONICLES

KILL OR CURE

Rebecca Levene

Price: £6.99 ★ ISBN: 978-1-905437-32-0

Price: $7.99 ★ ISBN: 978-1-905437-32-0

THE AFTERBLIGHT CHRONICLES

SCHOOL'S OUT

Scott Andrews

Price: £6.99 ★ ISBN: 978-1-905437-40-5

Price: $7.99 ★ ISBN: 978-1-905437-40-5

SNIPER ELITE

SPEAR OF DESTINY

Jaspre Bark

Price: £6.99 ★ ISBN: 978-1-905437-04-7

Price: $7.99 ★ ISBN: 978-1-905437-04-7

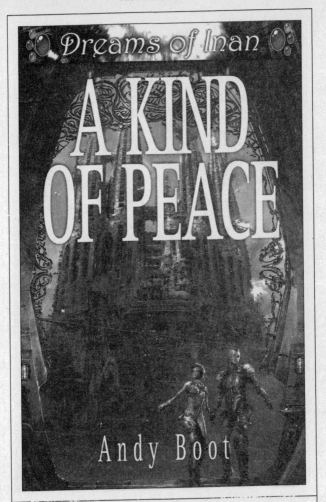

Dreams of Inan

A KIND OF PEACE

Andy Boot

Price: £6.99 ★ ISBN: 978-1-905437-02-3

Price: $7.99 ★ ISBN: 978-1-905437-02-3

Price: £6.99 ★ ISBN: 978-1-905437-12-2

Price: $7.99 ★ ISBN: 978-1-905437-12-2

Price: £6.99 ★ ISBN: 978-1-905437-53-5

Price: $7.99 ★ ISBN: 978-1-905437-53-5

TOMES *of the* DEAD

THE WORDS OF THEIR ROARING

Matthew Smith

Price: £6.99 ★ ISBN: 978-1-905437-13-9

Price: $7.99 ★ ISBN: 978-1-905437-13-9

Abaddon
Books

WWW.ABADDONBOOKS.COM